Beyond the Boardroom

by Maureen Child

From the desk of

Patrick Elliott, CEO

Shane,

Hard to believe it has been a year since I started this competition to name my successor. The family thought – and still thinks – I'm crazy to pit you all against each other, brother against brother against sister. But here we stand, at the finish line. And there can be only one winner.

The final reports are in. The profit margins have been tabulated for all the magazines, and I hold in my hand the name of the new CEO of Elliott Publication Holdings.

If you want to know who it is, come to my office tonight at seven. If you've got the guts…

Patrick

Available in November 2007 from Mills & Boon® Desire™

The Substitute Millionaire
by Susan Mallery
&
Surrogate and Wife
by Emily McKay

The Expectant Executive
by Kathie DeNosky
&
Beyond the Boardroom
by Maureen Child

Exposing the Executive's Secrets
by Emilie Rose
&
Expecting the Cowboy's Baby
by Charlene Sands

The Expectant Executive

KATHIE DENOSKY

Beyond the Boardroom

MAUREEN CHILD

All the characters in this book have no existence outside the imagination of the author, and have no relation whatsoever to anyone bearing the same name or names. They are not even distantly inspired by any individual known or unknown to the author, and all the incidents are pure invention.

First published in Great Britain 2007 by Harlequin Mills & Boon Limited, Eton House, 18-24 Paradise Road, Richmond, Surrey TW9 1SR

Special thanks and acknowledgement are given to Kathie DeNosky and Maureen Child for their contribution to The Elliotts series.

ISBN: 978 0 263 85606 4

51-1107

Printed and bound in Spain by Litografia Rosés S.A., Barcelona

THE EXPECTANT EXECUTIVE

by
Kathie DeNosky

Dear Reader,

I think at one time or another in life, we've all wished for a second chance to do something or wondered what choices we would have made if we could go back in time and do certain things differently. But other than a mulligan in golf or a "do over" in a neighbourhood ball game, there are very few times when we're given that opportunity.

That's why I was thrilled when I was invited to write a book for THE ELLIOTTS and learned that my story was all about second chances. I really enjoyed writing the journey Fin and Travis take as they find the courage to reach for their second chance at parenthood, family relationships and love. It is my fervent hope that you enjoy it, too.

All the best,

Kathie DeNosky

This book is dedicated to the authors of
THE ELLIOTTS.
You gals are awesome and it was a privilege
and an honour to work with you.

KATHIE DeNOSKY

lives in her native southern Illinois with her husband and one very spoiled Jack Russell terrier. She writes highly sensual stories with a generous amount of humour. Kathie's books have appeared on the Waldenbooks bestseller list and received the Write Touch Readers' Award from *WisRWA* and the National Readers' Choice Award. She enjoys going to rodeos, travelling to research settings for her books and listening to country music. Readers may contact Kathie at PO Box 2064, Herrin, Illinois 62948-5264, USA or e-mail her at kathie@kathiedenosky.com.

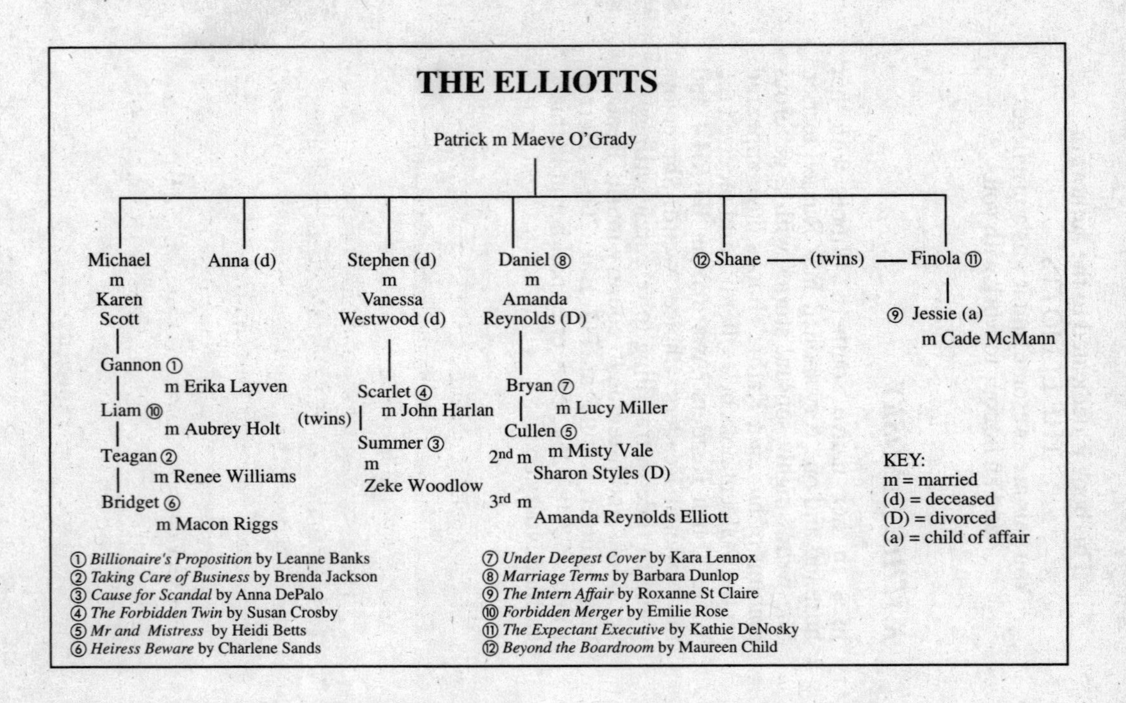
THE ELLIOTTS
Patrick m Maeve O'Grady
Michael m Karen Scott
Anna (d)
Stephen (d) m Vanessa Westwood (d)
Daniel ⑧ m Amanda Reynolds (D)
⑫ Shane — (twins) — Finola ⑪
Gannon ① m Erika Layven
Liam ⑩ m Aubrey Holt
Teagan ② m Renee Williams
Bridget ⑥ m Macon Riggs
Scarlet ④ m John Harlan
(twins)
Summer ③ m Zeke Woodlow
Bryan ⑦ m Lucy Miller
Cullen ⑤ m Misty Vale
2nd m Sharon Styles (D)
3rd m Amanda Reynolds Elliott
⑨ Jessie (a) m Cade McMann
KEY:
m = married
(d) = deceased
(D) = divorced
(a) = child of affair
① Billionaire's Proposition by Leanne Banks
② Taking Care of Business by Brenda Jackson
③ Cause for Scandal by Anna DePalo
④ The Forbidden Twin by Susan Crosby
⑤ Mr and Mistress by Heidi Betts
⑥ Heiress Beware by Charlene Sands
⑦ Under Deepest Cover by Kara Lennox
⑧ Marriage Terms by Barbara Dunlop
⑨ The Intern Affair by Roxanne St Claire
⑩ Forbidden Merger by Emilie Rose
⑪ The Expectant Executive by Kathie DeNosky
⑫ Beyond the Boardroom by Maureen Child

One

"I can't believe it's already the first of November," Finola Elliott muttered as she scanned the entries in her electronic planner.

There were only two months left before Patrick, founder and CEO of Elliott Publication Holdings and patriarch of the Long Island Elliott clan, retired and named one of his four children his successor to the magazine empire he'd built over the years. And Fin had every intention of being the indisputable winner of the competition he'd set up to decide who would best fill that role.

She'd spent her entire adult life working toward

taking over EPH, and even though her two brothers and one nephew were all equally qualified for the position, Patrick—she hadn't referred to him as her father in years—owed her the job and so much more. But when he reviewed the growth and profit margins of *The Buzz*, *Snap*, *Pulse* and *Charisma* magazines, Fin wanted there to be no mistaking that her "baby," *Charisma*, had outdistanced the others, hands down.

At the end of the second quarter, her fashion magazine had been in the lead. Unfortunately, in the past couple of months her twin brother, Shane, had pulled ahead with his show business publication, *The Buzz*. But Fin wasn't overly concerned. Everything was back on track and going her way again.

Smiling fondly, she glanced at the newly framed picture on her desk and the reason her attention had been diverted from the objective. She'd discovered that her intern, Jessica Clayton, was the baby girl Patrick had forced Fin to give up for adoption twenty-three years ago, and she and her daughter had been making up for lost time. Jessie was a wonderful young woman and they'd become quite close over the past couple of months. In fact, Fin had even accompanied Jessie to the Silver Moon Ranch in Colorado, to meet Jessie's adoptive father and see where she'd grown up.

But now that Jessie and Cade McMann, Fin's right-hand man at *Charisma*, were busy with the final preparations for their wedding later in the month, Fin needed to get back on track and regain her focus. She hid a yawn behind her hand. She just wished she wasn't so darned tired all the time.

As she switched to the month of October to review her notes on the magazine's growth projections for November, goose bumps skittered over her skin and a little chill streaked up her spine.

Something was missing. Where was the personal notation she made every month marking the start of her cycle?

Switching back to her entry in September, her heart slammed to a stop, then pounded hard against her ribs. She hadn't had a period in almost six weeks?

"That can't be right."

Surely she'd just forgotten to record the date for October. But as she thought back, she couldn't remember having had a period since well before accompanying Jessie to Colorado.

Stunned, Fin sat back in her high-backed leather chair and stared out the plateglass windows at the Manhattan skyline. The only other time in her life that she'd skipped her cycle had been at the age of fifteen when she'd gotten pregnant after her one night of passion with her sixteen-year-old boyfriend, Sebastian Deveraux. But there was absolutely no way she could be pregnant this time.

She almost laughed. For that to even be a remote possibility, she'd have to have a love life. And she didn't. She couldn't even remember the last time she'd been out with a man when the evening hadn't been business-related—either courting a potential advertising client or entertaining one of the many designers featuring his or her new line in *Charisma*.

Her social life had taken, and probably always would take, a backseat to the magazine that had become her obsession over the years. But a sudden thought caused her to catch her breath. There had been that one night at the party Travis Clayton, Jessie's adoptive father, had thrown in honor of Jessie and Cade's engagement.

Fin's cheeks heated at the thought of just what had taken place when she and Travis had gone into that charming old barn of his to check on a mare and her new foal. What had started out to be an innocent hug to express how grateful she was that Travis and his late wife, Lauren, had done such a wonderful job of raising Jessie, had turned into a passionate encounter that still left Fin feeling breathlessly weak. There had only been one other time in her life that she'd allowed herself to lose control and throw caution to the wind like that. The night she'd conceived Jessie.

She thoughtfully nibbled on her lower lip. She couldn't possibly have gotten pregnant from that one stolen moment with Travis, could she?

Shaking her head, she dismissed the idea outright. It might be possible, but it was most definitely improbable. She'd read somewhere that the closer a woman got to forty, the longer it sometimes took to become pregnant. And at thirty-eight, she was closing in on forty faster than she cared to admit.

Besides, fate couldn't possibly be that cruel. She'd conceived Jessie the night she'd lost her virginity to Sebastian. Surely the odds of her becoming pregnant again after making love with a man one time had to be astronomical.

No, missing her period had to be an indication that something else was wrong.

Swiveling her chair around, she reached for the phone to make an appointment with her gynecologist, but gasped at the unexpected sight of Travis Clayton leaning one broad shoulder against her doorframe.

"I know I'm not the best-looking thing to come down the pike, but I wasn't aware that I'd started scaring the hell out of pretty women and little kids," he said, his deep voice filled with humor.

The teasing light in his sinfully blue eyes sent a delicious warmth coursing throughout her body. If she'd ever seen a man as ruggedly handsome as Jessie's adoptive father, Fin couldn't remember when. Looking much younger than his forty-nine years, he was the epitome of the modern western man from the top of his wide-brimmed black cowboy hat all the way to his big-booted feet. Wearing a pair of soft-looking, well-worn jeans, chambray shirt and a western-cut sports jacket that emphasized the breadth of his impossibly wide shoulders, he could easily be one of the male models in an advertisement for men's cologne.

"Travis, it's good to see you again. I don't remember Jessie mentioning that you would be visiting this week." Rising to her feet, Fin walked around the desk to greet him. "Please, come in and sit down."

Giving her a smile that caused her toes to curl inside her Italian designer heels, he straightened to his full height and crossed the room with the confidence and grace of a man quite comfortable with who he was and what he was about. "When I talked to Jess the other day, she sounded a little hassled from all this wedding stuff, so I decided to surprise her," he said, settling into one of the chairs in front of Fin's desk.

"A little paternal support never hurts," she agreed, wondering what it would be like to have a father who was sensitive to his child's emotional needs. Patrick's approach to childrearing had been nothing short of dictatorial and he could have cared less how his issued orders affected his offspring's emotions—in particular, hers.

"How have you been, Fin?" Travis asked when she sat down in the chair beside him.

The warmth and genuine interest in his smooth baritone sent a little shiver up her spine. "Fine. And yourself?"

He shrugged. "Can't complain." Looking around her office, his curious gaze seemed to zero in on a stack of ad proofs on her desk. "When I asked Jess how you've been getting on, she said you're working like crazy to win this contest your dad set up."

Her stomach did a funny little flip at the thought that he'd been asking Jessie about her. "The competition and helping with Jessie and Cade's wedding arrangements have been keeping me pretty busy."

"I'll bet it has." He chuckled. "All this wedding hoopla makes me kind of glad I'm stuck off in no-man's-land until it's time to walk her down the aisle. Jess said all I have to do is go for the final fitting on my tux while I'm in town and that suits me just fine."

He wasn't fooling Fin for a minute. Travis and Jessie had a wonderful father-daughter relationship and he had to be feeling a little left out for him to fly all the way from Colorado.

"This is pretty tough for you, isn't it?"

He started to shake his head, then looking a bit sheepish, he grinned. "It shows that much, does it? I thought I was doing a pretty fair job of hiding it, but I guess I was wrong."

Fin nodded sympathetically. "I'm sure it's a difficult transition to suddenly be relegated to the number-two man in your daughter's life when you've always been number one."

"I can't believe she's old enough to get married," he said, removing his hat to run his hand through his thick dark blond hair. Replacing his hat, his expression turned wistful. "It seems like just yesterday I was kissing her skinned elbows and teaching her how to print her name for kindergarten."

A little pang of envy gripped Fin's heart. She'd been cheated out of so much when Patrick had forced her to give her baby daughter up for adoption.

They sat in silence for several long moments before Travis spoke again. "I know this is short notice, but I stopped by to ask if you'd like to join Jessie and me for supper this evening. We'll be meeting at some place she called the Lemon Grill."

He grinned. "If the name is any indication, it sounds like a place a man could get a decent steak."

Fin smiled. "I'm sure you can. It's a charming little bistro with excellent food."

"Then you'll join us?"

She should decline the invitation outright. She and Travis had absolutely nothing in common beyond their love for Jessie. But for reasons beyond her comprehension, Fin was drawn to Travis and had been since the moment they met.

"I don't want to intrude on your time with your daughter," she hedged.

He shook his head. "She's your daughter, too. Besides, I wouldn't have asked if I hadn't wanted you to join us. And I'm sure you want to spend as much time with her as you can now that you two have found each other."

Her heart filled with emotion when he referred to Jessie as her daughter, too. "You're sure you don't mind?"

When he took her hand in his much larger one, a tingling thrill streaked up Fin's arm at the feel of his work-callused palm against her much softer skin. "I'm positive." The warmth in his incredibly blue eyes assured her that he did indeed want her to have dinner with them. "What man wouldn't want to be out with the two best-looking women in this whole damned town?"

The truth was, spending the evening with Travis and Jessie was far more appealing than sitting alone in her too-big apartment eating take out and going over spread sheets filled with *Charisma*'s growth projections and profit margins. Surely one more night of putting off the task wasn't going to hurt her chances of winning the competition for EPH.

"Wh-what time should I meet you at the bistro?" Why did she suddenly feel like a teenage girl being asked to the homecoming dance by the best-looking, most popular boy in school?

"Eight." Still holding her hand, he rose to his feet, then pulled her up to stand beside him. "I guess I'd better let you get back to work if you're going to win your dad's contest."

"I suppose that would be a good idea." Why didn't she sound as resolute about it as she would have before he appeared at her door?

He leaned forward to press a soft kiss to her forehead. "Then I'll see you this evening, Fin."

Her skin tingled where his lips had been and before she could find her voice, Travis touched the wide brim of his cowboy hat in a gallant gesture and turned to walk away.

As she watched him disappear into the outer

office, she felt the need to fan herself. Dear God, the man was six feet four inches of pure sex appeal and could heat up a room faster than a blast furnace. His kiss had only been meant as a friendly gesture, but her heart had skipped several beats at the touch of his lips to her suddenly overly sensitive skin.

"Was that the model for Calvin Klein's new cowboy cologne?" Chloe Davenport asked, entering Fin's office. She glanced over her shoulder at Travis. "If so, could I sign up to be his cowgirl?"

Fin laughed at her executive assistant. "No. That's Travis Clayton, Jessie's father."

"You're kidding." Fin watched the young woman take another lingering glance before closing the office door. "He's the real deal, isn't he?"

"If by that you mean that he's a working cowboy, then yes, he's the real thing."

Chloe sighed wistfully. "If they grow them like that in Colorado, I just might have to head that way sometime."

Fin laughed. "And leave that cute little apartment you have in Chelsea?"

"Ooh, that would be a problem. I finally have it decorated just the way I want it," Chloe said, handing Fin the latest accounting reports. "I suppose

I'll just have to stay in New York and content myself with finding an urban cowboy."

Fin nodded, distracted by the report. "What's the latest word around EPH? Anything going on with the other magazines that I should know about?"

The young woman shook her head. "Not that I've heard. You and Shane are still the top contenders for CEO. *The Buzz*'s growth and profit margin is slightly better than *Charisma*'s, but the consensus in accounting is that *Charisma* could still come out the winner."

"G-good." Suddenly feeling a bit dizzy, Fin walked around her desk to sit in her high-backed chair. She definitely needed to see a doctor.

"Fin, are you okay?" Chloe asked, her pretty young face marred with concern.

Nodding, Fin gave her a weak smile. "I'm just tired, that's all."

"I'm worried about you, Fin. You've been working way too hard." Chloe frowned. "You've always been driven, but these past ten months you've made workaholics look like total slackers."

"I'll be fine, Chloe."

Her assistant looked doubtful. "Are you sure about that?"

Smiling, Fin nodded as she handed the report back to her assistant. "Now, go give these to Cade and tell him that I want to meet with him first thing in the morning to go over these figures."

"Anything else?"

Fin checked the clock. "No, I have a few phone calls to make, then I think I'm going to take off the rest of the day."

Chloe looked thunderstruck. "You're kidding. You never leave before eight or nine in the evening and more times than I care to count, I've found you sleeping on your couch when I arrive for work. Are you sure you're feeling all right? Should I call someone?"

"No, you don't need to call anyone." Smiling, Fin hid a yawn behind her hand. "I have a dinner engagement and I think I need a short nap to make it through the evening. Otherwise, I might fall asleep between the appetizer and the main course."

"That wouldn't be good for business," Chloe agreed, shaking her head as she walked to the door.

Fin didn't bother to correct her assistant as the young woman quietly closed the door behind her. Dinner this evening had nothing whatsoever to do with business and everything to do with pleasure. Her only concern was deciding which she was anticipating more—the pleasure of spending time with her newfound daughter or her daughter's adoptive father.

* * *

Travis felt like a fish out of water. The concrete and steel of New York City was a far cry from the wide open spaces he was used to and the Lemon Grill was to hell and gone from the little diner he sometimes frequented when he drove over to Winchester County for the stock auctions. Here he sat in an upscale café in the middle of Manhattan with a prissy little waiter sporting a pencil-thin mustache and slicked-back hair, hovering around him like a bumblebee over a patch of new spring clover.

"My name is Henri. It will be my pleasure to be your server this evening." The too-polished character smiled, showing off a set of unnaturally white teeth. "Would the gentleman like something to drink while he's waiting on his dinner partners?"

Travis frowned. The little guy sure spouted out a lot of words to ask a simple question. He was more used to being asked straight up what he wanted to drink instead of being referred to like he was some sort of third wheel.

"I'll take a beer."

"Would the gentleman like a domestic brand or imported?"

Unable to resist teasing the pretentious little man, Travis grinned. "I can't say what the gentleman would like, but I'll take domestic." As Henri started to leave the table, Travis added the name of a beer brewed exclusively in the Rocky Mountains.

"I'm sorry, sir. We don't carry that particular brand," Henri said, his apology as fake as his cap-toothed smile. Rattling off a list of the beer the restaurant had available, he asked, "Would the gentleman like to choose one of those?"

"Surprise me."

"Very well, sir."

As the waiter hurried away to get his drink, Travis spotted Fin entering the restaurant. She briefly spoke to the hostess, then when she headed his way, he couldn't help but marvel at what a beauty she was. With her straight, dark auburn hair stylishly brushing her shoulders, and looking like a model in her black form-fitting dress, she looked far too young to be the mother of his twenty-three-year-old daughter.

Standing when she approached, he thought his heart would jump right out of his chest when her perfect coral lips turned up in a warm smile. "I hope I'm not too late. The crosstown traffic was particularly heavy this evening."

"You drove?" He held the chair for her while she seated herself at the small table. "I remember Jessie telling me that you'd never learned to drive."

Fin's delightful laughter caused an unexpected

heat to settle in the pit of his belly as he sat back down. "Guilty as charged. I've never even been behind the wheel of a car."

"You're kidding, right?" Hell, he'd been driving around the ranch in either a truck or on a tractor since he was ten years old and he'd taught Jessie to drive when she was twelve. "You've never—"

"No. When my brothers and I lived at home, we always had drivers to take us wherever we wanted to go. Then, after I moved from the Hamptons into my Manhattan apartment, there was no need to drive. Everything I need is so close, I walk a lot. And when where I want to go is too far to walk, I use the corporate limo or take a taxi." Her eyes twinkled wistfully as she added, "But I've always thought it might be fun to learn how to drive a car."

"The next time you visit the Silver Moon, I'll teach you," he said, unable to wipe what he was sure had to be a sappy grin from his face.

Her eyes held a warmth that stole his breath. "I'd like that, Travis. Thank you."

The thought of Fin coming back to his ranch for a visit had his heart pounding like the bass drum in a marching band. But it was the slight blush on her porcelain cheeks and the warmth in her pretty green eyes that caused the region south of his belt buckle to tighten. She remembered what happened between them when she visited his ranch last month, the same as he did.

"Would the lady like something to drink before ordering dinner?" Henri asked, returning to their table with Travis's beer.

For reasons Travis didn't want to dwell on, the man's appreciative grin when he looked at Fin irritated the hell out of Travis.

"Just some water with a slice of lemon, please," Fin answered the prissy little guy. As he moved away to take care of her request, she asked, "Where's Jessie? I was sure she'd be here by now."

Travis shook his head. "I don't know. She said something about going with Cade to pick up airline tickets for their honeymoon after they got off work. But that was a good three hours ago. Surely it doesn't take that long to…"

His voice trailed off when he felt Fin's soft, delicate hand touch his. "I'm sure she's fine, Travis. I overheard her and Cade talking about a stop at the jeweler's to pick up gifts for their bridesmaids and groomsmen. Maybe it took longer than they had anticipated."

As he sat there trying to force words around the cotton suddenly coating his throat, Henri placed a glass of water on the table in front of Fin. "Sir, you have a phone call. If you'll follow me, you may take the call at the hostess's desk."

When Travis glanced at Fin, she smiled. "It's probably Jessie telling you that she's held up in traffic."

"I hope you're right." He briefly wondered why his daughter hadn't called his cell phone, until he remembered that he'd turned it off when he entered the restaurant.

Excusing himself, Travis quickly made his way to the front of the restaurant. Even though Jess had been living in New York City for the better part of a year, it still made him nervous to think of his little girl on the mean streets of a big city. He'd relaxed a little after meeting her fiancé, Cade McMann, and being assured that the man had every intention of keeping her safe and making her happy. But if something had happened to her, Travis would have Cade's head on a silver platter for not taking better care of her.

When the hostess handed him the phone, he was relieved to hear his precious daughter on the other end of the line. "Hi, Daddy."

"Where are you, angel? Are you all right?"

"I'm fine, but I'm afraid I won't be able to meet you and Fin for dinner this evening." There was a short silence before she added, "I've, um, got a headache and I think I'll turn in early. You don't mind having dinner alone with Fin, do you?"

"Of course not, princess." Travis glanced over at the beautiful woman waiting patiently at his table. He'd have to be as crazy as a horse after it got into a patch of locoweed to mind spending time with her.

"Good. I'm sure you'll both enjoy yourselves. The Lemon Grill has great food." Jessie's voice was a little too enthusiastic and she didn't sound the least bit under the weather. "Please give Fin my apologies and tell her that I'll see her at the office tomorrow morning."

"I'll do that, angel." She wasn't fooling him for a minute. Jess had been after him for the past couple of years to get out more and revitalize his social life, as she put it. And unless he missed his guess, his little girl was trying to play matchmaker between him and her biological mother.

"Oh, don't forget, Daddy. We're supposed to meet for lunch tomorrow, then go to the men's store to have you fitted for your tux."

"You're still going to make me wear that monkey suit, are you?"

"You'll be the best looking monkey at the wedding," she said, laughing. "I love you, Daddy. See you tomorrow."

"I love you too, Jess."

Handing the cordless phone back to the hostess, Travis walked over to the table where Fin sat waiting for him. "Looks like it's just the two of us for supper tonight," he said, settling into his chair.

She gave him a questioning look. "Jessie isn't coming?"

"Nope." He shook his head. "She said she has a headache and intends to go to bed early."

"Since your other dinner partner won't be joining you, would you care to order now?" Henri asked, suddenly appearing at Travis's elbow. The man had obviously been eavesdropping on their conversation.

Tired of the waiter's obtrusive presence, Travis gave him a look that had the little man quickly fading into the background without another word. "What do you say we go somewhere we can talk without old Ornery over there hanging on our every word?"

Fin looked puzzled. "Ornery?"

"Henri. Ornery." Travis grinned. "Same difference."

She gave him a smile that did strange things to his insides. "I think I know of a place where we can talk uninterrupted."

"Sounds good to me." Raising his hand, he motioned to Henri.

The little waiter was at Travis's side almost immediately. "Would the lady and gentleman like to order now?"

Fin spoke up before Travis had a chance. “No, we’ve changed our minds and won’t be dining with you this evening.”

Leaving Henri to hover over someone else, when they stepped out onto the street, Travis put his arm around Fin to shelter her from the chilly November wind. Her slender body pressed to his side sent his blood pressure up a good fifty points and brought back memories of the last time he’d held her close. His body tightened predictably and he felt as if his jeans had shrunk a size or two in the stride.

“What’s the name of this restaurant where the waiters leave the customers alone?” he asked when he finally got his voice to work.

“Chez Fin Elliott.”

His heart stuttered and he had to remind himself to breathe. “We’re going to your place?”

Nodding, she smiled. “If you don’t mind missing out on your steak, I thought we could go back to my apartment, order in some Chinese and talk without having someone else hanging on our every word.”

He wasn’t wild about egg rolls and chop suey, but he’d have to be a damned fool to pass up spending the evening alone with one of the most beautiful women he’d ever had the privilege to lay eyes on.

Before she had a chance to change her mind, Travis raised his arm and waved at an approaching yellow car. "Taxi!"

Two

As Fin phoned in a delivery order to her favorite Chinese restaurant, she watched Travis glance around her cavernous Upper East Side apartment and couldn't help but wonder what he thought of her personal space. Obscenely spacious for one person, it was a study in chrome and glass, black and white, and light-years away from his warmly decorated home in Colorado.

When she'd visited the Silver Moon Ranch, she'd found the house to be roomy and pleasantly cluttered, but it was also welcoming, cozy and everything her apartment wasn't. While Travis's rustic home had the unmistakable look and feel of being lived in and enjoyed—of love and family—her apartment appeared to be stark, cold and uninhabited in comparison.

Of course, that might have something to do with the fact that she was never there for more than a few hours at a time, nor had she made the effort to add anything to reflect her own personality after the interior designer had finished decorating the place. The really sad thing was, that had been several years ago and she still had no more interest in personalizing the place than she had the day she'd moved in.

"Mr. Chang assured me the food will be here in less than fifteen minutes," she said as she ended the phone call. "Would you like something to drink while we wait? I think I have a bottle of wine in the refrigerator or I could make a pot of coffee or tea."

"A cup of coffee would be nice."

When he turned to face her, Travis's smile sent a wave of goose bumps shimmering over her skin and a delicious little shiver straight up her spine. He was, without a doubt, one of the sexiest men she'd ever met. And she seriously doubted that he had the slightest clue of how handsome he was or the tantalizing effect he had on women.

Suddenly needing to put a little space between them before she made a complete fool of herself, Fin started toward the kitchen. He was her daughter's adoptive father, the man who had, along with his late wife, raised the little girl Fin had been forced to give up for adoption all those years ago. The last thing she needed to do was complicate the fledgling relationship she had with Jessica by lusting after Travis. Come to think of it, it was totally out of character for her to be lusting after anyone.

"I'll start the coffeemaker."

"Need help?"

She stopped in her tracks, then slowly turned to face him. Even as he stood all the way across the living room, his presence made the space feel decidedly smaller than it had when they'd first walked through the door. She could only imagine how minuscule the kitchen would seem with him in much closer proximity. Besides, having him join her would defeat the purpose of her much needed escape.

"No." To soften her hasty reply, she smiled. "By no stretch of the imagination am I domestic, but I think I can manage a pot of coffee without too much trouble." Waving her hand toward the white velour sofa, she added, "I'll only be a few minutes. Why don't you make yourself comfortable?"

"I think I'll do that." His grin sent a wave of heat from the top of her head to the soles of her feet.

As if riveted to the floor, Fin watched him remove his wide-brimmed hat and shrug out of his western jacket, then toss them on the back of an armchair. Years of listening to her mother recite the rules of proper etiquette went right out the window when she turned and entered the kitchen.

The proper thing would have been to step forward, take his hat and coat and hang them in the closet. But when Travis had unsnapped the cuffs of his chambray shirt and started rolling up the long sleeves over his tanned, sinewy forearms, she'd quickly decided there was a lot to be said for the old adage about retreat being the better part of valor.

Just the memory of those arms holding her so tenderly as they'd succumbed to passion that night in his barn last month was enough to cause her pulse to race and her breathing to come out in short, raspy little puffs. Everything about that night had been pure magic and she'd spent the past month doing her best to forget that it ever happened.

"You've got to get hold of yourself," she muttered when she noticed her hand trembling as she spooned coffee into the basket.

"Did you say something?" he called from the living room.

"No, just talking to myself."

Closing her eyes, she shook her head in an effort

to dislodge the disturbing memory. What on earth had gotten into her?

She was editor-in-chief of one of the top fashion magazines in the world, a shark in the corporate boardroom and had the ability to send the most fearless intern running for cover with nothing more than a raised eyebrow. But in Travis's presence, she seemed to be continually reminded of the fact that she was first and foremost a woman who had ignored her feminine wants and needs in favor of a rewarding career in the publishing industry.

Only, in the past couple of months she'd begun to realize that her career wasn't nearly as satisfying as she'd once thought it to be. Since learning Jessica Clayton was her long-lost daughter and meeting Travis, Fin had been reminded of what she'd given up in order to devote herself to making *Charisma* the premier magazine of the fashion world.

When she'd been a young girl, she'd wanted nothing more than to be a wife and mother, to have a family of her own. But that dream had been shattered when Patrick had forced her to give her baby girl away and had forbade her to ever see Jessie's father again. She'd never forgiven Patrick for denying her desperate pleas to keep her child, nor had she ever gotten over the loss. After she'd returned from the convent her parents had sent her to in Canada to hide her and her "shameful" condition from social and business acquaintances, she'd thrown herself into her schooling, then later into her career in an attempt to assuage the pain.

But it hadn't worked. She sighed heavily. All that she'd accomplished was finding that as she approached middle age, she was alone, childless and had become a hopeless workaholic.

"Are you all right?"

The sound of Travis's voice caused her to jump. Spinning around, she found him leaning one broad shoulder against the doorframe, much like he'd done this afternoon in her office. "Of course, why wouldn't I be?"

He pushed away from the doorframe and took a step toward her. "You were standing there staring off into space like your mind was a million miles away."

Shaking her head, she turned to slide the filled basket into the coffeemaker, then flipped the switch. "I was just thinking about the latest accounting figures for *Charisma*," she lied. "If my staff and I work hard enough, we should still be able to pull ahead of my brother Shane and his magazine, *The Buzz*."

"I don't think so."

"You don't think we'll be able to win?" she asked, frowning.

He shrugged. "I can't say if you will or not. I was

talking about what you were thinking. Whatever it was, you looked like your best roping horse had just pulled up lame, not like you were worried about winning a contest."

Shaking her head, she hoped her laughter didn't sound as hollow to him as it did to her. "I've never even ridden a horse, let alone owned one. And as for roping, I'm afraid I'd be a hopeless failure."

"You've never ridden a horse?" he asked, clearly shocked.

Grateful that she'd successfully diverted the conversation, she shook her head. "Not unless the rocking horse I had as a child counts."

His promising grin sent a wave of heat zinging throughout her body. "Looks like the next time you visit the Silver Moon, I'll have to teach you how to do more than just drive."

She swallowed hard as she tried not to think of the many other things he could teach her. And not one of them involved any type of horsepower—mechanical or otherwise.

Before she could think of something to say that wouldn't give her inner thoughts away, there was a knock on her apartment door. "I think our dinner has arrived," she said, thankful for Mr. Chang's habit of always being punctual.

"Why don't you set the table while I take care of the delivery guy?" Travis asked, starting toward the door.

As he walked across the living room, he wondered what in the name of hell he'd been thinking when he'd taken Fin up on her offer to eat at her place. They couldn't be within twenty feet of each other for more than a couple of minutes without the sexual tension around them becoming so thick it could be cut with a knife. And just the thought of how responsive she'd been to his touch that night in his barn was enough to make his body as hard as a chunk of granite.

But no matter how strong the attraction was between them or how great the sex, nothing could ever come of it. Not only was she Jessie's biological mother, Fin Elliott was a sophisticated career woman. She was city from the top of her pretty red head all the way to her perfectly polished toenails. Her lifestyle was glitz and glamour and that was a far cry from the simple life he led in the wide open spaces on the Silver Moon Ranch. While she attended formal galas and went to trendy nightclubs, he was more apt to be going to a stock auction or stopping in at the local honky-tonk for a cold beer.

As he paid the delivery boy, Travis took a deep

breath. The best thing he could do for his peace of mind would be to remove himself from the temptation that Fin Elliott posed to his suddenly overactive libido. He'd take the food into the dining room, make his excuses and head back to his hotel for room service and a shower cold enough to make him spit ice cubes.

But a few minutes later, when he set the bag on the chrome-and-glass table, Fin's warm smile had him settling onto a chair across from her. As he watched her pull white cartons with red Chinese symbols from the sack, he counted at least six, plus a couple of foam containers and some small waxed paper bags.

"How much did you order?" he asked, skeptically eyeing the amount of food in front of them.

She stopped fussing over the lids on the containers of what looked to be some kind of soup to give him a sheepish grin. "For some reason, everything sounded so good." She caught her perfect lower lip between her teeth. "But I think I might have gotten a little carried away."

"It looks like you're getting ready to feed an army." Laughing, he reached for one of the boxes. "Lucky for you, I've always had a pretty healthy appetite."

"I normally try to watch what I eat, but lately, I've

been absolutely ravenous," she said, spooning a heaping mound of rice onto her plate.

They ate in silence for some time, but Travis took little notice of the flavorful food. His mouth had gone as dry as a desert when he watched Fin delicately nibbling on a barbecue rib. But when her index finger disappeared between her kissable lips as she sucked away the last traces of sauce, his heart stalled and he felt as if he'd taken a sucker punch to the gut.

"That was good," he lied when, several minutes later, they settled down on the couch to drink their coffee. Truth to tell, he had no idea what he'd consumed, let alone how it had tasted. But it beat the hell out of telling her the truth—that he'd been so caught up in watching her, he'd practically forgotten his own name.

"I'm sorry you missed out on your steak dinner," she said apologetically.

"I wouldn't have enjoyed it anyway." He took a sip of the worst coffee he'd ever tasted in his entire life. Placing his cup on the coffee table in front of them, he decided that Fin might be beautiful and sexy as sin, but she couldn't make coffee worth a damn.

"You wouldn't have enjoyed your dinner because you missed getting to spend time with Jessie?"

"Not really." Shaking his head, he grinned as he

stretched his arm along the back of the couch behind her. "I'd had about all I could take of old Ornery and his hovering. That more than anything will put a man off his feed."

"He was a bit much, wasn't he?" The sound of Fin's delightful laughter sent a wave of heat streaking from the top of his head all the way to the soles of his size 13 boots.

Travis nodded as he touched the silky strands of her auburn hair with his index finger. "Old Ornery crossed the line between providing good service and being a pain in the butt."

When he moved his hand to lightly stroke the satiny skin at the nape of her neck, he felt her tremble. It was only the slightest of movements, but there was no mistaking that she was feeling the same overwhelming pull that he was.

As he watched, she closed her eyes and leaned back into his touch. "You know what Jessie was up to this evening, don't you?"

Putting his arm around Fin's slender shoulders, he pulled her closer to his side. "Our daughter is trying to set us up."

"That would be my guess." Fin's voice was softer than usual and she sounded a little breathless.

"Jess has been after me for quite a while to improve my social life." He chuckled. "Before she moved here, she even hinted that I'd been hiding out on the ranch ever since my wife died."

Fin nodded. "I've been accused of using my career to avoid becoming involved with anyone."

"Have you?" Realizing that she might be offended by his question, he shook his head. "It's really none of my business."

"I don't mind." She opened her eyes to look at him. "I haven't been using my career as an excuse. I'm just not good at relationships." She smiled. "As long as we're being honest about it, what about you? What's your excuse?"

He wasn't sure how to answer. It had taken him a few years, but he'd finally moved past the grief and accepted that he and his wife, Lauren, had been robbed of growing old together. But getting back into the dating pool seemed a little ridiculous at his age. And to be truthful about it, he hadn't really wanted to expend the energy to try.

"Some people might call it hiding out." He shrugged. "I think it's been more a case of not knowing how to be single again. I met my wife when I was nineteen years old and we were together until she passed away a few years back. If I have any dating skills left, they're pretty rusty. And besides, the rules of the game have changed quite a bit over the past thirty years."

She smiled. "Some of us were never good at the rules to begin with."

When his gaze met hers, he seriously doubted that Fin had any problems with dating protocol or with men asking her out. She most likely had them lined up from one end of the city to the other just waiting for any indication she'd be willing to grace them with her companionship.

"You're probably a lot better at it than you think, sweetheart."

Staring into her beautiful emerald eyes, Travis couldn't have stopped himself from leaning forward to press a kiss to her perfect lips if his life depended on it. But instead of the brief, friendly peck he'd intended, the feel of her lips as she kissed him back sent a wave of longing all the way to his soul and he didn't think twice about taking the kiss to the next level.

When Travis's firm masculine lips moved over hers with such tenderness that it brought tears to her eyes, Fin felt something warm and inviting blossom deep inside of her. The feeling quickly spread to fill every corner of her being. Never in all of her thirty-eight years of life could she remember a kiss being as enchanting, as compelling, as his gentle caress.

Without a thought to the consequences or the fact

that they were playing a game that could very well end in disaster, not to mention destroy her newfound relationship with Jessie, Fin didn't so much as hesitate to move closer and wrap her arms around Travis's broad shoulders. Is was totally insane, but she wanted to feel his strength surrounding her, needed to once again savor the taste of his masculine desire.

When he traced the soft fullness of her lower lip, she felt as if the blood in her veins turned to warm honey and she opened for him on a ragged sigh. Every detail of their night together in Colorado came rushing back as he tasted and explored her with tender care, and Fin felt her body tingle to life as he coaxed her to respond.

She'd never thought of herself as a sensual being, but in Travis's arms she felt more sexy, more alive than she'd ever felt in her life, and she tentatively met his demands by stroking his tongue with the tip of her own. His deep groan and the tightening of his arms around her was her reward. Feeling more feminine and powerful than she had in a very long time, she pressed herself to his wide chest. Heat flowed through her from the top of her head all the way to the tips of her toes as he stroked the tender inner recesses of her mouth. Fin could have no more stopped the insanity than she could stop her next breath.

Desire, sweet and pure, filled every cell of her being, but when he broke the kiss to nibble a path down the column of her throat, the building passion sent waves of delicious sensation coursing throughout her body. Her insides quivered and a soft moan escaped her lips as the heat flowed through her and began to gather in the pit of her stomach.

"Tell me to stop, Fin. Tell me to get the hell away from you before this goes any further," he said, his voice raspy with the same need overtaking her.

"I don't think…I can," she answered honestly.

His deep chuckle caused her to shiver with longing. "Then we may be in a heap of trouble, sweetheart, because I'm not sure I have enough strength to do the gentlemanly thing and leave on my own."

"You're right. We have a big problem, because I'm not sure I want you to be noble," she said before she could stop herself.

His chest rose and fell as he took a deep breath. "I haven't been able to forget that night back in October when you visited the ranch."

"I haven't, either."

"I don't know how it's possible, but I want you even more now than I did then."

Her breath caught and her heart skipped a beat when he slid his large hand along her ribs to the underside of her breast. "Th-this is insane."

"I couldn't agree more," he said as he cupped the soft mound through the layers of her clothing.

"I'm not good…at relationships," she reminded him when he began to trace slows circles over the tip of her sensitive breast.

"Like I told you earlier, I'm not looking for one," he said, his lips caressing the side of her neck as he spoke. "But I know what it's like to make love to you and I'd like to do it again."

"No strings attached?"

He nodded. "We've already opened that corral gate and the horse got out. I can't see the harm in having one last time together."

Resting her head against his shoulder, Fin did her best to remember all of the complications that being with this man could cause. But for the life of her, she couldn't think of a single one at the moment. And if she were perfectly honest with herself, she didn't even want to.

Before she could change her mind, she pulled from his arms, stood up and held out her hand. When he placed his callused palm on hers and rose to his feet, the look in his incredible blue eyes promised forbidden ecstasy and dark pleasure.

"One last night," she said as she led him into her bedroom and closed the door.

Three

Fin's heart raced and her knees had started to tremble, but calling a halt to what she and Travis were about to do wasn't a consideration. She felt as if she would burn to a cinder if she didn't once again feel the tenderness of his touch and experience the power of his passion.

"I know this is going to sound like I've lost my mind, but I have to know," he said, his voice low and intimate as he turned her to face him. "Are you sure about this, Fin?"

Just like everyone else, there had been several instances in her life when she'd been uncertain about her decisions. But this wasn't one of them.

"If we don't make love, I think I'll go up in flames, Travis."

"No regrets tomorrow?"

"Maybe." She caught her lower lip between her teeth to keep it from trembling a moment before she shook her head. "But not about you or our lovemaking."

She knew he was confused by her answer, but she wasn't sure how to explain what she didn't fully understand herself. How could she put into words that if she had any misgivings at all about what they were about to share, it wouldn't be about him or their night together? It was her inability to share more of herself than just her body that saddened her.

But she'd made a decision the day her father had forced her to give up her daughter. She'd vowed to concentrate on building a career that no one could take away from her. Very few men wanted to take a backseat to a woman's commitment to her work, let alone accept it and understand why she was so driven to succeed.

Of course, with Travis it was a moot point. He wasn't looking for a relationship any more than she was, nor did he have any expectations that they would ever have anything more than this one night together. Still, it seemed rather sad to think of all that she'd had to sacrifice in order to ensure her success.

Reaching up, she smoothed the lines creasing his forehead with the tip of her index finger. "Rest assured, I don't regret that night at your ranch, nor will I regret making love with you tonight."

"Then what—"

"It doesn't matter." She placed her finger to his firm lips to silence him. "Please hold me, Travis. I need you to kiss me and make love with me."

He stared at her for several long seconds as if trying to assimilate what she'd said before he took her into his arms. Slowly lowering his head to settle his mouth over hers, Travis kissed her with a thorough tenderness that brought tears to her eyes and curled her toes inside her chic black pumps.

Her pulse sped up and her stomach fluttered with anticipation when he deepened the kiss and she tasted his undeniable hunger for her. As she surrendered herself to the way he was making her feel, every nerve in her body sparked to life and a heavy warmth flowed through her veins, settling into a delicious coil deep in the pit of her belly.

As he teased her with a light stroking touch of his tongue to hers, she was vaguely aware that he'd moved his hands from her back to her waist. But when he slid his palms up over her ribs, her heart skipped several beats and her nipples tightened in anticipation of his gentle caress.

When they'd made love that night in his barn, their joining had been spontaneous and hurried—an unplanned union with the danger of being discovered. But tonight would be different. Although neither of them had intended for the evening to end with their sleeping together, tonight they had time to explore, time for the excitement of discovering what pleased each other. And they were completely alone. There was little or no possibility of anyone interrupting the coming together of two lonely souls in search of a few hours of comfort and companionship in each other's arms.

The exquisite sensations radiating from her breasts when he finally grazed the sensitive tips through her clothes sent liquid fire racing through her veins and caused her knees to wobble. The taste of his passionate kiss and the feel of his gentle touch were both thrilling and, at the same time, extremely frustrating. She wanted to feel his hands on her body without the encumbrance of satin and lace, wanted to experience the excitement of his firm lips and moist tongue savoring her sensitive skin.

"You feel so damn good," he said, raising his head. He drew in a ragged breath as he reached to turn on the bedside lamp. "But it's not enough. I'm a visual kind of guy. I want to see your beautiful body while I'm bringing you pleasure."

Captured by his intense stare, Fin felt as if he could see all the way to her soul and knew the degree of need he was creating within her. "I want to see and touch you, too, Travis."

With nothing more than a promising smile, he pulled the tail of the shirt from the waistband of his jeans, then took her hands in his and guided them to the snap closures. "Taking off each other's clothes was one of the many things we missed getting to do the first time we were together."

Her stomach fluttered with a delightful thrill at the thought of undressing him. "What else did we miss?" she asked as she unfastened the first gripper.

"We didn't get to take our time the way I would have liked," he answered, leaning forward to nibble on her earlobe.

"How long—"

"What I have in mind will take all night, sweetheart."

A shiver streaked up her spine and her fingers didn't seem to want to work as she fumbled with the next snap. "A-anything else?"

The look in his eyes seared her. "I didn't get to kiss you in ways that will make you blush from just thinking about it."

"I—I don't blush easy." Why couldn't she get her voice to work the way it should?

When he whispered what he intended to do, a jolt of pure electrified desire shot to every part of her being and she knew exactly why her vocal cords were freezing up. He was trying to send her into sensual meltdown and doing an excellent job of it.

"Is that what you want, Fin?"

Unable to get words past her suddenly dry throat, she nodded. She wanted everything this wonderful man was willing to give and had every intention of returning the favor in kind.

When she finally managed to unfasten the last snap on his shirt, she parted the chambray to gaze at his perfectly sculpted chest and stomach. A fine dusting of downy, dark blond hair covered sinew made hard from years of strenuous physical labor. She knew several male models who would kill to have Travis's muscle definition. But his perfectly padded pecs and rippling belly were results that no amount of time spent in a gym could accomplish.

"You're magnificent," she said, deciding he definitely had a point about their missing out on several enjoyable steps in the fine art of foreplay.

His low chuckle sent a wave of goose bumps shimmering over her skin. "I've been called a lot of things in my life—most of them pretty unflattering—but this is the first time anyone's ever referred to me as magnificent."

She grinned as she slipped off her shoes. "Trust me on this, darling. Your body is quite remarkable."

"I'll bet it can't hold a candle to yours," he said as he bent to pull off his boots. When he straightened he wrapped his arms around her to pull her against him. "But I'm damned sure going to find out."

His eyes held her captive as she felt his hands begin to gather the fabric of her dress. In no time at all, he pulled the clingy knit up and over her head. Then, reaching behind her, he unhooked her bra and slid the straps from her shoulders. The scrap of lace joined her dress on the floor.

When he stepped back to gaze at her, she hoped that he missed the fact that gravity had affected certain parts of her anatomy and things weren't as pert as they'd been ten years ago. Of course, they hadn't known each other then, so maybe he wouldn't notice that, although still slender and toned, she was approaching forty.

"My God, Fin, you're beautiful." From the appreciative gleam in his eyes, she had no doubt that he meant it.

Feeling more feminine and attractive than she had in a very long time, she pushed his shirt from his impossibly wide shoulders and tossed it on top of the growing pile of their clothing on the plush white carpet. Sparks of heat rushed through her at the speed of light when he pulled her back into his arms, and she had to force herself to breathe at the first contact of sensitive feminine skin meeting hair-roughened male flesh.

"You feel as good as I knew you would," he said, his breathing sounding quite labored.

"So…do…you." He wasn't the only one having trouble catching his breath.

His large hands splaying over her back felt absolutely wonderful and she marveled at how exciting his callused palms felt on her smooth skin. Closing her eyes, she reveled in the tiny tingles skipping through her at his touch. But when he leaned back to kiss the slopes of her breasts, the coil of need deep in her feminine core tightened to an empty ache and she felt as if she would melt into a puddle.

His firm lips nibbled and teased until she thought she would go mad if he didn't take the tightened tip into his mouth. But the moment his mouth closed over her, Fin's knees gave way and she had to grasp his hard biceps to keep from falling into an undignified heap at his feet.

"Easy, sweetheart." His lips grazing her sensitive

nipple as he spoke intensified the sensations racing through her body and she barely managed to suppress a moan from escaping. "We're just getting started."

"You really meant it…when you said our lovemaking would take…all night," she said, struggling to draw air into her lungs.

He raised his head, the promise in his dark blue gaze causing her heart to pound against her ribs. "I'm going to take my time and by tomorrow morning there won't be a single inch of you that I haven't kissed or made love to." His smile sent an arrow of heat straight to the most feminine part of her. "I'm not from New York, Fin. I'm a country boy with country ways. I take my time and don't get in a rush about much of anything. And especially when I'm loving a woman."

The sound of his smooth, steady baritone and the vow she detected in his navy eyes made her insides feel as if they'd turned to warm pudding. "Th-there won't be anything left of me but a pile of ashes," she said, barely recognizing the sultry female voice as her own.

His sexy grin as he guided her hands to his belt buckle increased the heat building inside of her. "Then I guess we'll go up in a blaze of glory together, sweetheart."

Slowly unbuckling the leather strap, Fin concentrated on unfastening the metal button at his waist. She delighted in the shudder that ran through his big body when her fingers brushed the bulge straining against his fly as she reached for the tab of his zipper. But instead of easing the closure open, she decided to treat him to a bit of the sweet torture he'd been putting her through.

"I think I'm going to enjoy this slow, country lovemaking," she said as she leisurely ran her finger along the top of his waistband. She allowed her knuckles to lightly brush his skin and watched his stomach muscles contract in response.

"I don't want you get the wrong idea." He drew in a deep breath. "I swear I'm not trying to hurry things along, but these jeans are getting damned uncomfortable in the stride."

"It does appear that you have a problem in that area," she teased. Taking pity on him, she eased the zipper down. "Does that feel better?"

"Oh, yeah." Brushing her fingers aside, he stepped back and made quick work of removing the denim from his muscular thighs. "You have no idea how painful a pair of jeans can be to a man in my condition."

When he straightened and reached for her, he hooked his thumbs in the elastic just below her waist. "As good as you look in this little scrap of satin, I think you'll look even better out of it," he said as he pulled her bikini panties down.

Her legs trembled and she had to brace her hands on his shoulders to steady herself as she stepped out of them. When she finally found her voice, she reached for the band at the top of his cotton briefs. "By the same token, I think you'll look fantastic out of these."

When she removed the last barrier separating them, her eyes widened and it felt as if the temperature in the room went up several degrees. That night in his barn they'd been in the shadows and there had been little time to pay attention to anything but their hurried coming together. But now she had the opportunity to study his incredible body and the perfection that was Travis Clayton.

His long legs and lean flanks were as well-defined as his upper torso, but it was the sight of his full erection that sent a shiver of anticipation and need straight to the heart of her femininity. He was an impressively built male, heavily aroused and looking at her as if she were the most desirable creature he'd ever seen.

"You may make me out to be a liar, sweetheart," he said, reaching for her.

"Why do you say that?" she asked, feeling as if

she'd go up in flames at the feel of his body touching hers from shoulders to knees.

"I promised you I was going to love you all night, but now I'm not sure that's going to be an option." He shook his head. "Just the sight of you has me hotter than a two-dollar pistol in a skid row pawnshop on Saturday night."

"That makes two of us." Her body quivered at the feel of his hard arousal pressed to her lower stomach. "I feel as if I'm going to go up in flames at any moment."

"I think we'd better take this to bed, while we still have the strength to get there," he said, swinging her up into his arms.

Smiling, Fin draped her arms around his neck. "I could have walked. The bed is only a few feet away."

He gave her a quick kiss and shook his head. "I know. But that would have required me turning loose of you and I didn't want to do that."

His candidness caused her heart to skip a beat. He knew just what to say to make her feel special and cherished. But more than that, she sensed that he really meant what he said. He didn't want to let her go and she didn't want him to.

When they reached the bed, he lowered her enough to pull back the black satin comforter, then placed her gently in the middle of the queen-size mattress. She watched him retrieve something from his jeans, then slide it under the pillow a moment before he stretched out beside her.

He gathered her to him and fused their lips in a kiss that caused her head to spin. She tasted his urgent male hunger and the depth of his passion and marveled at the fact that she was the object of this amazing man's desire.

As he broke the kiss to nibble his way down to her collarbone, Fin drew in a ragged breath. But when he continued to the slope of her breast, then on to the hardened peak, her breath caught. At the first touch of his tongue to her sensitive flesh, she held his head to her and wondered if she'd ever breathe again.

Taking her nipple into his mouth, he gently sucked and teased as he slid his hand down her side, then along her outer thigh. The delicious tension deep inside of her increased to an almost unbearable ache, but when he moved his palm up the inside of her leg to her nest of feminine curls, a jolt of need stronger than she could've ever imagined raced to every fiber of her being.

But nothing could have prepared her for the level of excitement Travis created within her when he parted her soft folds and, with a feather-light touch, stroked the tiny node hidden there. Her heart pounded against her ribs and she moved restlessly against him as wave after wave of intense sensation coursed through her.

Travis was taking her to heights of passion she'd never known existed and she was certain she'd spontaneously combust if he didn't make love to her soon.

"Please, Travis…I can't…take much more."

"What do you need, Fin?"

Driven to distraction by his continued stroking and the feel of his warm, moist lips brushing the puckered tip of her breast as he spoke, she had to concentrate hard on what she needed to tell him. "I need you…to make love to me. Now!"

"But I'm just getting started, sweetheart," he said, stroking her more deeply.

"I'll never…survive."

"Are you sure?"

"Yes."

Reaching down between them, she found him and used her palm to measure his length and the strength of his need for her. When a groan rumbled up from deep in his chest and his big body shuddered against her, she was overcome by a need like nothing she'd ever known.

He caught her hands in his to stop her. "I get the idea, sweetheart."

His breathing was labored as he moved away from her to find the foil packet he'd tucked under the pillow earlier. When he'd arranged their protection, he rose over her to nudge her knees apart and settle himself between her thighs.

"Let's do this together," he said, smiling as he took her hand in his and helped her guide him.

His gaze held hers captive as together they became one and Fin knew she'd never experienced anything quite so sensual or erotic. But as he eased his hips forward and her body stretched to welcome him, she gave herself up to the delicious feeling of their joining and abandoned all other thought.

She watched his jaw tighten as he moved farther into her. "You feel so damn good, sweetheart."

"So do you," she said, wrapping her arms around his broad back and her legs around his slender hips.

When he was buried completely within her, his heated gaze held hers as he set a slow pace of rhythmic thrusts. The weight of his lower body pressed intimately to hers and the exquisite friction of their movements sent tingling sparks skipping over every nerve in her body and in no time she felt the coil in the pit of her stomach tighten to the breaking point.

Holding him to her, Fin fought to prolong the feeling of being one with this amazing man. But all too soon the tension inside of her shattered into a million shards of sensation and she moaned his name as the sweet waves of release coursed through her.

Her satisfaction must have taken him over the edge because a moment later Travis's big body stiffened, then surged into her one final time as he released his essence with a shuddering groan.

As the light of dawn began to creep into the room, Travis lay holding Fin's slight body to his side. After making love again sometime in the middle of night, she'd drifted off. But he'd lain awake, thinking about one of, if not the most, exciting encounters of his life.

When Lauren had been alive, their coming together had been that of two people comfortable with each other. And although their intimacy hadn't been overly passionate, it had been satisfying.

But what he shared with Fin was nothing short of explosive. Her unbridled responses to his lovemaking fueled a fire within him that he'd never imagined possible. Hell, she made him feel more like a randy teenager than a man staring long and hard at fifty.

It was a real shame that with the coming of morning their time together would end. She'd resume her life as the glamorous editor-in-chief of a fashion magazine, while he went back to being a

Colorado rancher, chasing a herd of cattle all over hell's half acre.

When Fin moaned and stirred next to him, he glanced down to find her satiny cheeks had turned ashen and her emerald eyes were clouded by a mist of tears. "What's wrong, sweetheart?"

He watched her close her eyes and swallow hard. "I think...I'm going to...be sick." She'd no sooner gotten the words past her pale lips than she was bolting from the bed and running for the adjoining bathroom.

Following her, he supported her shoulders as she sank to her knees and lost her battle with the nausea. When she finally raised her head to take a breath, he released her long enough to grab a plush terry washcloth from a rack by the shower and dampen it with cool water.

"Th-thank you," she whispered brokenly as he bathed away the beads of perspiration from her forehead and helped her into the robe that had been hanging on the back of the bathroom door.

"Feeling better now?" When she nodded, he helped her to her feet and led her back to bed. "Do you have some seltzer?"

"I think there's some club soda...in the refrigerator behind...the wet bar," she said haltingly.

Quickly pulling on his jeans, Travis hurried into the other room. When he returned to the bedroom, he found her once again paying homage to the porcelain god.

"Do you think it was something you ate that didn't set well?" he asked as he knelt beside her and helped her take a few sips of club soda.

She shrugged her slender shoulders. "I've been queasy a lot lately, but this is the first time I've been sick."

Her words slammed into him like a physical blow and he had to force himself to breathe. "How long has this been going on?"

"I don't know," she said weakly. "Maybe a couple of weeks. I've been meaning to make an appointment with my doctor, but haven't gotten around to it."

His heart raced and a knot began to form in the pit of his stomach. "Have you had a period since you returned from your trip to the Silver Moon?"

As he watched her worry her lower lip between her teeth, he knew the answer even before she managed to get the single word out. "No."

The timing was right and the fact that they'd failed to use any kind of protection that night in his barn left him with only one conclusion. Taking one deep breath, then another, Travis felt light-headed and just a little queasy himself.

"Fin, I think there's a damned good possibility that you're pregnant with my baby."

Four

When the gravity of the situation finally began to settle in, Travis's words were as effective as a dose of smelling salts to Fin's cloudy brain. For the past week, she had purposely denied the telltale symptoms of pregnancy, but it was past time that she faced the facts.

She'd rationalized the occasional light-headedness and morning nausea as the result of stress from the competition and working grueling hours to win. But apparently that wasn't the case. It appeared that history was repeating itself and she was pregnant again after only one incidence of unprotected sex.

"This can't be happening," she moaned, burying her head in her hands. "Not again."

"It's going to be all right, Fin. Until you take a pregnancy test, we won't know for sure," Travis said, his voice gentle as he lifted her to his wide chest and carried her back into the bedroom. When he placed her on the bed, he sat down beside her and took her hands in his. "If you'll tell me where the nearest drug store is located, I'll run out and buy one of those home tests. Once we get the results, we'll know what we're facing and figure out how to handle it."

She raised her gaze to meet his. "We?"

He nodded without so much as a moment's hesitation. "If you are carrying my baby, you're not going to face the music alone. I'll be there with you every step of the way and whatever decisions have to be made, we'll make them together."

His vow to lend his moral support was very much appreciated, but until the stick turned blue, she had every intention of holding out hope that she wasn't pregnant. "Let's get that test kit and find out for certain one way or the other."

Giving Travis her key to let himself back in and directions to a pharmacy close by, she waited until he left before she allowed her tears to fall.

What on earth had she gotten herself into this time? And could the timing have been any worse?

She was in a fierce competition with her family, and especially her twin, Shane, to be named CEO of Elliott Publication Holdings when Patrick retired in a couple of months. Even if *Charisma*'s growth pushed it over the top and she became the clear winner of the contest, she seriously doubted that her self-righteous father would turn over the reins of his magazine empire to the daughter who made a habit of disgracing him with grandchildren born out of wedlock. And although times were different than they'd been twenty-three years ago and it was perfectly acceptable for a single woman to bear and raise her children alone, Patrick was from a different generation. There was no way he'd hand over his precious company to a woman he considered unable to manage her own life.

Her breath caught on a sob and she squeezed her eyes shut as she thought of all she stood to lose. "J-Jessie," she said aloud.

What would this do to her fledgling relationship with her daughter? They'd just found each other. How would Jessica react to the news that her biological mother and adoptive father had been unable to control themselves and now she was going to have a baby brother or sister?

Leaning back against her pillows, Fin tried not to think of the fallout an unplanned pregnancy would cause if what she and Travis suspected was true. The implications were endless and just thinking about them made her temples throb and a heavy feeling of dread fill her chest.

When she heard Travis unlock her apartment door, she sat up and wiped the moisture from her cheeks. She was no longer that frightened fifteen-year-old girl who'd had no recourse but to go along with whatever decision her parents made for her. She was a woman now and no matter what results the test showed, she would handle the situation with dignity, grace and a strength of will that she hadn't possessed twenty-three years ago.

"Is it showing anything yet?" Travis asked as he paced outside of Fin's bathroom door.

The pharmacist he'd talked to had assured him that the pregnancy test kit he purchased was the easiest, most accurate over-the-counter indicator on the market. If the digital display spelled out "pregnant," then he and Fin were going to have a baby together.

His heart thudded in his chest like an out of control jackhammer every time he thought of Fin being pregnant. He never in his wildest imaginings would have thought that at the ripe old age of forty-nine, he'd be anxiously awaiting test results to see if he'd gotten a woman "in trouble."

When he heard the bathroom door open, he stopped pacing. The look on her beautiful face answered his question even before he got the words out. "You're pregnant, aren't you?"

He watched her take several deep breaths as if she needed fortification, then nodding, she walked over to sit on the side of the bed. "It was such a strong positive that it didn't even take the entire amount of time the directions said it would for the results to show up."

Before his knees gave way, he sank down on the mattress beside her, then, putting his arms around her shoulders, he tried to think of something to say. Hell, what could he say? He felt as if he'd just been hit right square between the eyes with a two-by-four.

"I don't know how you feel about all this, but I'm going to keep my baby," she said suddenly. Emphatically.

He shook his head. "I never doubted for a minute that you wouldn't."

She straightened her shoulders and turned to face him. The only indication of her turmoil was the slight trembling of her perfect lips. "Patrick forced me to give up Jessica, but this time I won't let anyone take my child."

Travis could understand why she felt the way she did, given that her parents had made her put

Jessie up for adoption. But the baby was his, too, and he fully intended to be part of his child's life.

Only now wasn't the time to start discussing shared custody. Fin was about as fragile as he'd ever seen a woman and she needed his support. And he'd damned well give her the encouragement she needed or die trying.

"I give you my word that as long as I have breath in my body no one will separate you and the baby," he said gently.

Tears welled up in her pretty emerald eyes. "There's no way I could bear to go through that again, Travis."

"I know, sweetheart, and I promise you won't have to." He pulled her into his arms and held her close. "I'll be right beside you every step of the way and I'll walk through hellfire and back before I let anyone or anything harm you or our baby."

They sat in silence for some time before she pulled from his arms. "If you don't mind, I think I'd like to be alone for a little while."

He could understand her need for a little solitude. A lot had happened in the past hour or so and they both needed time to sort out their feelings.

"Are you going into the office today?" he asked as he rose from the side of the bed.

She shook her head. "My absence is going to

raise a few eyebrows and generate more than a little speculation, but I'll call Cade and have him take over for me today. Aside from the fact that I wouldn't be able to concentrate, I'd like to see my gynecologist as soon as possible. Hopefully, she'll be able to work me into her schedule sometime today."

As she walked him to the door, he shrugged into his coat and picked up his wide-brimmed hat. "Will you be all right on your own or do you want me to go with you to see the doctor?"

"You really meant what you said about being there for me." Her amazed expression and the sound of her voice left little doubt that he'd surprised her.

He caught her gaze with his as he touched her soft cheek with his index finger. "I never say anything that I don't mean, Fin." Giving her a quick kiss, he opened the door. "I'll be back this evening to check on you and see that you're all right."

Stepping out into the hall, he put his hat on and closed the door behind him. The last thing he wanted to do was walk away from her. But they both had a lot to think about and things they needed to do. Fin was going to try to get an appointment with her doctor and he had to call his housekeeper, Spud, to see how the ranch was faring in his absence. Then, after a quick lunch with Jessie, he had to get fitted for that damned monkey suit she was going to make him wear when he walked her down the aisle.

While he stood on the sidewalk waiting for a passing taxi, he couldn't stop thinking about the baby Fin was carrying. He shook his head in total disbelief. Most of his friends back home were becoming grandpas and here he was starting a second family.

When he and Lauren had discovered that she was unable to have children, they'd accepted the fact they would never have a child of their own and started the adoption process. And although Jessie wasn't his biological daughter, she was, and always would be, his little girl. From the moment he'd laid eyes on her bundled up like a little doll in her light pink baby blanket, she'd stolen his heart. He loved her more than life itself and that would never change.

But the baby growing inside of Fin would be his own flesh and blood—a child he never in a million years expected to have. That was going to take some getting used to, especially after all this time. It was also going to take awhile to wrap his mind around the fact that his adopted daughter and his biological child had the same mother.

And if he was struggling to come to grips with it

all, he couldn't even imagine how hard it was for Fin. Within the past couple of months, she'd found her first child and become pregnant by that child's adoptive father with her second child.

Sliding into the backseat of a taxi, he gave the driver the name of his hotel. As an afterthought, he asked, "Would you happen to know where I could order some flowers?"

"My cousin Vinnie's a florist," the man said. "His shop is a block down from your hotel. Tell him that Joe sent you. He'll give you a deal."

"Thanks, I'll do that."

Travis wasn't certain what the protocol was, or even if there was one, for waking up to find that he'd impregnated the woman he'd just spent the most incredible night of his life making love to, but he figured a nice bouquet of flowers surely wouldn't be considered offensive. He not only wanted to show Fin that he meant what he'd said about being supportive, he also wanted her to know how honored he felt that she was giving him a second go-round at fatherhood.

"What the hell's going on, Fin?" Her twin brother, Shane, barged into her apartment as soon as Fin answered the door.

"Good evening to you too, Shane," Fin said dryly.

She wasn't surprised that he stopped by on his way home from work. His apartment was only a few floors up from hers.

When he turned to face her, his expression was filled with concern. "Are you feeling all right?"

"I'm fine."

He frowned. "Then why didn't you come into the office today? I can't remember the last time you took an entire day off and neither can anyone else. Cade and Jessie have no idea what's going on and you have poor Chloe worried sick. She said you were having some problems with dizziness and she's convinced that you've worked yourself into physical exhaustion."

Fin had known that her absence would create a stir, but that couldn't be helped. "Would you like to sit down while you're taking me to task or would you prefer to stand?"

Her question seemed to erase much of the irritation from his handsome face. "Look, I'm sorry if I came across a little strong, but you'll have to admit that missing a day at *Charisma* is completely out of character for you. Especially when we're neck and neck in the competition for CEO."

Fin could understand her twin's confusion. She'd made it clear from the moment Patrick made his announcement about the contest that she had every intention of winning. But several things had changed in the past couple of months and she was having to realign her priorities.

"I appreciate everyone's concern and I truly didn't mean to cause you or anyone else any undue worry, but I had some personal business to attend to."

He cocked one dark eyebrow. "Would you care to elaborate?"

"No."

He looked taken aback. "But—"

"As I told you, it's personal."

She could tell he was more than a little mystified by her lack of details. But as close as she and Shane had always been and as much as they'd always shared, she wasn't about to discuss her pregnancy with him or anyone else. At least, not until she and Travis had the opportunity to talk things over and decide how to spring the news on everyone.

To soften her refusal to explain further, she smiled. "I'm sure there are things about yourself that you keep private, aren't there?"

A slow smile began to spread across his handsome face. "A few."

"Shall we agree to leave the matter alone, then?"

He nodded. "Agreed." As she watched, her brother turned his attention to the beautiful bouquet of two dozen long-stemmed red roses arranged in a crystal vase on top of her coffee table. "Do those have anything to do with the *personal* part of your time off?" he asked, his smile turning to a knowing grin.

Reaching down, she snatched up Travis's card before Shane had the opportunity to pluck it from the plastic pick and read it. "That, dear brother, is none of your business."

The cad threw back his head and laughed. "I'll take that as confirmation that it does."

"Don't you think it's past time that you went on up to your apartment and left me alone?"

"Expecting the sender of those flowers to show up soon, sis?" he teased. Before she could get the words out, he answered his own question. "I know, it's none of my business."

"Give the man a prize," she said, ushering him toward the door.

"All right, I'm going." Opening the door, he stepped out into the hall and turned back to face her. "Then you'll be at the office tomorrow?"

She nodded. "Of course. Where else would I be?"

His grin turn mischievous. "In the arms of whoever sent those flowers?"

"Mind your own business, Shane. And while you're at it, have a nice evening," she said, closing the door behind him.

She'd only made it halfway across the living room before a short knock had her turning back. "What part of 'it's none of your concern' don't you understand?" she asked as she jerked the door open.

"I take it that I'm not who you were expecting to see."

Fin's heart skipped a beat at the sight of Travis. He and Shane couldn't have missed each other by more than a matter of seconds.

"I'm sorry, Travis," she apologized, standing back for him to enter her apartment. "Shane felt it was his duty to give me the third degree about missing work."

He nodded as he removed his hat and coat, then tossing them onto one of the armchairs, he reached out to pull her into his arms. "Yeah, when Jess and I had lunch this afternoon, she said that you'd put Cade in charge for the day and wondered if you'd said anything about not feeling well at supper last night."

It was completely insane, considering the circumstances, but his strong arms surrounding her made her feel secure and more at peace than she could ever remember. "What did you tell her?"

"The truth."

Fearing Jessie's reaction, Fin's voice trembled. "Y-you told her I'm pregnant?"

"No." Stepping back, he kept his arm around her shoulders as he led her over to sit on the couch. "Jess asked if you'd mentioned it over supper, which you didn't. I made it a point not to say anything about knowing that the sickness thing didn't show up until this morning."

Fin breathed a sigh of relief. "I know how close you and Jessie are, but would you mind me telling her about the baby?"

"To be perfectly honest, I'd really like it if you did." He gave her a sheepish grin and hugged her close. "When Jessie was a teenager, one of my biggest fears as a father was that one day she'd tell me some pimple-faced kid had gotten her in trouble."

"Didn't you trust her?" Was Travis more like Patrick than she'd thought?

"Don't get me wrong," he said, shaking his head. "I've always had all the faith in the world in my daughter. It was the teenage boys with more hormones than good sense trying to talk the prettiest girl in the county into climbing in the back of their daddy's pickup truck that gave me nightmares."

Fin couldn't help but smile. "You're a wonderful father, Travis."

He shrugged one broad shoulder. "As hard as it

is to believe, I was a teenage boy once." He chuckled. "Hell, at the age of seventeen, I think I was hard about seventy-five percent of the time. And if the truth is known, I probably caused more than a few dads some sleepless nights myself."

If he was even half as good-looking in his youth as he was now, she could imagine that he had worried several girls' fathers. "I suppose it is rather ironic that the very thing you feared for Jessie has happened to you now."

He put some space between them in order to face her. "I know this was the last thing we expected to have happen and you have every right to blame me for not protecting you that night in the barn, but I've spent the day thinking about it." He ran his hand through his thick hair. "Hell, I haven't been able to think of anything else."

"Me, either," she said, reaching up to cup his face in her palm. "But I don't want you to think that I'm assigning blame or that I regret what's happened."

"You don't?"

"Not at all." Placing her hand on her still flat stomach, she smiled. "This is a second chance for me. I missed out on so much when I was forced to put Jessie up for adoption. I never got to see her take her first step or hear her say her first word."

"Horsey."

"Excuse me?"

His grin widened. "'Horsey' was the first thing she said."

Fin laughed. "Why doesn't that surprise me? She's always talking about her horse, Oscar."

"He loves her just as much as she loves him." Laughing, Travis shook his head. "I've never seen a horse mope around like he's on his last leg for weeks at a time, then perk up like a new colt the minute she comes home for a visit."

Uncharacteristic tears filled Fin's eyes and she cursed her hormones for making her so darned emotional. "Thank you for giving her such a wonderful childhood, Travis."

When he wiped a tear from her cheek with the pad of his thumb, her skin tingled from the contact and a warmth began to fill her chest. "Thank *you* for having her," he said, his voice sounding a little gruff. "I know that putting her up for adoption was the hardest thing you've ever had to do, but raising Jess and watching her grow up was the best thing that's ever happened to me. I wouldn't have had that if not for you."

"That's why having this baby is so important to me," she said, nodding. "I'm going to get to be a part of this baby's life the way I never was with Jessie."

She could tell by the look in his sky-blue eyes that he understood, but she noticed an underlying shadow of concern there as well. Anticipating what bothered him, she rushed to alleviate his fears. "I want you to be part of his or her life, too. You're the baby's father and I would never deny you your child."

The doubt disappeared immediately and she could tell he was relieved to hear that she wasn't going to cut him out of the picture. "How are we going to handle this? With you living here in New York and me living in Colorado, it's going to take some work."

"I'm not sure," she said honestly. "But we have eight months to discuss it and make plans."

"With Jessie and Cade's wedding coming up, the next couple of weeks are going to be pretty busy." He drew her into his arms, then leaned back against the couch. "What do you say we postpone any serious discussion until after the ceremony? That will give us a little time to think about it and see what we can come up with."

"That sounds like an excellent idea. And in the meantime, I'll find a way to break the news to Jessie." Snuggling against his shoulder, she hid a yawn behind her hand. "How do you think she'll react?"

His wide chest rose and fell a moment before he tightened his arms around her. "Your guess is as good as mine, sweetheart."

Five

Fin stared at the young woman seated across from her at the dining room table and wondered how on earth she was going to broach the subject of her pregnancy. To say she was a nervous wreck was an understatement.

She and Travis had hoped she'd have the chance to talk to Jessie before he left to go back to Colorado. Unfortunately, with the approaching wedding and all the last-minute details to pull together, there hadn't been enough time.

But when she learned that Cade was flying to the west coast for a few days to wrap up a lucrative advertising deal for *Charisma* the week before the wedding, Fin seized the opportunity and asked Jessie to have dinner with her.

"Fin, our relationship means a lot to me and I want it to continue to grow," Jessie said without preamble. Fin watched her lay her fork down and catch her lower lip between her teeth as if trying to gather her courage. Then, taking a deep breath, she asked, "Have I upset or offended you in any way?"

Her daughter's question was the last thing Fin expected and she hurried to put Jessie's mind at ease. "No, honey. You haven't done anything." She covered Jessie's hand with hers. "I know we've missed out on so much over the years, but you're still my daughter. I love you. You could never do anything that would change that."

"Thank God."

The relief on Jessie's face tore at Fin's heart. She hated that she'd caused her daughter any undue worry. But she wasn't sure how long the euphoria would last once Jessie learned about Fin's pregnancy and who the father was.

"You haven't been yourself since I canceled dinner with you and Dad last week." Jessie gave her a guilty smile. "I thought you might have been angry with me for trying to set you up with Dad."

Fin's heart beat double-time. This was her opening. She just hoped her announcement didn't cause irreparable damage to Jessie's feelings for her.

"I need to talk to you about that." Fin folded her napkin and placed it on the table, then rose to her feet and motioned toward the living room. "Let's get comfortable."

Jessie suddenly looked apprehensive. "You're beginning to frighten me, Fin."

As she led the way over to the sofa, Fin shook her head. "There's absolutely no reason for you to be afraid, honey." I, on the other hand, have every reason to be scared to death, she thought, dreading what she was about to tell her daughter.

Once they were curled into opposite corners of the plush sofa, facing each other, Fin took a deep breath. "If I've been a bit distracted lately, it's because something has happened—"

"Are you all right?" Jessie interrupted anxiously.

"I'm fine, sweetie." Fin hoped her smile was reassuring, but she was so nervous, she couldn't be sure. "In fact, when I saw the doctor last week, she said I'm in perfect health."

"Then what's the problem?" Jessie asked, clearly confused.

"It's not a problem as far as I'm concerned." Fin couldn't help but smile. "It was a shock at first, but

I've had time to get used to the idea and I'm actually quite happy about it." Taking a deep breath, she met her daughter's curious gaze head-on. "I'm pregnant."

Jessie's eyes widened and she covered her mouth with her hands as she let loose with a delighted little cry. "Fin, that's wonderful." She shook her head. "I didn't even know you were involved with anyone."

"I'm not…exactly." The next part of her announcement was what Fin had dreaded most—telling Jessie who the father was. "Travis is the father."

Jessie's mouth dropped open and she stared at Fin for several long seconds. "My dad? Your baby's father is my dad? My dad, Travis? Travis Clayton?"

Fin nodded slowly. She couldn't tell if Jessie kept repeating Travis's name out of shock or revulsion.

"It was that night at the Silver Moon, wasn't it?" Jessie guessed, her expression giving nothing away. "The two of you left the party to go into the barn to check on that mare and new colt."

Nodding, Fin tried to explain. "I gave Travis a hug to show my appreciation for raising and taking such good care of you and…it just happened."

"This is wonderful," Jessie said suddenly, leaping forward to throw her arms around Fin. "I suspected that something was going on between the two of you." Leaning back, she beamed. "I could see the attraction from the moment you met."

"You're not upset?" Fin asked cautiously as she hugged her back.

Jessie shook her head and sat back to give her an encouraging smile. "I'll admit that it's a huge shock, but I'm thrilled for both of you. I know how much you missed getting to see me grow up and Dad is the best father, ever. This baby is extremely lucky to have the two of you for parents."

Relief washed through Fin at Jessie's emphatic tone, leaving her feeling weak and emotional. "I'm so glad to hear you aren't upset."

"Why would I be upset? I'm ecstatic that I'm finally going to have a sibling," Jessie said, grinning from ear to ear. "And I'll bet Dad is excited beyond words." She stopped suddenly. "You have told him, haven't you?"

Fin nodded. "I discovered that I'm pregnant last week, while he was in town visiting and getting the last fitting for his tux." She purposely omitted they were together when she'd taken the pregnancy test and the fact that they'd spent the night before making love.

"I wonder why Dad hasn't said anything."

"I asked him to let me tell you about the baby because if our predicament upset you, I wanted the brunt of your anger directed at me," Fin explained. "I thought if I took the majority of the blame it would keep from damaging your relationship with your father."

Jessie reached out and took Fin's hands in hers. "That is so sweet of you. But I'm in no way upset by this." She grinned. "Far from it."

Fin felt as if a huge weight had been lifted from her shoulders. "You don't know how many times I've wanted to talk to you about this, but there was never a good time."

"Everything has been so busy with the wedding and all, I'm surprised we were able to find time to have dinner this evening," Jessie agreed, nodding. "Have you told anyone else?"

"No. We felt that you should be the first to know."

"I know I'm just full of questions," Jessie said, her expression turning serious, "but have you made any decisions about how you're going to raise the baby? Are you going to try to share the responsibility?"

"It's only fair that we do." Fin sighed. "But I have no idea how we're going to work this out."

"You have *Charisma* and I can't see Dad leaving the Silver Moon to move to New York," Jessie said, shaking her head.

"We're going to review our options while he's

here for the wedding and hopefully come up with a workable plan." Smiling, Fin reached out to hug her beautiful, understanding daughter. "Keep your fingers crossed that we find a solution and that when we make the announcement about my impending motherhood the rest of the family is as enthusiastic as we are."

Tears filled Fin's eyes as she watched Travis, looking incredibly handsome in his black tux, escort their beautiful daughter down the sweeping staircase at The Tides. Jessie was utterly stunning in her pure white satin-and-lace wedding gown and if the captivated look on Cade's face was any indication, the groom thought so, too.

Glancing over at her mother and Patrick, Fin was thankful they'd welcomed their long-lost granddaughter back into the Elliott clan and insisted the wedding be held at their estate in the Hamptons. All things considered, it was the very least they could do for Jessie.

When Travis walked his daughter down the aisle between the rows of chairs assembled in the large living room, Fin's heart went out to him as he kissed Jessie's cheek, then stepped back for Cade to take his place beside her. It had to be one of the most difficult things Travis had ever had to do—placing the care and happiness of his beloved child in the hands of someone else.

"That was tough," he whispered, his voice gruff as he sat in the seat beside her to watch Jessie and Cade exchange vows.

Unable to get words past the lump clogging her throat, Fin reached over to give his hand a gentle squeeze. She wasn't at all surprised when he held onto it as the ceremony proceeded.

By the time Jessie and Cade had been pronounced husband and wife and everyone started making their way to the heated tent that had been adjoined to the family room to accommodate the reception, Fin needed a few moments alone to collect herself. "If you'll excuse me, Travis, I think I need to freshen my makeup."

"I could use a couple of minutes myself," he said, his need for solitude reflected in his tight expression and the gruff tone of his voice. "If you don't mind, I think I'll step outside to catch my breath."

"I'll see you a bit later," she said, kissing his lean cheek.

As she stood watching Travis walk to the front door, she couldn't help but wonder what it felt like to have a father who loved his child as much as Travis loved Jessie. She'd never had that, never known what it was to have a father who loved unconditionally. Placing her hand over her stomach, she knew her baby was extremely lucky to have Travis for his or her father.

"Fin, are you feeling well? I noticed you look a bit pale."

At the sound of the soft Irish lilt beside her, Fin glanced over at Maeve Elliott. "Mom, could we speak in private?" she asked, deciding there was no time like the present to tell her mother about the baby.

A look of alarm widened Maeve's soft green eyes and Fin knew her mother anticipated bad news. "Of course, dear." Leading the way into the library, she closed the door behind them. "What is it, Finola? What's wrong?" The use of Fin's given name was an indication of the level of Maeve's concern.

"There's nothing wrong," Fin said, placing her hand on her mother's arm to reassure her. "Actually, everything is the way it should be for the first time in twenty-three years."

The worry lines creasing her mother's kind face softened into a smile and she gathered Fin into her arms. "'Tis the way I feel, too, Finny."

Fin held onto her mother for several moments before she led her over to the tall leather armchairs facing the fireplace. "Please sit down, Mom. I have something I need to tell you." When they were both seated in the comfortable chairs, Fin met her mother's questioning gaze. "I'm pregnant. I'm going to have a baby with Jessie's adoptive father, Travis."

Maeve stared at her a moment before covering her eyes and breaking into soft sobs.

A feeling of déjà vu swept over Fin. Her mother's reaction was much the same as it had been the night Fin had told her she was pregnant with Jessie. The only difference between then and now was that Patrick wasn't present for this announcement.

"I had hoped you would be happy for me this time," Fin said, sighing heavily. "But it appears that I've once again disappointed you."

"Oh, no, Finny." Her mother reached out to take Fin's hands in hers. "My tears are those of joy. You never got to hold Jessie, to watch her grow into a beautiful young woman. 'Tis past time that you got to hold and raise a wee babe of your own."

"I should have been allowed to raise Jessie." Try as she might, Fin couldn't keep her bitter tears in check. "Why, Mom? Why didn't you stop Patrick from forcing me to give my baby away? You of all people should have known what it felt like to lose your child. To have her taken away without being able to…stop it from happening." Struggling to control her voice, she shook her head. "Didn't you feel as if your heart had been ripped from your chest when Anna died?"

The emotional pain that clouded Maeve's eyes tore at Fin's heart. She hadn't meant to mention her sister. It had to have been devastating for her mother to lose a seven-year-old child to cancer, but what Fin said was true. Maeve should have known what it would be like for Fin to have her baby taken from her with no say in the matter.

"Oh, Finny, 'tis sorry I am that you had to go through that," Maeve said, her Irish accent becoming more pronounced, as it always did when she was upset or overly emotional. Wiping her tears with a linen handkerchief, she shook her head. "'Twas a sad day for this family and one I have regretted all these years since."

"Then why did you let Patrick do that to me? Couldn't you have stopped him?"

Her mother shook her head. "I did try. But your da wouldn't listen and when it became a threat to our marriage, I backed down."

"You and Patrick had problems because of my situation?" It was the first Fin had heard of it if they had.

Maeve nodded. "Your da is a stubborn man. He put his pride ahead of what was right for you and this family."

"I never knew." Fin had always thought her mother supported every decision Patrick made. "The two of you always presented a united front and I thought you let him force me to give up my child without lifting a finger to help me."

"'Twasn't for you to know," Maeve said, smiling sadly. "What happens between a husband and wife behind closed doors is no one's affair but their own."

"I'm so sorry, Mom." Letting go of the last traces of her misguided anger at her mother, Fin knelt down and put her arms around Maeve's thin shoulders. "I know how much you've always loved Patrick. It must have torn you apart to be caught in the middle of all that."

"'Tis done and past." Her mother soothingly stroked Fin's hair. "Since we are all gathered for Jessie's wedding, I think you should tell the family about the wee one you carry," she said softly as they continued to embrace.

Leaning back, Fin shook her head. "I don't think it's the right time. This is Jessie's day and I don't want to cause a scene or detract from her happiness in any way."

"Does she know?"

Fin nodded. "I didn't want her to hear it from someone else."

"Was she happy for you and her da?"

"She's thrilled."

"'Tis rare when we all gather at the same time." Smiling, Maeve rose to her feet, then tugged on Fin's hand for her to stand. "We should celebrate a new babe on the way, as well as a wedding."

Fin tried to swallow her apprehension. "I don't want Patrick ruining this day for Jessie because of me."

Maeve shook her head. "You needn't worry, Finny. Your da is different now."

"Since when?"

"Give him a chance," Maeve said, her smile encouraging.

As they walked out of the library and down the hall, Fin found Travis standing by the staircase. She needed to warn him about her mother's request, as well as find Jessie and Cade and see if they had any objections to her announcing her pregnancy.

"We'll join the reception in a moment, Mom," Fin said, waiting until Maeve disappeared down the hall before she turned to Travis. "Since everyone is here, my mother thinks we should tell the family about the baby," she said, careful to keep her voice low. "Are you okay with that?"

He nodded. "I'm fine with it. The question is, how do you feel about it?"

"I'm not sure," she said truthfully. "I couldn't be

more excited and I want to tell everyone how happy I am that I've been given a second chance at motherhood. But at the same time, I'm apprehensive about Patrick's reaction. I don't want him putting a damper on Jessie and Cade's big day."

Travis shook his head. "He won't."

"You don't know Patrick Elliott the way I do." She sighed. "And thank your lucky stars you don't."

"He's all about appearances, isn't he?"

"That's *all* he's about," she said, unable to keep the disgust from her voice.

Nodding, Travis smiled. "Then don't you think he'll keep his mouth shut to keep from airing the family laundry in front of all these people?"

The more she thought about it, the more she realized that Travis was right. Not all of the guests were family. And Patrick would never dream of saying anything in front of outsiders that would throw the family in what he perceived to be a bad light.

"You might have a point."

Touching her elbow, he guided her toward the happy sounds coming from the direction of the reception. "Let's find Jess and Cade and clear it with them."

"I want you to promise me you'll let me know if this yahoo doesn't treat you right," Travis said as he and Jessie moved around the dance floor during the father-daughter dance. "I'll hop the first plane east and by the time I'm done with him, there won't be enough of him left to snore."

"Oh, Dad, you're such a cowboy," Jessie said, laughing and hugging him close.

He hugged her back. "I just want you to be happy, angel."

"The only thing that would make me happier would be if Mom was here," she said softly.

Time had eased his loss, but he hated that Lauren couldn't have been here to see their little girl on her special day. "Your mom would have been right in the middle of all this fuss and loving every minute of it."

A tear slipped down Jessie's cheek. "I know."

They were silent for a moment before he asked, "Are you and Cade sure you're all right with Fin letting the family know about the baby here at the reception?"

She nodded. "I think this is the perfect time. In fact, if you don't mind, I'd like to have the honor of telling everyone. Do you think Fin would mind?"

"To tell the truth, I think she'd be relieved that someone else let the cat out the bag." Travis glanced over at the Elliott patriarch. "She's dreading the head honcho's reaction."

"I can't imagine Fin being afraid of anything," Jessie said, frowning.

"I don't think it's a matter of her being frightened as much as it is a case of nerves," he corrected. "She just wants this day to be perfect for you and Cade." He chuckled. "I have a feeling if old moneybags over there gets his drawers in a wad, she'll take into him like a she-bear protecting her cub."

Jessie smiled fondly. "That's so sweet of her." She paused for a moment. "I don't think Granddad will say a single word after I make the announcement. You just stick close to Fin. I'm sure she could use all the moral support she can get."

Travis had no idea what Jess had planned, but she had a good head on her shoulders. He trusted her judgment and if she said she could spring the news and keep Elliott from raising a ruckus, he had no doubt she could do it.

"All right, angel. This is your day. Do what you think is best."

When the dance ended, Travis kissed her cheek and, stepping back for Cade to take his place, walked over to sit at the table with Fin and Shane. "Jessie's going to take care of telling everyone the big secret," he said close to Fin's ear. "Any objections?"

She shook her head and her silky auburn hair

brushing her creamy shoulders fascinated the hell out of him. "I don't mind, but when is she going to do it?"

"Your guess is as good as mine." He covered her hand where it rested on the white linen tablecloth. "But if I know Jess, it won't be long."

He'd no sooner gotten the words out than Jessie and Cade walked over to one of the band's microphones. "If I could have your attention, my wife has an announcement to make," Cade said, giving Jessie a look that left Travis with no worries about how much he adored her.

When all eyes turned her way and the room fell silent, Jessie gazed lovingly at the man standing beside her. "This is one of the happiest days of our lives and Cade and I would like to thank you all for helping us celebrate our marriage." Turning her attention toward the table where Travis sat with Fin, she smiled. "I would also like to announce that we have another reason to celebrate. My dream of being a big sister is finally going to come true. Fin and my dad have just learned they're going to give me a brother or sister in the summer."

The stunned silence that followed was suddenly interrupted by a round of applause and Travis found himself and Fin besieged by a herd of well-wishing Elliotts. As Fin's brothers, their wives and what seemed like an endless line of nieces and nephews congratulated them, he couldn't help but notice that Fin's gaze kept returning to the tall, silent, white-haired gentleman standing as stiff and straight as a marble statue on the opposite side of the room.

It appeared that Patrick Elliott was none too happy about the news, even though his wife, Maeve, looked just the opposite. As Travis watched, Maeve said something to Patrick, then took the old gent by the arm and led him toward the crowd congratulating them. Putting his arm around Fin's shoulders, Travis drew her close as he met the older man's steely gaze head on, sending a clear message that Travis wasn't going to tolerate Fin being bullied or upset in any way.

When the elder Elliott approached, it was like watching the parting of the Red Sea. The family divided into two groups, and just as Travis imagined happened thousands of years ago, a hushed silence reigned. Not even the smallest child present made a sound.

"A wee babe is a grand event and we welcome another addition to the family," Maeve said, breaking the uncomfortable silence.

Stepping forward, Fin smiled and hugged her mother. "Thank you, Mom."

The crowd seemed to wait for Patrick to add his

blessings, but it never came. The man remained as stoic as ever.

Although Fin's expression never changed, Travis could have sworn he saw a shadow of pain in her pretty green eyes. But it was gone in a flash, replaced with a defiance that matched her father's.

The uneasy silence was almost deafening and just when Travis thought they'd all pass out from holding their collective breath, Maeve turned to her husband. "'Tis time you told them why you put them at odds to win the company, don't you think?"

A frown creased the man's forehead as he shook his head. "Leave it be, Maeve," Patrick said gruffly. "They'll understand soon enough." And with that, the Elliott patriarch tucked his wife's hand in his arm, turned and walked away.

"Don't let the old man get you down, sis," Shane said, hugging her.

Fin didn't look the least bit surprised by her father's reaction. "I expected nothing less from him," she said, shaking her head as she hugged her twin brother in return.

As the crowd began to recede and the band commenced playing, Travis noticed a young blond-haired woman slip up beside Shane. When she whispered something in his ear, the man let out a whoop loud enough to wake the dead, then wrapped her in a bear hug and, grinning like an old possum, swung her around in a circle.

When everyone stopped to stare at them, Travis had to choke back his laughter at the red flush creeping up from Shane's collar all the way to his forehead. The little blonde beside him was just as embarrassed and looked as if she were ready to dive under the table at any moment.

"Travis Clayton, this is Rachel Adler, Shane's executive assistant," Fin said, grinning as she made the introductions.

"It was nice to meet you, Mr. Clayton," Rachel said, her cheeks still bright red. "If you'll all excuse me, I need to be going now. I'll see you at the office on Monday, Shane."

As they watched Rachel hurry to the family room door, Fin turned to her brother. "Would you care to explain that emotional display and the huge grin on your face?"

"No."

"You want to know what I think?" Fin asked.

"No, I don't care what you think," Shane said defensively.

"Tough." As she winked at Travis, her smile caused a warmth to spread throughout his chest and he didn't think he'd ever seen her look more beautiful. "I'm going to tell you anyway, dear brother."

Shane frowned. "I'd rather you didn't."

"I don't know what Rachel told you, but I think you're to the point where you'd use any excuse to finally have her in your arms," Fin said, clearly ignoring her brother.

"You, dear sister, need to shut up and mind your own business," Shane said irritably as he turned to walk away.

"You just confirmed my suspicions, Shane," Fin called after him.

For reasons he didn't even want to begin to analyze, her delightful laughter had a strange effect on Travis's insides. "Let's dance," he said suddenly, taking her by the hand to lead her out onto the dance floor.

"I thought Jessie mentioned one time that you didn't like dancing," she said, sounding a little breathless as he pulled her to him.

"I don't." He smiled at the shiver he felt course through her when he whispered, "Your brother isn't the only man here who'll use whatever excuse he can find to have the most beautiful woman in the room in his arms."

Six

"I don't think I've ever seen a more lovely couple," Fin said, settling into the back of the EPH corporate limo for the ride back to the city. She sighed happily. "Jessie was absolutely stunning."

"She looked just like you," Travis said, reaching over to take her hand in his.

"A much younger version, maybe," she said, laughing.

His smile heated her all the way to her toes. "I don't think I had the chance to tell you how sexy you look in that slinky green dress." He lightly touched the teal silk of her Versace gown with his index finger. "You and Jessie were the two most beautiful women at the wedding."

"Well, you clean up pretty good yourself, cowboy." She placed her hand on the arm of his black tuxedo. "You look incredibly handsome in formal attire, Travis."

He grunted. "I feel like a trained monkey in a side show."

"I think you're a very handsome monkey," she said, laughing.

"Well, take a good look because I won't be wearing this thing again," he said, putting his arm around her shoulders. "I'll take it home and hang it in the closet, never to see the light of day again."

"Never say never."

"I think this is one time it's a sure bet to say never." His arm tightening around her to draw her close and his low chuckle caused every cell in her body to tingle to life. "A jackass will sprout wings and fly before you see me in this thing again."

As they left the lights of The Tides behind and the intimacy of the night closed in around them, Travis reached over and pushed the button to raise the privacy panel between them and the driver. "How are you doing?" he asked. "I know today was an emotional roller coaster for you and you have to be drained."

"I probably should be, but surprisingly I'm

feeling pretty good." Slipping off her high heels in an effort to get comfortable for the two-hour drive, she added, "Now that my pregnancy is no longer a secret, I'm more relaxed than ever."

When he gathered her close, a wave of goose bumps shimmered over her arms at the feel of his warm breath stirring the fine hairs at her temple. "I told you your dad wouldn't say anything."

"There wasn't a lot he could say after Jessie made her little speech." Touched beyond words at the enthusiasm and support her daughter had shown for her pregnancy, Fin smiled. "She's going to be a wonderful big sister."

"She'll have the poor little thing spoiled rotten."

"And you won't?"

He chuckled beneath her ear and tightened his arms around her. "I didn't say I wouldn't."

They rode along in a comfortable silence for several minutes before Travis spoke again. "Have you come to any conclusions about how we can handle your pregnancy and the distance between us?"

"With all of the last-minute details for the wedding, I haven't had time." She shook her head. "What about you? Have you come up with anything?"

"No, but we're going to have to figure out something." He touched her chin with his index finger to tilt her head back. When their gazes met, he gave her a smile that had her toes curling into the thick carpet on the limo floor. "This is all pretty new for me, but when I told you I'd be there with you every step of the way, I meant it. And I wasn't just talking about raising the baby once it gets here. I intend to be there for you through the pregnancy, as well."

Before she could respond, he lowered his head and captured her lips in a kiss so gentle it brought tears to her eyes. The soft caress of his mouth as it moved over hers had her quickly feeling as if the temperature in the car had gone up several degrees. But when he coaxed her to part for him and used his tongue to mimic a more intimate mating, a spark ignited deep in her soul and the heat flowing through her veins spread throughout her body.

Sparkles of light danced behind her closed eyes and a longing began to build in the most feminine part of her when he slipped his hand inside the plunging neckline of her evening gown and pushed the built-in cup aside to caress her breast. The work-hardened calluses on his palm chafed her sensitive nipple, sending tingling streaks of pure delight to every cell of her being. But when he traced the puckered tip with his thumb, her heart skipped several beats and her breathing became extremely difficult.

As he gently rolled the peak between his thumb and forefinger, he continued to tease her inner recesses with his tongue and her insides quivered with need like nothing she'd ever known. Heaven help her, but she couldn't have stopped a tiny moan of pleasure from escaping if her life depended on it.

"Does that feel good, sweetheart?" His smooth baritone vibrated against her lips and fed the pool of desire gathering in her lower belly.

"Mmm."

Lifting her to sit on his lap, she felt the hard ridge of his erection against her thigh, and her own body's answering need left her feeling light-headed from its intensity. The tension building inside of her was maddening and she wanted nothing more than to surrender herself once again to Travis's masterful brand of lovemaking.

His groan of frustration penetrated the sensual haze surrounding her when he tried to shift them into a more comfortable position. "It's been a long time since I made out in the backseat of a car, sweetheart." He eased her back to sit beside him on the limo's plush velour seat. "And for what I want to do to you, we'll need more room than there is in the backseat of this damned limousine."

"When are you leaving to return to Colorado?" she asked breathlessly.

"Tomorrow afternoon." He kissed his way to the hollow at the base of her throat. "Spend the night with me, Fin," he said, nibbling at her wildly fluttering pulse.

If she'd stopped to think about it, she might have thought of all the reasons they should back away from whatever was going on between them. Even though they were going to have a baby together, he lived thousands of miles away on his quiet, charming ranch in Colorado and her life was in the most exciting, glamorous city in the world.

But without a second thought, she snuggled against the most incredible, giving man she'd ever met. "Your bed or mine?"

"Why the hell can't these places have regular metal keys?" Travis muttered as he fitted the little plastic card into the lock on his hotel room door.

The ride from the Hamptons to the hotel had been the longest trip of his life. Coupled with the fact that he and Fin hadn't been able to keep their hands off of each other, he was hotter than a blast furnace in the middle of an August heat wave. And Fin wasn't much better off. Her porcelain cheeks wore the blush of unfulfilled passion and he didn't think she'd ever looked sexier or more desirable.

When the tiny light on the lock finally flashed to

green, he pushed the door open and quickly ushered her inside. The door had barely swung shut before he had the light switched on and reached to pull her back into his arms.

"You know what I've discovered about these designer dresses?" he asked as he slid the back zipper down below her waist.

"What's that?" she asked, sounding as winded as he felt.

"They're designed to drive a man out of his mind with lust."

Peeling the dress from Fin's luscious upper body, he took her into his arms as the evening gown floated down to form a green pool of silk around her trim ankles. As he pressed kisses across her collar-bone, then down the creamy slope of her breast, he could have cared less that he'd just sent thousands of dollars worth of dress to lie in a tangled heap on the floor.

She shivered against him when he took her pebbled coral nipple into his mouth. Tasting her sweetness, feeling the nub tighten further, he felt his lower body harden to an almost painful state.

"You're driving me insane," she said, sagging against him.

"I'm right there with you, honey." He drew in a ragged breath. "Let's get out of the rest of these glad rags before I do something stupid and rip them off of both of us."

Fin's laughter sent a shock wave of heat coursing through him at the speed of light. "At the moment, I think you're the only one with an over abundance of clothing, Mr. Clayton."

Glancing down, he grinned at the sight of her standing before him in nothing but a little triangle of lace and silk. The dress Fin had been wearing not only had a built-in bra, it had some kind of underskirt, as well. He wasn't sure who came up with the idea of combining women's undergarments with a dress, but he'd bet his last dime that men all over the world were singing their praises.

"I think you might have a real good point there, Ms. Elliott." Tugging his shirt from the waistband of his trousers, he could have cheerfully throttled whoever thought it would be better to use studs instead of buttons on formal wear.

"Let me help you with those," she said, stepping forward.

To his relief, within no time Fin was pushing the shirt apart to place her hands on his chest. At the first contact of her soft palms on his flesh, it felt as if a bolt of lightning shot from the top of his head to the soles of his feet.

Jerking as if he'd been zapped by a cattle prod,

he shook his head and backed away from her. "I think I'd better take care of getting undressed or else the race will be over before this old horse leaves the starting gate."

"That wouldn't be good," she said, kicking out of her high heels and reaching for the elastic band that held the tiny patch of lace material covering the apex of her thighs.

When Fin tossed her panties on top of her dress, then slid beneath the covers of the king-size bed, he swallowed hard and did his best to concentrate on getting himself out of his clothes. By the time he crawled in beside her, he was breathing as if he'd run a marathon and he was pretty sure he'd just set some kind of speed record for disrobing.

As he put his arms around her and settled his mouth over hers, her eager response sent blood surging through his veins and his arousal was so intense it made him feel light-headed. He needed her with a hunger that robbed him of breath and he wanted nothing more than to join their bodies in the age-old dance of love. But what shocked him down to the core was his deep desire to join their souls—to make her his in every way.

It should have been enough to scare the living hell out of him. But the feel of her soft body pressed to his and the taste of her sweet lips as she returned his kiss made rational thought all but impossible.

As he continued to kiss her, he felt her hands slide down his chest as if she were trying to map every individual muscle. But when her fingers touched his puckered nipple, Travis broke the kiss as he struggled for his next breath. Falling back against the pillow, he clenched his back teeth together so hard he figured it would take a crowbar to pry them apart as he tried to slow his runaway libido.

"Does that feel as good to you as it does for me when you touch me like this, darling?" Fin asked.

"Oh yeah." The blood rushing through his veins caused his ears to ring and sent a flash fire straight to his groin.

If he'd had the presence of mind, he would have stopped her before things went any further, but her hands on his body felt so damned good he didn't even consider it. Then, when her hand drifted lower to trace the narrow line of hair that arrowed down to his navel and beyond, he couldn't for the life of him force words past his suddenly dry throat.

But as her talented little fingers closed around him to measure his length and girth, then teased the softness below, he felt as if his head might just fly right off his shoulders and he had to concentrate hard on maintaining what little control he had left. A wave of need stronger than anything he could ever imagine threatened to swamp him and when he finally found the strength, he caught her hands in his to stop her tender assault.

"Honey, I don't want you thinking that I don't like what you're doing because believe me, I sure as hell do." His voice sounded like a rusty gate hinge and he had to clear his throat before he could finish. "But I'm hotter than a young bull in a pen full of heifers and I'm not going to last any longer than a June frost if we don't slow down."

Wrapping her arms around him, she smiled. "I love your quaint country sayings, even if I don't always understand them."

He laughed, releasing some of the tension that held him in its grip. "One of these days, we'll have to sit down and I'll give you a crash course in cowboy lingo. But right now I have other, more pleasurable activities in mind."

With his hormones better under control, Travis lowered his head to kiss her at the same time he parted her legs with his knee and moved over her. He'd wanted to go slow, wanted their lovemaking to last. But the two-hour ride back to the city in the limo had taken its toll. By the time they'd arrived at his hotel, he and Fin were both aroused to the point of no return and taking things slow wasn't an option.

He gazed down at the woman in his arms, the woman who was carrying his child. He didn't think he'd seen a more beautiful sight than the passion glazing her emerald eyes and the soft, welcoming smile curving her lips. "Show me where you want me, Fin."

The blush of desire painting her porcelain cheeks deepened as without a word she reached down and guided him to her.

As he eased into her and her supple body took him in, his chest swelled with an emotion he wasn't ready to identify. He felt as if he'd found the other half of himself, the part he'd been missing since the death of his wife. Trying not to think about it, or what it could mean, he set a slow pace and concentrated on bringing them both the satisfaction they needed.

The feel of her surrounding him and the motion of their bodies as they rocked in perfect unison had them racing toward completion. All too soon, he felt Fin's feminine inner muscles tighten around him a moment before she found her release.

Determined to ensure her ultimate pleasure before he found his own, he thrust into her deeply and watched her eyes widen a moment before she came apart in his arms. Gathering her to him, he let go of his rapidly slipping control to join her. His body shuddered as he gave up his essence and he was certain he felt fireworks light up the darkest corners of his soul.

His breathing harsh, Travis closed his eyes and buried his face in the cloud of her dark auburn hair. He had no idea where they would go from here or how they would work out raising the child they'd created together. But he knew as surely as he knew his own name, he was going to do everything in his power to find the right answers.

And if he had his way, he'd not only be a part of the baby's life, he'd be a big part of Fin's life as well.

The following Friday afternoon, Fin sat in her office listening to Chloe fill her in on the current projections from the accounting department and the latest EPH gossip. She was normally interested in anything that could help her push *Charisma* over the top and make her the new CEO when Patrick retired. But for the past few weeks, she'd been thinking less about her fashion magazine and more about a tall, ruggedly handsome cowboy from the wilds of Colorado.

When they'd parted ways the morning after Jessie and Cade's wedding, they still hadn't arrived at any conclusions concerning the distance separating them or how they were going to handle it during her pregnancy and after the birth. In fact, they hadn't even discussed it after he'd kissed her in the back of the limo.

Her body tingled to life from just the memory of his masterful kisses, but it was the thought of their lovemaking that quickly had her insides feeling as if they'd turned to warm pudding. Their coming together might have started out as two lonely people finding comfort and physical release in each other's arms, but somewhere along the way it had changed into something far deeper, far more meaningful.

It was completely insane, considering they had nothing whatsoever in common except for the baby she carried and their love for Jessie. But Fin hadn't been able to think of anything but Travis's request that she come out to Colorado for a visit as soon as possible. And what surprised her more than anything was that she desperately wanted to go.

"Fin, have you heard a word of what I just told you?" Chloe asked. Her assistant's tone drew Fin back to the present.

"I'm sorry, I guess I was daydreaming," she apologized. She needed to get a grip on herself or she could kiss winning Patrick's contest goodbye. "What were you saying?"

Chloe's exasperated expression indicated that Fin had missed something the young woman had thought was extremely significant. "I said that you still have a good chance of beating out Shane for the CEO position." Chloe's expression changed to one of excitement. "Word around the accounting department water cooler is that *Charisma*'s numbers have closed the gap and at the rate we're going, we'll pull ahead of *The Buzz* just before the deadline."

"Really?"

A month ago, Chloe's information would have been the best news Fin could have received. It would have sent her into overdrive to make it happen and she had no doubt that it would have. But now?

She wasn't sure whether her lack of enthusiasm was due to her pregnancy and the fact that the job of CEO would keep her from devoting as much attention to her child as she knew she would want to do, or if it was the discovery that since Travis returned to his ranch, she'd been more lonely than ever before. But either way, it was clear that her priorities had changed and she was no longer as driven to be named Patrick's successor as she once had been.

"Fin, what's wrong with you?" Chloe asked, clearly confused. "I thought you'd be doing the happy dance over the news."

Smiling at her executive assistant, Fin shrugged. "I am quite pleased to hear that *Charisma* is doing so well. And I hope with all my heart that we win."

"But?"

"That's it." Fin handed a stack of ad copy to the woman and motioned toward the door. "Put these on Cade's desk with a note for him to look over them as soon as he and Jessie return from their honeymoon."

She could understand Chloe's confusion as she scooped up the stack of papers and quietly left Fin's office. But that couldn't be helped. Fin wasn't about to reveal to her executive assistant, or anyone else for that matter, that she was just the same as conceding the race for CEO to Shane.

With her decision made, she swiveled her chair to gaze out at the western side of the Manhattan skyline. She really would like to win the competition, but not because she coveted Patrick's title. If *Charisma* did pull ahead of *The Buzz*, she had every intention of declining the position. But winning would certainly prove to Patrick that she wasn't quite the disappointing failure he'd always thought her to be.

Quite content with herself for the first time in years, she relaxed and thought about her lack of plans for the weekend. Her OB/GYN had advised that getting the proper amount of rest was essential to the health and well-being of both her and the baby. And for the past week, she had cut back on the hours she spent at the office. But the thought of rattling around in her huge apartment by herself for the entire weekend was extremely unappealing.

Nibbling on her lower lip, she wondered how Travis intended to spend the time. He had told her that he hoped she planned to visit the Silver Moon at her earliest convenience.

She turned her chair to face the desk, then typed a quick search into her computer. When the information she wanted appeared on the screen, she reached for the phone and dialed the number for the airlines.

When the booking agent answered, Fin's heart skipped a beat and she couldn't believe the level of excitement coursing through her as she made her request. "I need to reserve a first-class seat on the first available flight from New York to Denver, Colorado, please."

Seven

Parking his truck in short-term parking at the Denver airport, Travis impatiently checked his watch as he started walking toward the terminal. He'd been tied up in a traffic jam on the interstate while the authorities cleared away a fender bender and the longer he'd had to sit there, the more he'd realized how much he'd missed Fin since leaving New York.

It didn't matter that it had only been a few days since he'd said goodbye to her at his hotel the morning after Jessie's wedding or that they barely knew each other. It felt as if it had been an eternity since he'd seen her. And when she'd called this morning to see if he had plans for the weekend, he hadn't been able to tell her fast enough that he didn't.

He refused to think about why he was so anxious to be with her again or why he'd been as irritable as a grizzly with a sore paw since his return. All that mattered was the three days they'd have together on his remote ranch. Alone.

As soon as his housekeeper, Spud Jenkins, heard that Fin was on her way, he'd suddenly remembered that he had plans to visit his brother's family down in Santa Fe. Travis knew the old geezer had made up the excuse. Spud and his brother had been on the outs for well over twenty years. But Travis hadn't bothered to point that out to the old cowboy.

The truth was, he needed time alone with Fin to figure out what was going on between them. And he wasn't just thinking about how they were going to manage his role in her pregnancy and, later on, the raising of their child.

When he entered the baggage claim area, he spotted Fin immediately as she waited for her luggage to tumble out of a chute and onto the revolving carousel. Damn, but she looked good in a pair of jeans and that oversized tan sweater.

It was the first time he'd seen her in anything but dress clothes or formal wear and he wasn't the least bit surprised that he found her attractive in more casual attire. Hell, it didn't matter what she wore, she knocked his socks off every time he saw her.

Dodging a couple of teenagers with battered backpacks and an older woman pulling a suitcase big enough to hide a body in, he walked over to wrap his arms around Fin and lift her to him. He kissed her like a soldier returning from war and when he finally set her on her feet, they were both left gasping for some much-needed air.

"I don't remember you greeting me like this the first time I came for a visit," she said, her voice sounding breathless and sexy as hell.

He felt like a damned fool, but for the life of him he couldn't stop grinning. "We didn't have a history then, sweetheart."

She laughed as she reached for a medium-sized bag that had just come down the chute. "Your definition of history is knowing each other for a month?"

Shrugging, he reached down to take hold of the luggage before she could lift it from the carousel. "If you want to get technical, what happened yesterday is history."

As they walked through the terminal, her sweet smile sent his blood pressure up a good fifty points. "I suppose you have a point."

When they reached the automatic doors at the

exit, he shook his head. "Wait here out of the cold, while I get my truck."

"You don't have to do that," she said, taking a step forward. "I don't mind walking. I'm used to walking a lot and I'm sure it's not that far."

"It's pretty cold out there and you're not used to the altitude." He dug his truck keys from the front pocket of his jeans. "It might not be good for you or the baby."

She looked at him as if he might not be the brightest bulb in the chandelier. "Travis, being pregnant isn't a disability."

"I know that." Planting a kiss on her forehead, he smiled and shook his head. "But you're in my neck of the woods now, honey. And if I want to be a gentleman and take care of you while you're here, I'll damned well do it."

Fin snuggled into the crook of Travis's arm as they sat on the leather sofa in front of a blazing fire in the big stone fireplace in his living room. She loved the cozy feel of the Silver Moon ranch house. From the rich wood and leather furniture to the colorful Native American accents, it was warm, inviting and felt exactly the way a home was supposed to feel. Something her apartment was sorely lacking.

When she returned to New York, the first thing

she intended to do was call an interior designer to have her apartment redecorated. The ultramodern, museum look wasn't in the least bit child-friendly and she wanted a comfortable, relaxed place like the Silver Moon ranch house for her baby to call home.

"I'll give you a quarter for your thoughts," he said, resting his head against hers.

"I thought that was supposed to be a penny for your thoughts," she said, feeling more relaxed and at peace than she could ever remember.

"Inflation, sweetheart." He drew her a little closer and kissed the top of her head. "I've heard that even the tooth fairy is having to pay a buck a tooth these days."

She leaned back to look up at him. "What was the going rate when Jessie was growing up?"

"Fifty cents." His smile made her tingle all the way to her bare toes. "At least it was until she learned the fine art of negotiation."

"You're kidding."

"Nope." Chuckling, he shook his head. "One time, when I went to get her tooth from beneath her pillow and leave a couple of quarters, I found a note for the tooth fairy."

Curious to hear more about what Jessie had been like as a child, Fin asked, "What did the note say?"

"Something to the effect that since it was a little

farther back in her mouth and because she used it for chewing, she thought it was worth at least seventy-five cents."

Laughing, Fin shook her head. "She didn't."

"She sure did." He grinned. "The tooth fairy laughed so hard, he damned near woke her up."

"Did she get the seventy-five cents?"

"No, that tooth netted her a cool five bucks." He shook his head. "I figured the note alone was worth that much."

"You're a wonderful father," Fin said when they stopped laughing.

He shrugged, but she could tell from the sparkle in his incredible blue eyes that her comment pleased him. "I did what I thought was best." He kissed her cheek and placed his hand over her stomach. "The same as I'll do with this baby."

Emotion filled Fin's chest and she had to swallow around the huge lump that formed in her throat. "I'm so glad you're my baby's father."

His tender smile increased the tightness in her chest. "*Our* baby. Remember, we're in this together, Fin."

She couldn't keep a lone tear from sliding down her cheek. "Thank you."

He looked taken aback. "For what?"

Reaching up to cup his lean cheek with her hand, she smiled. "For being you."

Her stomach fluttered with anticipation at the slow, promising smile curving his firm male lips. He was going to kiss her and, if the look in his intense gaze was any indication, more.

When his mouth covered hers, Fin surrendered herself to the moment and the overwhelming sense of belonging that she'd come to associate with being in Travis's strong arms. Never in her entire existence had she felt more wanted or cherished than she did when he held her, made love to her.

It didn't seem to matter that they'd only known each other a short time or that they had very little in common. She'd never felt anything as right or as real as she did when she was with him.

Her heart pounded hard against her ribs. Was she falling in love with him?

She really didn't have a lot of experience at being in love, so she wasn't certain how it was supposed to feel. She'd been positive that she loved Jessie's young father, Sebastian Deveraux. But that had been a long time ago and she suspected every fifteen-year-old girl was convinced that she loved her first boyfriend. Unfortunately, in the years since, she'd concentrated all of her energy toward building her career instead of personal relationships and she had nothing else to compare to the way she felt about Travis now.

As his lips moved over hers, coaxing her to open for him, encouraging her to respond, she abandoned all speculation and gave herself up to the delicious sensations beginning to course through her. She could analyze her feelings once she'd returned to New York.

When he slipped inside to tease her inner recesses, sparkles of light danced behind her closed eyes. But as he stroked her tongue with his it felt as if a starburst lit the darkest corners of her soul. The hunger of his kiss, the taste of his passion, sent heat surging through her veins and made every cell in her body tingle to life.

Shivers of delight slid up her spine when she felt his hand slip beneath the bottom of her sweater to caress her abdomen, then come to rest just below her breast. Restless anticipation filled her when he paused his exploration long enough to unfasten the front clasp of her bra. She needed to feel his hands caressing her, wanted his moist kisses on her sensitive skin.

The hard muscles of his arms suddenly bunched as he lifted her, then stretched them both out on the long couch. She reveled in the rapid beating of his heart and the hard ridge of his arousal against her thigh where their legs tangled, but when he created a space between them to cover her breast with his large palm, her own pulse began to race and a moist heat began to gather at the apex of her thighs.

Needing to touch him as he touched her, she unsnapped his chambray shirt to trace the steely sinew of his broad chest and abdomen. The light sprinkling of hair covering the thick pads of his pectoral muscles tickled her palms and she marveled at the exquisite differences between a woman and a man. But when she traced his flat male nipple with the tip of her finger, the tiny nub's puckered reaction was much the same as when he touched her breasts.

His groan of pleasure thrilled her and as she continued to memorize every ridge and valley, she decided Travis's body was perfect in every way. Taut and unyielding, his muscles held a latent strength that belied his gentle touch and contrasted perfectly with the softer contours of hers.

"There isn't enough room on this damned couch to kiss and taste you the way I'd like," he said, nibbling the hollow beneath her ear.

His low drawl and the promise of his words sent quivers of excitement shimmering through her. "It is rather restrictive, isn't it?"

"Damn straight." He sat up, then pulled her up

beside him. "Let's find a place with more room to move."

"That looks inviting," she said, eyeing the colorful Native American rug on the floor in front of them. She shrugged one shoulder at his questioning expression. "I've never made love in front of a fireplace."

A slow smile began to appear on his handsome face as he glanced at the rug, then back at her. "It does look fairly comfortable, doesn't it?"

Before she had the chance to agree with his observation, he was easing them onto their knees on the floor. "I'm going to love the way your body looks in the glow from the fire," he said, switching off the lamp at the end of the couch.

With nothing but the muted light from the fire, the room suddenly became incredibly intimate, and as his smoldering gaze held her captive, he slipped his hands beneath her sweater to slowly push it upward. Raising her arms to help him slip it over her head and toss it aside, she slid the straps of her bra down her arms and handed it to him. His sharp intake of breath and the darkening of his blue eyes, made her insides quiver and her breathing grow shallow.

"I've dreamed of you like this every night since that evening in your apartment." His deep baritone, rough with passion, and his appreciative look sent a honeyed warmth flowing through her veins.

Pushing his opened shirt off his broad shoulders and down his muscular arms, she smiled as she dropped the garment on top of her clothing. "And I've dreamed of you." She placed her hands on his chest. "I've wanted to touch you like this again."

He cupped her face with his hands and kissed her deeply, letting her taste a hungry need that matched her own. "I intend to touch and taste every inch of you, sweetheart. And when I'm finished, I intend to start all over again."

As he nibbled his way down her neck to her shoulder, then her collarbone, Fin's head fell back as she lost herself to the delicious sensation of having his lips on her skin. But when his hot mouth closed over her tightened nipple and he flicked the bud with his tongue, she trembled from the waves of pleasure flowing through her and the empty ache of need beginning to form deep in her lower region.

By the time he finally lifted his head, she felt as if she'd melt into a wanton puddle at any moment. "This isn't fair. I want to kiss you like this, too."

"What do you say we get the rest of these clothes off?" he asked, standing up, then helping her to her feet.

Once he'd finished stripping both of them and

they knelt facing each other on the rug in front of the fire, he took her into his arms. The feel of skin against skin, his male hardness pressed to her female softness, sent tiny currents of electrified desire to every part of her.

"You feel so damned good," he said roughly.

Delightful shivers of excitement coursed through her at the passion in his voice. "I was just thinking the same thing about you."

The sultry quality of her voice amazed her. She'd never thought of herself as a sensual creature, but with Travis it seemed all things were possible.

When he lowered them to the rug and gazed down at her, the heated need and the promise of complete fulfillment she saw in his eyes sent hot, dizzying desire flowing to the most feminine part of her. As his mouth covered hers and he slipped his tongue between her lips the pulsing ache in her lower belly increased and she gasped from the intensity of it.

But when he trailed kisses down to the valley between her breasts, then beyond, her breath caught. Surely he wasn't going to…

"T-Travis?"

Raising his head, he gave her a look that caused her heart to skip several beats. "Do you trust me, Fin?"

Incapable of speech, she could only nod. No other man had ever made love to her the way Travis was doing now and heaven help her she never wanted it to end.

As his lips blazed a trail down her abdomen, she closed her eyes and tried her best to remember to breathe as wave after wave of heated pleasure washed over her. But when he gave her the most intimate kiss a man could give a woman, the sensations threatened to consume her.

"P-please…I can't stand…much more."

He must have realized the depth of her hunger, because he moved to gather her to him, and gazing down at her, tenderly covered her lips with his. His callused palm smoothed over her skin with such infinite care, it brought tears to her eyes and she felt branded by his touch.

Her body trembled with longing as he slid his hand down her side to caress her hip, then her inner thigh. But when he cupped the curls at the apex and his finger dipped into the moist folds to stroke and tease, spirals of sheer ecstasy swirled through her. The feelings were so intense, she couldn't have stopped her body's reaction if her life depended on it.

Arching into his touch, she fought for sanity as waves of excitement flowed through her. "P-please—"

"Does that feel good, sweetheart?" His low whisper close to her ear only added to the sweet tension gripping her.

"I…need…you."

In answer to her broken plea, he spread her thighs with his knee and rose over her. She felt the tip of his strong arousal against her, but instead of joining their bodies, he commanded, "Open your eyes, Fin."

The blaze of need in his dark blue gaze took her breath. He was holding himself in check as he slowly, gently pressed forward to fill her completely. He remained perfectly still for several long seconds and she instinctively knew he was savoring the moment, savoring her.

When he pulled his lower body away from hers, then thrust forward, time stood still. He set a slow, rhythmic pace that built her excitement faster than she'd ever dreamed possible. The heat spiraling throughout her body burned higher and brighter with each stroke and she wrapped her arms around his broad back to keep from being lost.

But all too soon, the delicious tension inside of her let go and wave after wave of fulfillment washed over her. Her moan of satisfaction faded to a helpless whimper as her body relaxed and she slowly drifted back to reality.

Only then did she hear Travis groan, then felt

him shutter as the spasms of his release overtook him. When he buried his face in the side of her neck and collapsed on top of her, Fin tightened her arms around him, holding him to her in an effort to prolong the feeling of oneness she had with this wonderful man.

As his breathing eased and he levered himself up on his elbows, he gently brushed a strand of hair from her cheek. “Are you all right?”

Smiling, she cupped his strong jaw with her palm. “That was, without a doubt, the most incredible experience of my life.”

His low chuckle as he rolled to her side and gathered her to him sent a fresh wave of heat coursing through her. “If I have my way, it’s just the first of many incredible experiences we’re going to have this weekend.”

A shiver of delight streaked up her spine. “I’m going to hold you to that, cowboy.”

“I’d rather have you hold *me* to *you*,” he said, brushing her lips with his. “And while you’re holding me, we’re going to have another one of those incredible experiences.”

She felt his body stir against her thigh and her own body answered with a delicious tightening in the pit of her stomach. Wrapping her arms around his shoulders, she smiled. “I’m holding you against me.”

His promising grin caused her heart to race. "Honey, I'm about to amaze both of us."

And to her delight, he did just that.

Holding Fin as she slept, Travis stared at the ceiling above his bed and tried to figure out what was going to become of them. They were treading in an area that could very well spell disaster for all concerned.

If it was just between the two of them, the stakes wouldn't be nearly as high. They could explore what was happening between them and if it didn't work out, they could go their separate ways with a minimum of fuss.

But it wasn't just the two of them. There was Jessie and the baby to think about. Whatever happened between him and Fin affected them as well.

Fin had told him up front that she wasn't good at relationships and he'd told her the truth when he'd said he wasn't looking for one. And he hadn't been.

After his wife died, he'd been sure that he'd never care for another woman the way he had for Lauren. But he was beginning to think that he might have been a little hasty in that assumption.

From the minute he'd laid eyes on Fin, he'd been drawn to her like a bee to honey. And apparently, it had been the same for her with him. Her first visit to the ranch was proof of that. They hadn't been able to keep their hands off of each other. But was great lovemaking enough of a base for a long-term relationship?

The way he saw it, they only had three things in common—Jessie, the baby Fin was carrying and an insatiable need for each other. Other than that, their lives were about as different as night and day.

He was country from his wide-brimmed Resistol hat to the soles of his Justin boots. His life was hard, grueling hours of work spent outside in all kinds of weather, and at night he slept with nothing to listen to but the crickets and an occasional coyote howling off in the distance. And he was much more comfortable in a honky-tonk where the music was loud, the beer was cheap and wearing a new pair of jeans and a clean shirt from the local Wal-Mart was considered dressed up than he'd ever be putting on a suit to go to a Broadway production or some trendy nightclub.

And as foreign as his life was to Fin, her life was just as foreign to him. She lived and worked in a city that never slept. Hell, how could it? With taxis honking and sirens blaring all the time, it was no wonder people were up around the clock. And that was just the tip of the iceberg.

Day in and day out, she worked in a climate-controlled office where the only time she felt the warmth of the sun on her face was when she stood close to the window, and every piece of clothing she owned had some famous designer's name stitched into the label. Even the jeans she'd been wearing at the ranch had some guy's name plastered across the back pocket.

When Fin stirred in her sleep, he tightened his arms around her and pressed a kiss to the top of her head. On her first visit to the Silver Moon, she'd mentioned that she loved the wide open space, but after a while the novelty would wear off and she'd go stir-crazy from missing the hustle and bustle of New York. He had no doubt, he'd be just as unhappy if he had to live in a crowded city.

As he felt sleep finally begin to overtake him, Travis closed his eyes and wondered how they were possibly going to share the raising of a child. Kids needed stability and permanence, not being bounced back and forth between two entirely different worlds.

As he drifted off with no more answers than he'd had before, his dreams were filled with images of sharing his life on the Silver Moon with a green-eyed, auburn-haired woman and child.

Eight

"What do I do first?"

Smiling, Travis handed Fin the keys to the old truck he used for hauling hay. "Put the key in the ignition and your right foot on the brake."

"That's simple enough," she said, doing as he instructed. "What's next?"

Fin's pleased expression caused his chest to tighten. He couldn't get over how excited she was at the prospect of learning to drive and he wouldn't have missed teaching her for anything in the world.

"Turn the key toward the dashboard. When you hear it start, let go of the key."

When the truck's engine fired up, she beamed. "I can't believe I'm actually going to do this."

"I think that's what you said last night when we—"

"You have a one-track mind, cowboy," she interrupted, laughing.

Feeling younger than he had in years, he grinned. "It's incredible, as well as amazing, wouldn't you agree?"

"Your mind or last night?"

"Both."

When she took her foot off the brake, the engine died. "What happened?"

He gave her a kiss that left them both needing resuscitation and when he finally raised his head, she gave him a look that was supposed to be stern, but only made her look more adorable. At least, to him.

"Back to business, cowboy. You're supposed to be teaching me how to drive."

"You have to keep your foot on the brake until you put it in gear or the engine will die."

She frowned. "This is going to start getting complicated, isn't it?"

"Not at all. Before you know it, it'll be second nature to you." He pointed to the ignition. "Put your foot back on the brake, start it up and take hold of the gearshift. Then, without taking your foot off the brake, pull the shift slightly forward and then down until the little indicator on the dash lights up the 'D'."

"Done," she said, looking more confident as she followed his directions.

"You're doing great. Now lightly step on the gas feed." He'd no sooner gotten the words out than she stomped on the gas and the truck shot forward at what seemed like the speed of light.

"This is fun."

"Holy hell!" They spoke at the same time.

It had been ten years since he'd taken Jess out in the same pasture for her first driving lesson, but he remembered it as if it were yesterday. They'd raced across the field and barely missed running off into a small pond.

As the truck bounced across the pasture, Travis tightened his shoulder harness. It seemed that mother and daughter were similar in more ways than just their looks. They both had a foot made of pure lead.

"You might want to take your foot off the front bumper and slow down a little, honey," he said, pulling his hat down tight on his head. He felt like he had in his younger days when he'd ridden broncs in the local rodeo.

When she eased off the gas a bit, Travis breathed

a little easier. The pond had been filled in a few years ago, and even though the pasture was wide open and there was nothing Fin could crash into, he was still glad the horses were safe in their stalls in the barn.

"I should have learned to drive years ago," she said, her cheeks flushed with excitement. "This is a lot more fun than having a driver take me where I want to go."

"I've created a monster," he groaned. His stomach clenched into a tight knot just thinking about her trying to drive in New York City traffic. "You aren't thinking about getting a license and a car, are you?"

"Hardly. There isn't enough room in the city for all the cars now. And parking is an absolute nightmare." She gave him an indulgent look. "I'll limit my driving to the Silver Moon and this pasture."

His heart stalled, then took off at a gallop. She was talking as if she'd be visiting the ranch quite frequently and that pleased him to no end.

"That makes me feel somewhat better," he said when she turned the truck in a tight circle and headed back the way they'd come. As they barreled toward the barn, he decided the horses might not be as safe as he'd first thought. "When you put your foot on the brake, give yourself plenty of room. These things don't stop on a dime."

Apparently, she took him at his word because in the next instant, Fin planted her foot on the brake and the truck skidded to a bone-jarring halt. "I suppose there's a trick to making a smooth stop," she said, frowning.

Reaching over to the steering column, he turned off the key and put the truck in Park. "We'll work on that the next time," he said, thanking the good Lord above for whoever invented antilock brakes.

She surprised him when she unbuckled her shoulder harness, then leaned over and wrapped her arms around his neck. "Thank you, Travis."

"For what?"

"I'm learning all kinds of incredible things this weekend," she said, giving him a smile that sent his temperature skyward.

He grinned as he pulled her close. "Is that so?"

The impish sparkle in her emerald eyes as she nodded fascinated him. "Some of what I learned was particularly amazing."

Lowering his head, he kissed her soundly. "What do you say we go back to the house for a while?"

"Did you have something in mind?" Her whispered words in his ear had him harder than hell in about two seconds flat.

Nodding, he unbuckled the shoulder harness, got out of the truck and walked around the front to slide in behind the steering wheel. "I want to show you something."

She grinned. "Is it incredible?"

He started the truck and, putting it into gear, laughed as he drove toward the house. "Honey, prepare yourself to be downright amazed."

"Have you given any thought to our situation?" Fin asked as she and Travis prepared dinner together. She was supposed to return to New York tomorrow morning and they still hadn't discussed anything about the baby, let alone made a decision.

"A little, but I haven't come to any conclusions," he said, tending to a couple of breaded steaks he was frying in a big cast-iron skillet.

"Me, either." Cutting up vegetables for a garden salad, she thoughtfully nibbled on a sliver of carrot. "I think it's only fair that we have equal time with her."

"Or him." Travis gave her a grin that sent her pulse racing. "There's a fifty percent chance the baby is a boy."

"True."

She turned back to the task at hand before her hormones diverted her attention from the subject. It seemed that with nothing more than a look or a touch, she and Travis gave in to the electrifying passion between them and found themselves in each other's arms.

Slicing a cucumber, she arranged the circles on top of a bed of lettuce. "I don't think we'll have much of a problem with equal time until he or she reaches school age."

He chuckled. "You're ahead of me. I can't think past how I'm going to juggle being in New York for your visits to the obstetrician and here, too." He arranged the steaks on two plates, then spooned milk gravy over the tops. "It gets real busy around here in the spring and summer."

"What's it like here in the spring?"

She loved hearing Travis talk about the ranch. From everything she'd seen and heard, it had to be one of the most tranquil places on earth.

"After the snow melts, everything is green." He smiled. "Then, when the wildflowers start to bloom, there's all kinds of colors mixed in."

"It sounds absolutely beautiful."

He nodded. "With the snowcapped mountains in the distance it looks a lot like the postcards they sell at the tourist places over in Colorado Springs."

"I'd love to see it," she said, unable to keep the wistful tone from her voice.

When he slipped his arms around her waist from behind, she leaned back against his solid frame. "If you'd like, after the baby comes, I'll take you on a trail ride up to some of the upland meadows."

Turning to face him, Fin put her arms around his shoulders, raised up on her tiptoes and kissed his cheek. "I'd love that, Travis. But I still haven't learned to ride a horse."

"And you're not going to until after the baby's born." He shook his head. "I'm not willing to take the chance of you falling. It might cause you to lose the little guy."

It was completely ridiculous, but his statement caused her heart to squeeze painfully. She knew this would be his only biological child, and therefore as important to him as it was to her. But was the baby the only one he was worried about?

It was an undeniable fact that they were extremely attracted to each other physically. That was the reason they found themselves in their current set of circumstances. But was that as far as it went for him? Was the baby the only one he cared for? And why was she suddenly obsessing over it now?

"Honey, are you all right?"

"I'm a little tired." She stepped back from his embrace. "If you don't mind, I think I'll skip dinner and lay down for a nap."

Fin could tell her sudden mood swing confused him, but that couldn't be helped. She needed time to think, time to sort through her feelings and try to understand why it was suddenly so important that the baby wasn't his only concern.

Wanting to get away from him before she did something stupid like burst into tears, she hurried down the hall and started up the stairs. But she suddenly had the strange sensation of flying a moment before she landed in a heap on the hardwood floor.

As she lay there wondering what on earth had happened, a sharp pain knifed through her left side, taking her breath, causing her to draw her legs into a fetal position. Her pulse thundered in her ears and as the room began a sickening spin, she felt herself being drawn into a fathomless black abyss.

She thought she heard Travis call her name, but the beckoning shadows refused to release her. As she gave in to the mist closing around her, her last thought was of losing the baby she wanted so desperately and the man she'd come to love.

Seated in the waiting area at the emergency room, Travis was about two seconds away from tearing the hospital apart if somebody didn't tell him something, and damned quick, about Fin's condition. When he'd brought her in for treatment, they'd run him out of the examining room and he hadn't been allowed back in there since.

He let out a frustrated breath and scrubbed his hands over his face. When he'd heard the loud thump in the living room, followed by an eerie silence, his heart felt as if it had dropped to his boot tops. He'd called her name as he started down the hall to see what happened, but at the sight of her crumpled body lying at the bottom of the stairs the blood in his veins had turned to ice water and he was pretty sure it had taken a good ten years off his life.

"Mr. Clayton?"

When he looked up, a woman in a white lab coat stood at the swinging double doors leading to the treatment area. Jumping to his feet, he walked over to her. "What's going on?"

"I'm Doctor Santos, the on-call OB/GYN," she said, shaking his hand.

"Is Fin going to be all right?" he demanded. If she lost the baby, he'd mourn. But if it came down to her life or the baby's, there was no choice. He wanted the best care humanly possible for Fin.

Smiling, the doctor nodded. "Ms. Elliott cracked a rib when she fell, but I think she and the baby will both be fine. She's healthy and the pregnancy seems to be a normal one, so I don't foresee any problems."

"Thank God." The degree of relief he felt was staggering and his knees wobbled as if they'd turned to rubber.

"She'll need to be on bed rest for the next few days and I wouldn't advise traveling for a couple of weeks. But after that, if she doesn't experience any more problems, she should be able to resume normal activities." The woman scribbled something on the chart she held, then she looked up and her brown-eyed gaze met his. "And it would be best to refrain from sexual intercourse until she goes back for her next prenatal check."

"Can I see her?" he asked, anxious to see with his own eyes that Fin was okay.

"She's getting dressed now," Dr. Santos said, turning to go back through the swinging doors. "You might want to go get your truck and bring it around to the patient pick-up area."

He frowned. "You're sending her home? Shouldn't you keep her for observation or something?"

It wasn't that he didn't want to take Fin back to the ranch. He did. But he wanted the best care possible for her.

"Relax, Mr. Clayton." The woman's dark eyes twinkled. "Believe me, she'll get a lot more rest at home than she would here. And of course, bring her back if she experiences any further problems."

Five minutes later, when he parked outside of the doors designated for discharged patients, a nurse pushed Fin in a wheelchair out to the truck. Once he had her comfortably settled on the bench seat, he slid in behind the steering wheel and started the thirty-mile drive back to the Silver Moon.

"Did the doctor tell you that I'm going to have to extend my stay with you?"

Fin's voice sounded weak and shaky and it just about tore him apart. She was one of the strongest women he'd ever met and it took a lot to bring her down. But he had a feeling that she was shaken more by the thought that she could have lost the baby than from physical pain.

"I wouldn't mind if you wanted to spend the rest of your pregnancy on the Silver Moon," he said, taking her hand in his.

She gave him a tired smile. "That would be nice, but I need to get back to the magazine."

Her words were like a sucker punch to his gut and a definite wake-up call for him. Of course, she'd want to get back to that damned magazine and the contest for CEO of her dad's publishing company. Jess had told him that Fin lived and breathed *Charisma*. She was the first one in the office in the morning and the last one to go home at night.

He'd lost a lot of sleep speculating on whether

anything could ever come of the attraction between them. It looked as if he'd just gotten the answer.

"Ooh. That doesn't feel good at all," Fin said, holding her side as she rose to her feet and took a tentative step toward the dresser. She'd known that moving around was going to hurt, but she hadn't realized how much.

Sitting on the side of Travis's bed for the past several minutes, she'd been trying to work up the courage to walk over and get her purse. She'd needed to call the office and talk to Cade. He was going to have to assume her duties for the next two weeks and keep *Charisma* on track to win Patrick's contest. Even though she had no intention of accepting the position, she wanted to win and prove to Patrick, once and for all, that his daughter wasn't a complete disappointment.

"What the hell do you think you're doing?"

Travis's booming voice made her jump and the movement jarred her sore ribs, causing them to hurt more. "I need my cell phone."

"Why didn't you ask me to get it for you?" Placing the bed tray he carried on top of the dresser, he helped her back to bed. "Is it in your purse?"

"Yes." As she reclined against a mountain of pillows, she took shallow breaths until the ache in her side receded. "I need to call the office and have Cade take over for me until I get back."

He handed her the purse. "Isn't this his and Jessie's first day back from the honeymoon?"

Nodding, she dug around in the bottom of the bag for her cell phone. "What a thing to come home to. He's still basking in the glow of being a newlywed and I'm going to tell him he has to put his nose to the grindstone and not look up until I get back."

Travis chuckled. "Jess might not take too kindly to that, either."

"I can almost guarantee that she'll stay at the office with him." Laughing, she held her side. "Even laughing hurts."

His teasing expression changed immediately. "Are you sure you're all right? No other signs that something else could be wrong?"

"None," she said, shaking her head. She concentrated on the phone in her hand so he wouldn't see the disappointment she felt at his concern for her pregnancy and not her.

She could feel his eyes watching her for several long moments before he finally cleared his throat and hooked his thumb over his shoulder toward the dresser. "I'll take your breakfast back to the kitchen and keep it warm for you. Let me know when you get off the phone and I'll bring it back up."

"Thank you," she mouthed as Chloe answered on the other end of the line.

While her assistant went through the spiel of which office she'd reached and whom she was speaking to, Fin watched Travis glance her way once more as he carried the tray from the room. She could tell he wasn't happy that she was conducting business instead of resting, but he was wisely keeping quiet about it.

"Chloe, it's Fin," she said, interrupting the young woman.

"Where are you? Why aren't you here at the office? Is everything okay?" The rapid-fire questions were typical Chloe.

Smiling, Fin answered, "I decided to take a weekend trip to Colorado."

"Ooh, you went to see Jessie's father, the cowboy, didn't you?"

"Yes." She listened for a moment as Chloe gushed about how handsome Travis was and how thrilled she was to hear about the baby before Fin interrupted. "Is Cade in his office?"

"He and Jessie arrived an hour ago, disappeared into his office and they haven't been seen since." Chloe giggled. "You know how newlyweds are."

Fin winced. She hated having to be the one to break up their bliss, but this was a business call. She needed to speak to him as his boss, not his new mother-in-law.

"Transfer this call to his office."

"When are you coming back, Fin?" There was an excited edge to Chloe's voice and Fin could tell her assistant had something she wanted to share.

"Probably not for a couple of weeks."

Chloe gasped. "You're kidding, right?"

"Unfortunately, no." Pinching the skin over the bridge of her nose, she tried to ward off the tension headache that threatened. "Now, ring Cade's office for me." She'd put just enough firmness in her voice to let Chloe know that the social part of her call was over.

"Cade McMann." From the slight echo, Fin could tell that he was using the speakerphone.

"Cade, it's Fin. I have something I need you to do."

"Do you need me to come down to your office?" he asked.

Fin sighed. "It wouldn't do you any good. I'm in Colorado."

"You're with Dad at the ranch?" Jessie asked excitedly.

"Yes."

"How long have you been there? Are you staying for a while?" Jessie's excitement seemed to be building.

"Three days. And yes, I'll be staying for the next two weeks."

"Two weeks!" Cade's voice forced Fin to hold the phone away from her ear. "With the competition as tight as it is you're not going to be here?"

"First of all, calm down and listen." When it came to *Charisma*, taking charge and getting results were second nature to her. "You'll be acting editor-in-chief until I return at the end of the month, Cade. Don't let anyone slack off on the push to bring profits up. Have Chloe give you a daily report of what she learns from the accounting department. And go over all ad copy with a fine-tooth comb to make sure it's in order before you send it to production."

"Anything else?"

"Call me every day and let me know how we're doing." She paused. "I don't have to tell you how much I want to win this competition."

"No, Fin. You've made it clear from the start how important this is." There was a long pause and she could tell he was trying to figure out how to word his next question.

"What?"

She could almost see him blow out a frustrated breath. "You haven't taken a vacation in years. Why now? Why couldn't it have waited until January after you've won the CEO position?"

"Believe me, I'd be there if I could."

"Fin, what's wrong?" The concern in her daughter's voice touched her as little else could.

"I'm fine, sweetie. Honest." Explaining what had happened and the doctor's advice, she added, "But I'm not so sure about your dad."

"He's hovering, isn't he?" Jessie guessed. "He doesn't like not being in control and when something like this happens, he always makes a big fuss."

"That's an understatement. He's waiting right now for me to get off the phone so that he can bring me breakfast in bed."

"You do realize he's going to drive you nuts?"

Looking up, Fin watched Travis walk into the room with the bed tray laden with every kind of breakfast food imaginable. "He already is, sweetie."

Nine

Travis cautiously watched Fin walk over to the couch and sit down. He'd tried to get her to take another day to lounge around, but she'd pointed out that the doctor had told her to take it easy for a couple of days and it had already been four since her fall. He hadn't liked it, but he'd reluctantly agreed to her being up as long as he was in the same room with her when she got up and started moving around.

She'd given him a look that would have stopped any of her male coworkers dead in their tracks. But it hadn't fazed him one damned bit. She was on his turf now, not some corporate boardroom where she said "jump" and the people around her asked, "How high?"

"Travis, will you please stop watching me like you think I'm going to fall apart at any moment?" She shook her head. "Aside from my ribs being sore, I'm as healthy as one of your horses."

He shrugged. "You don't look like a horse."

"Thank you." She frowned. "I think."

"Miss Fin, would you like for me to fix you somethin' to eat or drink," Spud asked, walking into the room.

"No, but thank you anyway, Mr. Jenkins," Fin answered politely.

"Well, anything you need, you just give me a holler," Spud said, giving her a toothless grin. "I'll see that you get it."

"I appreciate your kindness," she said, smiling.

Travis eyed the old man as he walked back into the kitchen. Fin had charmed his housekeeper's socks off the first time she'd visited the ranch, and when Spud learned she'd be staying with them for a while, he'd been happier than a lone rooster in an overcrowded hen house.

"I think there's something I need after all." She rose to her feet before Travis could get across the room to help her off the couch.

"Where are you going?" He pointed toward the stairs. "If you need something from the bedroom, I'll get it."

Shaking her head, she walked over to the coat tree by the front door. "I'm going outside for a breath of fresh air."

"Do you think that's a good idea?" he asked, following her.

He knew better than to try to talk her out of it. If there was one thing he'd learned when he was married, it was never tell a woman she couldn't do something. It was a surefire way to get a man in hot water faster than he could slap his own ass with both hands.

Holding her jacket for her, then shrugging into his own, he tried a different angle. "The temperature has dropped a good ten degrees since this morning and we've had a few snow flurries. You might get a chill and shivering would probably cause your ribs to hurt."

"Give it up, cowboy. You and Mr. Jenkins won't let me do anything and I'm going stir-crazy." She smiled. "Now are you going to stand here and argue, or are you coming with me?"

Resigned, he reached around her to open the door. "As long as we're going outside, we might as well check on the horses and see that they have hay and plenty of water." At least if they were in the barn, she'd be sheltered from the wind.

Her green eyes twinkled merrily and she looked so damned pretty, he felt a familiar flame ignite in the pit of his belly. "We're returning to the scene of the crime?"

Laughing out loud, he nodded. "Something like that." He didn't tell her, but be hadn't been able to go into the barn one single time since that night and not think about her and their lovemaking.

"How is the colt?" she asked as they walked across the ranch yard.

He didn't even try to stop his wicked grin. "You actually remember there was a colt?"

"You're incorrigible, Mr. Clayton. Of course, I remember the colt. That's the reason we went into the barn that night in the first place." Her smile did strange things to his insides and reminded him that he hadn't been able to make love to her in what seemed like a month of Sundays. "I'll bet he's changed a lot in the past month."

"All babies, no matter what their species, grow faster in their first year than any other time," he said, nodding. Pushing the barn door open, he waited for Fin to step inside. "When Jess was a baby, she grew so fast there were times I could have sworn she changed overnight."

"Unfortunately, the only memory I have of Jessie as an infant was seeing the nun carry a small bundle away," Fin said, walking up to the over-sized stall where he kept the mare and colt. "Patrick gave them strict orders that he didn't even want me knowing whether I'd had a boy or a girl. But one nurse told me I'd had a perfect little girl before she left the delivery room with Jessie."

Travis's chest tightened at the thought of Fin having to watch her baby being taken away, of never knowing whether she would see her little girl again. "You'll get to watch this baby grow up from the moment he's born, Fin." Slipping his arms around her, he held her close. "We both will."

Nodding, she remained silent and he figured she was struggling to hold her emotions in check.

It just about tore him apart to think of anything causing her such emotional pain and he knew right then and there that he wanted to spend the rest of his life making sure that she never knew another sad moment.

He took a deep breath, then another as the realization spread throughout every fiber of his being. There was no more doubt and no more denial. Whether they came from two different worlds or not, he'd fallen in love with Fin.

It scared the living hell out of him to think that

she might not feel the same. But he knew beyond a shadow of doubt that he had to lay his heart on the line and take that chance. Whether they lived on the Silver Moon or in New York, Fin and the baby were more important to him than taking his next breath. And he had every intention of telling her so.

Lowering his mouth to hers, he gave her a kiss that threatened to buckle his knees and had them both breathing heavily by the time he raised his head. Then, releasing her, he took a step back to keep from reaching for her again.

"As soon as I finish feeding the horses, we're going back to the house for a long talk, sweetheart."

"Cade, are you sure about this?" Fin asked, pacing the length of the living room. "*Charisma* is tied in the competition with *The Buzz*?"

When she and Travis returned from the barn, Spud had informed her that her cell phone had, as he put it, "chirped like a cricket with four back legs" about every five minutes since she'd walked out the door. After checking the caller ID, she'd immediately phoned the office to find out what was so important that Cade had called her four times in less than thirty minutes.

"Chloe heard it first when she was on break this morning. Then Jessie overheard someone from accounting talking about it in the hall." Cade paused. "I'm trying to get the official word on it, but from all indications we've made up the difference and we're in a dead heat with Shane and *The Buzz*."

The information should have excited her beyond words. But as Cade's news sunk in, she found that, although she was proud that it looked as if the hard work she and her team had put into making *Charisma* number one was paying off, it wasn't nearly as important to her as it would have been three weeks ago.

"As soon as you get the information confirmed one way or the other, I want you to call me." She glanced at Travis, standing ramrod straight across the room. He was watching her closely, his expression guarded. "I have to go now. Give Jessie my love."

When she closed the phone and set it on the end table by the couch, Travis nodded. "I take it that your magazine is doing well in your father's competition?"

"At this point, we're holding our own," she said, nodding. "With a little more work, I have no doubt that we'll pull ahead and win."

She watched his broad chest expand as he drew in a deep breath. "Then you'll take over as CEO of your dad's company in January?"

"That's the way Patrick has it set up," she said,

careful to be as noncommittal as possible. She hadn't told anyone that, in the event she won the competition, she'd step down in order to spend as much time as possible with her child.

Travis shook his head. "You didn't answer my question."

Should she tell him that it was no longer as important to her as it had once been? Should she admit that her priorities had changed and she wanted nothing more than to be his wife and their baby's mother?

"I…that is…we—"

She snapped her mouth shut as she struggled to find an answer. It wasn't in her nature to lie. But she wasn't certain she was brave enough to tell him the truth, either.

Would he believe her if she admitted that she'd only used *Charisma* all these years as a substitute for the family she really wanted? How could she put into words, without risking the humiliation of a rejection and a broken heart, how she felt about him? What if he wanted the baby, but not her? What would happen if she told him she'd fallen hopelessly in love with him and wanted to abandon her cold, lonely apartment overlooking Central Park to live with him and their child on the Silver Moon Ranch? Could she survive if he didn't feel the same?

He took a step toward her. "Fin?"

She gave herself a mental shake. What was wrong with her? She was Fin Elliott, a fearless executive who could face any challenge set before her and come out the victor. Why was it so hard for her to find the courage to tell the man of her dreams how she felt and what she wanted?

As she stared into his incredible blue eyes, she knew exactly why she was finding it difficult to express herself. Travis was far more important to her than *Charisma* or the CEO position at EPH had ever been or ever would be.

But when she opened her mouth to tell him so, Travis shook his head. "Before you say a word, I have something to tell you."

"I have something to say to you, too," she said, wishing that he would take her in his arms and give her the slightest indication they were in the same place emotionally.

"You can have your say, after I've had mine." He pointed to the couch. "You might want to sit down. I'm not very good at stuff like this and it could take awhile."

Lowering herself to the leather couch, she held her breath as she waited for him to tell her what was so important to him.

"When Jessie first talked about trying to find you, I was dead set against it."

Fin felt certain that her heart shattered into a million pieces and she wasn't entirely sure that she'd be able to draw her next breath for the devastating emotion tightening her chest. "I…didn't know. Jessie never said how you felt about our meeting."

"I was dead wrong and she was right not to tell you." He rubbed the back of his neck as if to ease tension. "You've got to understand, Fin. I wasn't sure you'd be all that receptive to meeting a daughter you gave up for adoption all those years ago. You were extremely young and some women want to forget something like that ever happened to them." He gave her an unapologetic look. "And from the minute my wife and I adopted Jessie, I dedicated my life to protecting her from anything that would harm her physically or emotionally."

Fin swallowed hard. Jessie couldn't have been placed with a better family than the Claytons. And although it had been the hardest thing Fin had ever had to do, Jessie had fared far better having Travis for her father than she would have with Fin raising her alone.

She could understand his reasoning, but it still hurt to think that if Jessie had listened to him, they might never have met. "You were afraid I'd reject her," Fin whispered brokenly.

He nodded. "I spent many a sleepless night

before Jess called to tell me how happy you'd been when she finally told you who she was."

Tears filled Fin's eyes. "I loved and wanted her from the moment I discovered I was pregnant."

"I know that now." He smiled. "In fact, the first time I laid eyes on you, I knew you were nothing like what I'd feared you would be."

"Really?" she asked cautiously.

He sat down on the raised stone hearth in front of her. "Instead of a corporate executive with a killer instinct, you were warm, personable and sexier than sin."

She almost choked. She'd never associated herself with the word sexy. "Me?"

"Honey, you've had me turned wrong side out ever since I first laid eyes on you."

His laughter warmed her, but she tried not to let her hopes build. Sexual attraction was one thing, but he hadn't mentioned anything about loving her.

"I don't think there's ever been a doubt for either of us that we share an irresistible chemistry," she said, nodding.

"But we've had some huge problems from the get-go," he said, his expression turning serious. "You live in New York and my life is out here in God's country. Your career is glamorous and impressive as hell." He shrugged his wide shoulders. "I'm nothing more than a rancher, leading a simple, uncomplicated life. I couldn't see anything coming of the attraction between us."

Her heart sank. Was he trying to tell her all the reasons that a relationship between them wouldn't work? That he wasn't even willing to give them a fair chance?

His gaze dropped to his loosely clasped hands hanging between his knees. "Then we put the cart before the horse. We discovered that I'd gotten you pregnant before we'd even really gotten to know each other."

She swiped at an errant tear as it slid down her cheek. "You see our baby as a problem?"

"Hell no." There was no hesitation in his adamant answer. "I couldn't be happier about our having a child together." He stood up and walked over to where she sat on the couch. "But what I'm not happy about is trying to juggle time and distance in the raising of him."

"Or her."

"Right." He dropped down to one knee and took her hands in his. "I've never done anything half-assed in my entire life and I'm not about to start now. I don't want to be a part-time dad any more than you want to be a part-time mother."

Her heart skipped several beats. "What are you saying, Travis?"

"I want us to get married, Fin," he said seriously. "I want both of us to be full-time parents and raise this baby together."

He'd talked about wanting their baby and his desire to be with the child, but he hadn't mentioned anything about loving and wanting her. "I…don't know what to say."

He leaned forward and gently pressed his lips to hers. "'Yes' would work for me, honey."

She had to clear her suddenly dry throat before she could get her vocal cords to work. Being Travis's wife was what she wanted more than anything, but not without his love.

Touching his cheek, she shook her head. "Unfortunately, it doesn't work for me."

Ten

Travis felt like a damned fool. He'd laid his heart, as well as his pride, on the line and Fin had just the same as stomped all over them.

Releasing her hand, he took a deep breath and stood up. In all of his forty-nine years, he'd never dreamed that he could hurt so much and not have something physically wrong. Gathering what was left of his dignity, he squared his shoulders and met her gaze head-on.

"Well, I guess all there is left to do now is figure out who gets the baby on holidays and where he—"

"Or she."

He nodded. "Or she will spend the summers."

Suddenly needing to put distance between them, he turned toward the door. "Let me know whatever you think is fair and I'll go along with it."

"Hold it right there, cowboy." Fin's hand on his arm stopped him cold.

Her touch burned right through his shirt and the pain in his chest tightened unbearably. Glancing down at her soft palm on his arm, then back at her beautiful face, he wanted nothing more than to take her in his arms and try to convince her that they belonged together. But he'd never begged for anything in his life and, God help him, he'd never been tempted to do so—until now.

"You've had your say, now I'm going to have mine." Her green eyes sparkled with determination and he loved her more in that moment than life itself.

"What do you want from me, Fin? I offered marriage and you turned me down."

"That's just it." She rose to her feet, then pushing him down on the couch, she planted her fists on her slender hips as she glared down at him. "You didn't ask me to marry you. You offered."

Damn, but she was gorgeous when she pitched a hissy fit. But as her words sank in, he frowned. "It's the same thing."

"No, it's not." She started pacing. "There's a big difference. Huge even."

He noticed that Spud had walked in to see what all the commotion was about. But one quelling look from the incensed female giving Travis hell had the old geezer retreating back to the safety of the kitchen as fast as his seventy-plus years and arthritis would allow.

"Did it ever occur to you that I might want a marriage proposal that sounded more personal and less like a business merger?"

He frowned. "I didn't mean for it to sound like—"

She held up her hand. "Save it. I'm not finished." Looking every bit as commanding as he knew she had to be in the boardroom, she narrowed her pretty green eyes. "It's all or nothing with me, cowboy. I want it all. Marriage, a cozy home and this baby. And maybe one or two more."

The tightness in his chest eased a bit. "I can give you all of that."

"Yes, you can." Pausing, her voice softened. "But can you give me what I need most of all?"

The tears in her eyes caused a tight knot to form in the pit of his stomach. He couldn't bear to think he'd caused her to cry.

Rising to his feet, he walked over and took her

in his arms. "What do you want, sweetheart? Name it and it's yours."

"I want you to want me, as well as the baby. I want to be your wife. I want to share your life here on the Silver Moon." Her voice dropped to a broken whisper. "I want…your love, Travis."

If he could have managed it, he would have kicked his own tail end. He might have been proposing marriage, but he hadn't bothered to tell Fin how much she'd come to mean to him, how he loved her and needed her more than he needed his next breath.

Holding her close, he lowered his mouth to hers and gave her a kiss filled with the promise of a lifetime of everything she wanted. "I'm sorry, honey. I told you I wasn't good at this stuff." Using his index finger to tip her chin up until their gazes met, he smiled. "I love you more than you'll ever know. I have since the minute I first saw you."

"Oh, Travis, I love you, too. So very much." Wrapping her arms around his waist, she laid her head against his chest. "I was afraid you wanted the baby, but not me."

He kissed her silky auburn hair. "I never again want you to doubt that I want and love you. You own my heart, Fin Elliott. The baby is an extension of that love." Leaning back, he smiled. "Even though

I don't deserve you, will you do me the honor of being my wife, Fin?"

"That's more like it, cowboy." She gave him a watery grin. "Yes, I'll be your wife."

He felt like the luckiest man alive. "I promise to spend the rest of my life making sure you don't regret it, sweetheart. But are you sure you want to live here on the ranch? What about your career? Your apartment in New York? Won't you miss them?"

"No." She placed her soft palm along his jaw and gazed up at him with so much love in her eyes it stole his breath. "When I was a child, my dream in life was to have a husband and family. But after Jessie was taken from me, I made *Charisma* my baby. I nurtured it and watched it grow. But it's time to let my 'baby' go. I've raised her to be a strong force in the fashion industry. Now it's time for me to step back and let someone else guide her while I devote myself to my first dream."

"You won't miss New York?" he asked, still unable to believe that she wanted to give up life as she knew it to marry him and raise their child under the wide Colorado sky.

She shook her head. "I belong here with you on this beautiful ranch." Her smile caused him to go weak in the knees. "I want to raise our children here in this wonderful place. I want to make love with you every night in that big bed upstairs. And I want to sit with you on the swing on the front porch and watch our grandchildren playing in the yard."

He would have told her that he wanted all those things, too, but he couldn't have forced words past the lump in his throat if his life depended on it. Instead, he showed her by placing his lips on hers and kissing her with all the emotion he couldn't put into words.

When he finally raised his head, he smiled. "Who do you think your dad will appoint as editor-in-chief at *Charisma*?"

"I'm not sure." She grinned. "But he'd better do it soon because other than occasional visits to see Jessie and Cade and the rest of the family, I'm not going back."

"How do you think your dad will take the news?"

Fin nibbled on her lower lip as she thought about her father. She'd held a grudge against him all these years, but it truly had been a waste of spirit and energy. It hadn't brought her baby girl back to her. Only time had taken care of that. And if she were perfectly honest with herself, she wouldn't have met the love of her life and had a second chance at motherhood if Patrick hadn't insisted that she give Jessie up for Travis and his wife to adopt.

"Why don't you give him a call?" Travis asked, as if reading her mind.

She sighed. "I'm not sure what to say."

"Start by saying hello." He led her over to the phone. "The rest will take care of itself."

As she dialed her parents at The Tides, Travis disappeared into the kitchen and she knew he was giving her the privacy he thought she needed for the difficult phone conversation. She loved him for it, but he needn't have bothered. She didn't intend for there to be any secrets between them.

"Hi, Mom." Fortunately, instead of the maid answering the phone, her mother had picked up on the second ring.

"Finny, 'tis good to hear your voice." The sound of her mother's Irish lilt caused Fin to smile. Maeve had always been the glue that held the Elliott clan together, despite their share of problems.

"It's good to hear you, too." After exchanging a few inconsequential pleasantries, Fin asked, "Is Patrick home from the office?"

"Yes, dear. He returned from the city about an hour ago."

Fin closed her eyes as she gathered her courage. "Could I speak with him, please?"

When her mother handed the phone to Patrick, his booming voice filtered into her ear. "Hello, Finola."

Taking a deep breath, she forced herself to bring up the subject that had driven them apart over twenty years ago. "I want you to tell me the truth, Patrick. Have you ever regretted forcing me into giving Jessie up for adoption?"

His sharp intake of breath was the only sound she heard from him for several long, nerve-wracking seconds. When he finally spoke, there was a gruffness in his voice that she'd never heard. "I thought I was doing what was best for you at the time, Finola. But in hindsight, it was quite possibly the worst decision I've ever made."

Patrick's admission that he'd been wrong was the last thing she'd expected him to say. "You never told me."

There was a short pause before he spoke again. "I never knew how to tell you how sorry I was that I put my pride and concern for social appearances ahead of your happiness."

"In all fairness, I don't think I ever gave you the chance," Fin said, admitting her own part in the rift.

"I'm—" he stopped to clear his throat "—glad that we've finally got this out in the open, lass."

His use of the pet name he'd called her when she was a little girl caused tears to pool in the corners of her eyes. "I am, too, Dad."

"I...love you, Fin. Can you ever find it in your

heart to forgive me?" The hitch in her father's voice sent tears streaming down her cheeks.

"Yes, Dad. I forgive you."

There was a long pause as if they both needed time to get used to the fact that they'd finally made their peace with the past.

"I'm going to marry Jessie's adoptive father," Fin said, breaking the silence.

"Does he make you happy, lass?" Patrick's voice held a fatherly concern that she knew for certain she'd never heard before.

"Yes, Dad. He makes me very happy."

"I'm glad you found him. He seems like a good, hard-working man. And he did a wonderful job raising Jessica." Her father surprised her further when he added, "I also think it's wonderful that we'll have a new grandchild soon."

"You don't know how much that means to me, Dad," she said, meaning it.

"How are you going to juggle time at the office with a new baby?" he asked, giving her the perfect opportunity to tell him the second reason she'd called.

"I'm not even going to try." She took a deep breath as she prepared to end her career and kiss the CEO position goodbye once and for all. "Effective immediately I'm no longer the editor-in-chief of *Charisma*."

"Are you sure that's what you want?" From the tone of his voice, she could tell her father already knew the answer.

"Yes, Dad. I want what Mom always had—time to be with her babies."

"I can't fault you for that, lass."

"Dad, there's one more thing."

"What's that?"

"I think Cade McMann would be an excellent candidate for my position. He knows the magazine inside out and he has fantastic instincts. You can trust him and his judgment to keep *Charisma* on the right track."

"And he's part of the family now," her father said, sounding thoughtful.

After telling her parents again that she loved them and that she'd see them at the New Year's Eve party they were holding at The Tides, she hung up the phone and went in search of Travis. She felt more at peace than she had in twenty-three years and finally ready to start the rest of her life.

"You look absolutely beautiful, Fin."

Smiling at her daughter, Fin asked, "Is your dad ready?"

"I think he's going to wear a hole in the floor from pacing so much," Jessie said, laughing as she finished with the tiny buttons at the back of Fin's wedding dress. "Cade and Mac have both threatened to tie him down and Spud offered to supply the rope."

Fin laughed. "He asked me two days ago if we couldn't just elope."

Tears filled Jessie's eyes as she nodded. "Dad loves you so much. We all do."

"And I love all of you." Fin gave her daughter a watery smile. "Here we go again. We're both going to ruin our makeup if we don't stop crying."

Dabbing at her eyes with a tissue, Jessie smiled. "I'm just so happy for both of you."

Fin hugged Jessie close. "I'm happy for all of us. I have a beautiful daughter, a wonderful son-in-law and I'm marrying the man I love."

"It's time, Aunt Finny."

Looking up, Fin smiled at her niece. Marriage to Mac Riggs definitely agreed with Bridget. There was a sparkle in her eyes and a glow about her that hadn't been there before she met the tall, dark-haired sheriff of Winchester County.

"We'll be right there," Jessie said, hugging Fin again. "Let's go take pity on Dad before he has to have the floor resurfaced."

As Fin followed the two young women down the stairs of the Silver Moon ranch house, her heart skipped a beat when she saw Travis, standing straight and tall in the tuxedo he'd worn for Jessie and Cade's wedding. When she'd asked him what he was going to wear for their wedding, he'd just smiled and told her not to worry about it.

When he met her at the bottom of the steps, she touched his handsome face. "You said your tux would hang in the closet, never to be worn again."

He grinned. "Do you remember what you told me when the kids got married?"

"I said you looked handsome and—" her cheeks heated and she smiled as she realized why he'd worn the tux "—incredible."

His low chuckle sent waves of longing throughout her entire body. "That's right. And since the doctor gave you a clean bill of health yesterday—"

"You wanted to amaze me?" Fin asked, laughing delightedly.

"Honey, I intend to amaze both of us tonight after we're alone." The promise in his blue eyes made her tingle from head to toe. "But right now I want to make you mine."

She smiled at the man she loved more than life itself. "I am yours, Travis. For now and always. Never doubt that."

"And I'm yours, sweetheart." He gave her a kiss so tender, she thought she might melt into a puddle right then and there. When he raised his head, he offered her his arm. "Let's mosey on over to the fireplace and let Mac make it official."

And as they took the vows that made them husband and wife, Fin looked forward to an amazing future filled with love and happiness beneath the wide Colorado sky.

* * * * *

New York Times bestselling author
Linda Lael Miller is back with a new romance
featuring the heartwarming McKettrick family
from Special Edition.

Sierra's Homecoming
by Linda Lael Miller

On sale December 2007,
wherever books are sold.

Turn the page for a sneak preview!

Sierra's Homecoming

by

Linda Lael Miller

Soft, smoky music poured into the room.

The next thing she knew, Sierra was in Travis's arms, close against that chest she'd admired earlier, and they were slow dancing.

Why didn't she pull away?

"Relax," he said. His breath was warm in her hair.

She giggled, more nervous than amused. What was the matter with her? She was attracted to Travis, had been from the first, and he was clearly attracted to her. They were both adults. Why not enjoy a little slow dancing in a ranch-house kitchen?

Because slow dancing led to other things. She took a step back and felt the counter flush against her lower back. Travis naturally came with her, since they were holding hands and he had one arm around her waist.

Simple physics.

Then he kissed her.

Physics again—this time, not so simple.

"Yikes," she said, when their mouths parted.

He grinned. "Nobody's ever said that after I kissed them."

She felt the heat and substance of his body pressed against hers. "It's going to happen, isn't it?" she heard herself whisper.

"Yep," Travis answered.

"But not tonight," Sierra said on a sigh.

"Probably not," Travis agreed.

"When, then?"

He chuckled, gave her a slow, nibbling kiss. "Tomorrow morning," he said. "After you drop Liam off at school."

"Isn't that…a little…soon?"

"Not soon enough," Travis answered, his voice husky. "Not nearly soon enough."

BEYOND THE BOARDROOM

by
Maureen Child

Dear Reader,

Being asked to be a part of a continuity series for the Desire™ line is a real treat. Being asked to write the last book in a series is both a challenge and a treat.

Beyond the Boardroom, the final book in the Elliott family continuity, was great fun to write. I love the idea of setting a book in New York City at Christmastime. And I absolutely adored my hero, Shane. He's so focused on his job for the family company, he never notices the one woman – Rachel Adler – who has been keeping his world in order for years. Until Rachel does the unthinkable and actually quits her job.

I hope you have all enjoyed reading about the Elliotts as much as the twelve of us did writing the books.

And until next time, I wish you good books, great joy and always, more time to read!

Love,

Maureen

MAUREEN CHILD

is a California native who loves to travel. Every chance they get, she and her husband are taking off on another research trip. The author of more than sixty books, Maureen loves a happy ending and still swears that she has the best job in the world. She lives in Southern California with her husband, two children, and a golden retriever with delusions of grandeur.

For my husband, Mark,
because really, all of my books should be
dedicated to him. I love you, honey!

One

"Okay then," Rachel Adler said, keeping her voice pitched to be heard over the thumping of running feet and the hum of the treadmill. "I've got you booked for dinner with Tawny Mason tonight at eight."

"At Une Nuit?" Shane Elliott asked, reaching for his water bottle, tucked beneath the cord at the head of the machine.

"Where else?" Rachel muttered with a little shake of her head. Why in heaven would he even ask? she wondered. Hadn't she been taking care of every detail of Shane's life for four years now?

"Good." Shane took a long drink of water and Rachel's gaze locked on the bobbing motion of his Adam's apple. Seriously, even the man's *neck* was sexy.

When he'd finished off the last of the water, he wiped sweat from his face with the towel looped around his neck and tossed Rachel the empty bottle. "And call ahead. Have Stash order in some flowers for, um…" He waved one hand in a silent attempt for help.

"Tawny," Rachel provided dryly as she set the empty bottle down on the floor beside her. For heaven's sake, the man couldn't even remember his date's name.

Plus, he knew as well as she did that Stash Martin, manager of Une Nuit, never missed a beat when getting the Elliott family table ready. There would, she knew, be flowers, champagne and some delicious appetizers just waiting for Shane and Tawny.

Tawny.

What kind of woman named her daughter Tawny? A stage mother, hoping for a starlet daughter? Or had the woman taken one look at her newborn baby girl and decided…future bimbo?

"Right." Shane nodded. "Tawny. She says her mother named her for the color of her eyes."

Rachel rolled her own green eyes.

Shane grinned at her and Rachel's stomach did a quick dip and spin.

If she could have managed it without looking like a complete idiot, she'd have kicked her own ass. Honestly. Why was it Shane Elliott who could turn her insides to mush with a simple smile?

The first three years she'd worked with the man, everything had been fine between them. They'd had a good working relationship and Shane even appreciated Rachel's sometimes quirky sense of humor, when most of her previous employers hadn't. Then she'd had to go and ruin the whole thing by falling for him.

For the last year she'd suffered silently, wanting him every day, dreaming about him at night, all the while knowing that he thought of her only as Good ol' Rachel.

Idiot.

"What do you think?" he asked, clearly oblivious to her thoughts. "Roses?"

"Huh?" She blinked, shook her head and reminded herself to concentrate on the moment. "Right. Flowers. Roses are boring."

"Really?"

"Trust me."

"I always do," he said, giving her another of those smiles that had the power to zap an unwary female at twenty paces.

She couldn't do this much longer, she thought. Couldn't keep working with him every day and dying a little more every day. Couldn't set up his dates with other women and imagine him in bed with every one of them. Couldn't keep wasting her life away waiting for the wrong man to wake up and stumble on her.

Sighing, Rachel flipped through her memo book, scanned the notes she kept on the legions of Shane's women and found what she was looking for. "Tawny prefers daisies."

"Sure, I remember now. Such a simple girl."

"Simple*ton*, you mean," she muttered again, keeping her voice low enough that her boss's running feet would drown out the comment.

"What was that?"

"Nothing." She automatically handed him the second bottle of water she'd brought with her to the executive area of the company gym on the fifth floor.

"Rachel, what would I do without you?" he mused, not really expecting an answer.

But oh boy, could she give him one. Rachel was Shane's right hand at *The Buzz,* one of the magazines in the Elliott family empire. As a weekly entertainment magazine, *The Buzz* covered all the new movies, did interviews with up-and-coming directors and fawned over whichever actor or actress was the current hot topic. And as editor in chief of *The Buzz*, Shane did his best to keep on top of everything going on around him.

Of course, when she'd first come to work for him, he hadn't been so involved. Instead he'd tried to avoid the office as much as humanly possible. But slowly, Rachel had convinced him to enjoy his job more.

Back then, he'd resented being pulled into the family business. But Rachel had seen just how good he was at not only handling the day-to-day running of the magazine but at dealing with people and managing disasters. She'd eventually convinced him that he was meant to run this business.

And he'd really come into his own over the last

several months—ever since his father, Patrick, had kicked off a competition among his children.

Old man Elliott had determined that the best way to name a new CEO of Elliott Publication Holdings was to see who was willing to work hardest to earn it. At the end of the year the editor in chief of whichever one of the magazines showed the most proportional profit growth would become Top Dog.

And *The Buzz* was the front-runner.

Shane's father was due to announce the winner any day now.

Patrick was a sneaky old man, in Rachel's opinion. Nice, sure, but sneaky. He'd found a way to make his grown children admit just how much they wanted to succeed. By pitting them against each other, he'd been able to sit back all year and watch them discover themselves.

And there had been plenty of discoveries, she thought, remembering all of the turmoil over the last year.

"Did you put that call in to Fin for me?" Shane asked, breathing hard as he picked up the pace on the treadmill.

"Yes," Rachel said, flipping back a page in her memo book. Smiling, she read off, "Fin says and I quote, 'Tell Shane he needs to get away from the city and smell some fresh air. Come to Colorado and I'll teach him to ride a horse.'"

Shane laughed. "A month on a ranch and she's Annie Oakley?"

Rachel chuckled along with him. She couldn't

help it. Shane's twin sister had been sad for so long, it was good knowing that she was finally happy. She'd reconciled with Jessie, the daughter she was forced to give up for adoption so many years ago. She was married to a man she was clearly nuts about and her newly discovered pregnancy was the icing on the cake. "She's happy."

"Yeah," Shane said, his running steps slowing a little as he thought about the sister he was so close to. "She really is. But damn, I miss having her around."

His eyes narrowed thoughtfully as he stared straight ahead, out the bank of windows overlooking Park Avenue.

"I know," Rachel said. "But she'll probably come back home for Christmas."

"Christmas." He shut off the treadmill, stepped neatly to one side and used his towel to wipe his face again. "It's December, isn't it?"

"All month," she agreed.

"Have I started shopping yet?"

"No."

"Damn." Grabbing the second bottle of water, he chugged down the liquid, then handed off the empty bottle. "No time to worry about it now, though. I'm gonna grab a shower, then I'll see you back in the office in half an hour. I'd like to take a look at the new copy for the magazine before it heads out to production."

"Right." Rachel winced as she thought about one column in particular that he'd be going over.

As if reading her mind, he turned and called back, "The new Tess Tells All column was turned in on time, right?"

"Oh, yeah. She's very dependable."

From across the room, Shane winked at her. "Just like you, Rachel."

She watched him disappear into the men's locker room and as the door swung shut behind him, she whispered, "You have *no* idea."

A few hours later, Shane listened with half an ear as his art director, Jonathon Taylor, laid out plans for next summer's Fourth of July edition even as snow flurries dusted the windows. On a weekly magazine, they usually operated months in advance. And the specialty editions required even more in-depth planning.

Jonathon really thrived on the rush of trying to outdo himself with every holiday issue. And damned if he didn't pull it off most of the time. Right now Jon was in the midst of describing, with wildly waving hands, his salute to patriotism, centering on celebrities dressed in red, white and blue. Not original, but knowing Jon, it would be great.

Sandy Hall, the managing editor, was practically frothing at the mouth. No doubt she had a complaint or two about the money Jonathon was budgeting for his blowout edition.

And Shane would have to listen to both sides and make a decision. Used to be that he hated being here, listening to all of the day-to-day drama of the magazine's inner circles. Now, though, he was enjoying himself.

Amazed him to admit it, but there it was. He'd been getting a charge out of running *The Buzz* for months now. Surprisingly enough, Shane realized he was pleased. Proud, even, of how well *The Buzz* was doing. He'd gone into this contest with halfhearted enthusiasm. But as the months had worn on, Shane had found himself being swept up into the competitive spirit. Nothing an Elliott liked better than a contest.

"So—" Jonathon was wrapping up his speech "—I figure if we shell out top dollar to a few of the biggest celebrities, the rest of 'em will come along, too. Nobody wants to feel left out."

Before Shane could respond, Sandy stood up, brushed her short blond hair back from her eyes and narrowed her gaze on Jon. "And if we pay top dollar for a handful of celebs, who's going to offset that expenditure?"

"You have to pay to play," Jon said smugly, shooting a glance at Shane as if knowing he'd back him up.

And he did. "Jon's right, Sandy," he said, holding up one hand to keep his managing editor's temper in check. "We get the right people into that issue, the advertisers will line up to be a part of it. Plus, we'll sell more copies."

"The budget's already stretched pretty thin, Shane," Sandy said, sneering at Jon's gleeful chortle.

"Bull." Shane stood up behind his desk, swept the

edges of his jacket back and stuffed his hands into his pockets. "You know as well as I do that the profit margins are way up. We're beating the pants off the rest of the Elliott magazines. And we're going to keep doing it. And the way we're going to keep doing it is by *not* cutting corners."

Jon slapped one hand to his chest and bowed his head as if in prayer. "Brilliant, my king, brilliant."

Shane laughed at the dramatics, but hey, it was good to be king.

"You're only saying that because you won," Sandy pointed out.

"Sure," Jon said, grinning at her now that he'd made his point.

"Before the bloodletting starts up again," Shane interrupted, looking from one editor to the other, "has either of you made any headway on the job I gave you?"

Jon and Sandy looked at each other, shrugged, then turned back to Shane.

"Nope." Sandy spoke first, clearly reluctant to admit that she'd failed. "I've talked to everyone I know and *nobody* has a clue about this woman's identity."

"I second that," Jon said, obviously disappointed. "Our little Tess is like Spider-Man or something, keeping her secret identity so secret, there's not even a whisper of gossip about her."

Just what Shane hadn't wanted to hear. Damn it. Tess Tells All was the most popular column in his magazine. They'd picked up thousands of new readers thanks to the anonymous woman's talent for being both funny and insightful.

Seven months ago *The Buzz* had carried the very first of the mystery woman's columns.

The response had been immediate. Calls, e-mails, letters, all from people who wanted to read more from Tess. But the woman was untraceable. She faxed her monthly column in from a different location in the city every time and her checks were sent to a PO box and then forwarded to yet another.

As well as *The Buzz* was doing, Shane knew it would be doing even better if he could just talk this woman into writing a weekly column. But she hadn't answered any letters he'd sent and all other attempts at communication had failed.

Making him one very frustrated man.

"Fine," he said on a sigh. "Never mind. Just keep looking for her." Then he sat down behind his desk, waved one hand at them dismissively and picked up the latest column by the mysterious Tess. He didn't even look up when his co-workers left his office.

He read every issue of *The Buzz* before it was laid out for production and eventual printing. The only way to keep a handle on what his magazine was doing was for him to stay involved. From the ground up.

But reading this particular column was always a pleasure. He leaned back in the black leather chair and swung around until he was facing the snow-dusted bank of windows overlooking Manhattan. He smiled ruefully as he read.

Tess says, the secret to surviving your boss is to never let him know you understand him. The poor guy's got to have a few illusions.

My boss thinks he's mysterious. Right. About as mysterious as a pot of chicken soup. The man, like all others of his gender, is so very predictable.

Just last week, I set up two "first dates" for him. At the same restaurant, with the same meal, the same wine. Only the names of the women were changed. Mysterious? Hardly.

I juggle his women just like I juggle his business meetings. The man has made me a good enough juggler that I could be making twice as much money working at a circus—and hey, the co-workers wouldn't change that much!

Shane chuckled. Tess was good, but he felt sorry for her. Working for a man like that couldn't be easy.

When it comes to business, though, he's at the top of his game when everything around him is falling to pieces. Which, I suppose, is why I'm still here after all this time. Despite having to run the man's social life, I do enjoy being at the top. I like being the right hand woman—even if sometimes I feel invisible.

Invisible? Shane shook his head. How could a woman like Tess go unnoticed by anyone?

Maybe it's the time of year that's got me thinking about my life. Sure, you're reading this column sometime in March, but as I write this, it's December. Snow's falling outside, turning Manhattan into a postcard. Wreaths are up on the shop windows, twinkling lights are everywhere and people are ice skating in Rockefeller Center.

The old year is winding down and a new one's getting ready to roll. And I have to ask myself if I really want to maintain the status quo. Is this all there is? Do I really want to keep working for a man who treats me like a well-trained dog? Toss me a treat every now and then so I'll keep running and fetching?

He frowned, wondering why the tone of Tess's column had suddenly changed. Usually she was funny, lighthearted. Making jokes about her boss and underlining, apparently, how every other assistant in the country felt about his or her job.

When he read the next line, he sat up straight in his chair and scowled at the page.

Wonder what he'd do if I quit?

Quit?

She couldn't quit. Hell, her column was too damn popular for her to quit working. If she walked away from her job, she wouldn't be writing this column anymore and where did that leave *The Buzz*?

The truth is, my boss probably wouldn't even notice I was gone until his dry cleaning went unclaimed or until he had to make his own reservations for dinner with the latest wide-eyed blonde. So why'm I still here?

I think we all know the answer to that.

I've let him become too important to me.

I spend more time living his life than I do living my own.

Shane really didn't like the sound of this.

What do you readers think? Should I give it up and stop torturing myself? Should I finally realize that he's never going to look up and notice me? The real me? Should I accept that all I'll ever be to him is an excellent assistant?

Shane grumbled and finished reading the column with a snarl on his face.

The answer to that question is no. The time has come to leave my job and move on to something else while I still can. To all of you assistants out there—all of you who've written to me over the last several months, telling me your own stories—I guess this is goodbye.

Goodbye?

By the time you read this, I'll probably be long gone. I'll miss you guys. I'll miss this column. Heck, I'll miss the boss, too.

I wish you all the best of luck with your own bosses and I'll never forget any of you.

Two

Shane hit the intercom button and when Rachel answered a second later, he snapped, "Come in here for a minute, please."

A moment later the double doors opened and Rachel stepped in, carrying a steno pad. "What's up?"

"Did you see the Tess Tells All column for March?"

"Yeeesss..." One word came out in four distinct syllables.

"So you know she's thinking about quitting her job?"

Rachel took a deep breath and turned her back on him for a second. Deliberately she schooled her features into a politely interested mask. Deciding to quit her job hadn't been an easily reached decision, but she knew it was the right one. Asking her readers for their votes had merely been a way of breaking the news about that decision.

Quietly she shut the door then walked across the thick red carpet toward his desk. "I read it. What's the problem?"

"The problem?" Shane dropped Tess's column onto his desktop and stood up. "She's too popular with our readers, that's the problem. She can't quit her job. We need her column."

Rachel wondered if Shane would be this concerned when she turned in her resignation. And if he were, would that change her mind? No. She had to leave EPH. Had to get out into the world and find someone else to care for. Hopefully someone who would care for her in return.

She shook her head as she sat down in the black leather armchair opposite his desk. Taking another deep breath, she steadied her voice. "I doubt this is a whim. She's obviously done a lot of thinking. Probably some soul searching. People don't just walk away from a good job without a lot of thought."

Which she knew for a fact, since she'd spent the last five months talking herself into doing just that.

He narrowed his gaze on her. "Do you know something you're not telling me?"

"Why would you think that?" Oh, good one, she told herself. Stall without actually lying.

She blew out a breath and tucked a loose strand

of honey-blond hair behind her right ear. She worried her bottom lip and said, "Honestly, Shane, I don't see how you're going to keep her from quitting her job when you don't even know who she is."

"We have to find out."

Rachel tucked her pad against her chest and folded her arms over it. "Haven't you had people working on that for months now?"

"Yes," he muttered, then turned toward the bank of windows. Staring down at the snow-covered street eighteen floors below, he added, "I can't understand how she can stay so hidden. Hell, you'd think her *boss* would recognize himself in her articles."

Rachel mmm-hmmed. "You would, wouldn't you?"

"How could he not?" Shane wondered, more to himself than to her.

"It's surprising, all right," Rachel said dryly. She knew darn well Shane had read every one of the articles she'd written as Tess. And yet, here he stood, completely clueless.

He glanced at her and Rachel caught the glint in his clear green eyes and recognized it. He'd had the same look in his eyes when this competition with his brothers and sisters was just getting started. Shane Elliott simply did *not* lose well. But this time, he was going to have to deal with it.

"Do you know something about Tess you haven't told me?"

She paused just a fraction of a second, then shook her head firmly again even as she skipped around his question. "She faxes those columns in from all over the city. No one knows where the next one's coming from."

He stared at her for a minute or two longer. Long enough to worry Rachel just a little. Good thing he couldn't read her mind. Although, if he *could* read her mind, she wouldn't have to quit her job, because he'd *know* that she loved him and then he'd either be pleased about it or fire her.

"Right," Shane said. "Right." Walking back to his desk, he slid Tess's column into the manila envelope with the rest of the layout for the March issue. Handing it to her, he said, "Get these to production for me, will you, Rachel?"

"Sure." Glad to be on safer ground, she asked, "Anything else?"

He dropped into his chair, braced both arms on his desk and said, "Just find the mysterious Tess. If she's looking for a new job, we'll give her one."

Rachel turned and left the office and when she'd closed the door behind her, she leaned back against it. Hah. Shane wanted to offer Tess a job? Ironic? Oh, yeah.

She walked past her desk and on down the hall toward production. She glanced to either side of her as her heels sank deeply into the rich scarlet carpet. It was going to be hard to leave this place. It was familiar. Comfortable.

Maybe *too* comfortable, she reminded herself.

The gleaming glass and chrome offices on either side of the wide aisle were bustling with sound as the staff of *The Buzz* worked on various tasks. Phones rang, someone laughed and the scent of coffee floated on the warm air drifting from the central heating system.

Rachel smiled at Stacy, the receptionist, as she strolled through the main waiting area. The walls were a clean, pure white, and the art on the walls mostly enlarged, chrome-framed covers of *The Buzz*. The effect was startling, but eye catching. The idea was to make this floor look up to the minute, fresh. Exciting. And it worked.

Every floor of the EPH building had its own color scheme and was decorated according to whichever magazine it was trying to promote. Rachel was probably prejudiced, but she'd always thought the eighteenth-floor home of *The Buzz* was the nicest.

Rachel kept walking, tossing a glance into the small meeting rooms as she walked, smiling in at one or two of the people she passed. The photography lab door was closed and she smiled wryly. Ferria—no last name—was notoriously territorial about her office. Even Shane had a hard time getting past the lead photographer's doorway.

At Production, Rachel stepped through the open door and handed over the manila envelope to the head man's assistant, Christina. Fiftyish, Christina was a single mother of four boys who took no crapola off of anyone—least of all her boss. Her snow-white hair was cut into extremely short layers that hugged her head and highlighted bright blue eyes.

The older woman pushed her silver wire-framed glasses up on her nose and grinned. "I'm thinking about heading out to Lucci's Deli for lunch. Want to join me?"

"Love it," Rachel said, realizing that Christina was only one of so many people she'd miss when she left. "I'll meet you at the elevator at twelve, okay?"

"Excellent."

Walking back to her desk, she felt almost as though she were already saying goodbye. Her gaze swept over the familiar fixtures and faces and she hugged the electrical hum of activity close. She was really going to miss this place.

She loved her job. Loved working for Shane and feeling as though she were a part of something special. Working on a weekly magazine, there was always something happening. An air of excitement, urgency that she would probably never find anywhere else.

But she knew she had to go.

She couldn't stay at *The Buzz*, working with Shane every day, loving him as she did. It was just too hard. Too hard to make his dates for him, to see him look at every other woman in the world with more interest than he would ever show her. So whether she liked it or not, it was time, Rachel thought, that she left EPH.

Both she and her alter ego Tess were going to quietly disappear from Shane's life.

And there was nothing he could do to change her mind.

By seven o'clock, most of the magazine's employees were gone. Shane walked through the empty office and listened to the sound of his own footsteps on the carpet. Only a few of the overhead lights were on, splashing the shadows with occasional bursts of light. The reflected lights shone against the black expanse of windows and mirrored Shane as he walked toward the elevator.

During the day, this office thundered with the noise of productivity. People laughing, talking, computer keys clicking, phones ringing. But at night…it was like a house emptied of its children.

Quiet to the point of spooky.

He passed reception, where an acre of desk sat dead center of a waiting area. Twin couches in matching shades of white faced each other across the expanse and on the far wall, the elevator gleamed dully in the overhead light.

Sighing, Shane stabbed the up call button and waited impatiently for the elevator to arrive. If he hadn't answered that phone call from his father a few minutes ago, he'd have been pushing the down button and heading for home to get ready for his date with… He frowned. What the *hell* was that woman's name?

Shaking his head, he pushed that question away to concentrate on another one. Why did his father want to see him? And why now, after the business day?

Patrick Elliott was a hard man. Always had been. More focused on building an empire than a family, over the years he'd become a stranger to his own children. Shane's mother, Maeve, was the glue that held the Elliott family together. Hell, *she* was the only reason he and his siblings were still speaking to Patrick.

The elevator opened in front of him and he stepped inside with all the enthusiasm of a man heading to a tax audit. Generic Muzak filtered down all around him, but he did his best to ignore it. He punched the appropriate floor button, and as the doors slid shut again, Shane let his mind drift back over the years.

In all the memories he had of growing up, Patrick was no more than a blurred image on the fringes of his mind. Until one memorable year.

He and his twin, Finola, were the youngest of the Elliott children. And, since they'd been born nine years after their brother Daniel, Shane and Fin were even closer than twins usually were. Growing up, they'd been each other's best friend. They'd fought each other's battles, celebrated each other's victories, and shared the hurts and pains that came along.

And maybe, Shane told himself, that was the main reason he just couldn't bring himself to get close to his father now. Patrick was trying to make up for his failures as a parent and slowly, each of the Elliott kids was coming around. But Shane held back—because he'd never been able to forgive the old man for what he'd put Fin through when she was just a kid.

He leaned back against the cool, slick chrome of the elevator wall and closed his eyes, remembering. Shane could see Fin as she'd been at fifteen, beautiful, trusting, with bright green eyes filled with anticipation. Until she'd made the mistake that Patrick wouldn't countenance.

She'd become pregnant by the son of another wealthy family, and neither side wanted their children getting married for the sake of a child they hadn't planned.

Though their mother had cried and sided with Fin—something none of the children knew until recently—Patrick had been adamant about saving the family's "good name." He'd shipped Fin off to a convent in Canada with as much feeling as a man who dropped off an unwanted puppy at the pound. No one had been able to reach Patrick. The old man never backed down from a damn thing if he believed he was right—and he *always* believed he was right.

Fin was forced to give up her daughter at birth and Shane would never be able to forget her pain, her misery. Just as he was pretty sure he'd never be able to completely forgive Patrick for causing it.

The elevator dinged as it reached the executive level of the EPH building and the doors slid open with a whoosh.

"Might as well get this over with," Shane muttered and walked into a very different atmosphere than the one found on the eighteenth floor. On the twenty-third, the carpeting was subdued, the walls a soft beige with cream trim and the furniture was elegant antiques. Even the air smelled different up here, he thought, more…rarified, he supposed.

But then, that's what Patrick had always been concerned about. How things looked. The perception of the Elliott family. Which was why it had taken Fin too many years to reconnect with her long lost daughter.

At least *that* had come around and turned out well. Now that Jessie was finally where she'd always belonged—with them—Patrick had at last accepted and welcomed the girl. And the pain Shane had seen in Fin's eyes for too many years was finally gone.

Knowing Fin was so happy had made dealing with Patrick easier than it used to be.

Shaking his head, he wondered where all the philosophical thoughts were coming from. Hell, he was wasting time. He still had to get home and change for his date with…what was her name?

Grumbling, he knocked briefly on the closed door to Patrick's office and waited.

"Come on in."

Opening the door, he stepped into an elegantly appointed office and looked directly at his father, seated behind a mahogany desk fit for a king.

At seventy-seven, Patrick Elliott looked at least ten years younger than his age. Still had most of his hair, though it was completely gray now. Tall, with squared shoulders and a defiant tilt to his chin, the old man continued to look like he'd be able to take on the world, if necessary.

Shane walked across the office and dropped into a burgundy leather club chair opposite his father's desk. Absently he noted that the chair was built to be lower than Patrick's desk, leaving whoever sat in it at a disadvantage. That was his father, though. Never miss a trick. "What can I do for you, Dad?"

Patrick leaned back in his chair, braced his elbows on the padded arms and steepled his fingers. "In a hurry, are you?"

"Not really." Of course he was, but if he admitted as much, Patrick was contrary enough to slow this meeting down. Crossing his legs, Shane rested his right ankle on his left knee and idly tapped his fingers against the soft leather of his shoe.

Nodding, the old man said, "That's all right. I am in a hurry. Your mother's got us tickets to some play or other."

Shane smiled. "A musical?"

Patrick shuddered. "Probably."

This time Shane dipped his head to hide a broader smile. His parents were sharply divided on the theater. His father hated it and his mother loved it. One thing he could give Patrick Elliott. The man was crazy enough about his wife that he'd actually suffered through seeing *Cats* twelve times.

"God knows what she's gonna make me endure tonight. But she's meeting me here in twenty minutes, so I'm gonna make this short."

"All right." Back to business, then. "Let's hear it."

Patrick leaned forward in his chair and gave his son

a broad smile. "The final reports are in. All of the profit margins on each of the magazines has been tallied."

"And…?" Shane's heartbeat quickened and a sense of expectation filled him. Hell, just a year ago, if someone had told him he'd care this much about being named CEO of Elliot Publication Holdings, he would have laughed himself sick.

Now?

Hell, he wanted that position more than he cared to admit. And even more, he wanted to *win* the competition his father had instigated.

"Congratulations," Patrick said.

Shane let out a breath he hadn't realized he'd been holding. "Yeah?" He grinned and stood up. "Thanks."

The old man stood, too, and held out one hand. Shane grabbed it and gave it a shake.

"You did a good job, son."

A surprising zip of pleasure shot through Shane. Apparently, he thought wryly, no one outgrew the need for approval from a parent. Even one who'd been as absent from his children's lives as Patrick.

"Appreciate it," Shane said, reeling in his thoughts as they careened wildly through his mind. CEO. It meant a world of responsibilities that only a year or so ago he would have done anything he could to avoid. Weird how a man's life could change.

He couldn't wait to tell Rachel. All the work they'd been doing for the last few years had finally culminated in winning the grand prize.

"I'll make the official announcement at the family

New Year's party," Patrick was saying as he came around the edge of his desk. "But I wanted you to know now. You earned it, Shane."

"Damn straight I did," Shane said, still feeling the hum of excitement. Gratification. "But I couldn't have done it without my staff. The people at *The Buzz* have worked their asses off this last year. Especially Rachel, my assistant."

The older man nodded, pleased. "I'm glad you realize that no man succeeds alone."

Shane slanted his father a look. "Oh, I know it. I'm just sort of surprised that *you* know it."

Patrick sighed and shook his head. "A man reaches a certain age and he gets to know all sorts of things, Shane. Things he should have realized a long time ago."

"Yeah, well," Shane said, suddenly uncomfortable. "Better late than never, I guess."

"I suppose. At the first of the year, I'll clear my stuff out of this office and you can move in."

"Seems strange. Thinking about me, working up here."

"Seems damn strange to me, too, son," Patrick said, wandering across the room to stare at the plaques and framed awards EPH had won over the years. "I'm so used to coming here every day," he murmured, "I can't really imagine *not* working."

"Hell, I can't even remember the last time you took a vacation."

The older man glanced over his shoulder at Shane. His eyes flashed with something that might have been regret, but it was gone so fast, Shane couldn't be sure. And even if it was regret, he told himself, what did it change?

"I made mistakes," Patrick admitted, turning around now to face his son. "I know that."

Shane stiffened slightly. He didn't want to head down Memory Lane with his father. Especially since those memories would no doubt douse the feeling of victory still rushing through him. Over the last year, Patrick had made a sincere effort to get to know his children. But the bottom line was, one good year didn't offset a lifetime. "Dad—"

"I know. You don't want to talk about it. Well, neither do I." Shoving both hands into the pockets of his well-tailored dark blue suit, the older man said, "But I can't help thinking about it. I can't rewrite the past, though I wish to hell I could. All those years, I focused on my work. Building a legacy for you and your brothers and sisters."

"And you did it."

"Yes, I did. But along the way," he said, his voice suddenly sounding tired, "I missed what was really important. It all slipped out of my reach and I let it go. Did it to myself. No one else to blame."

"There doesn't have to be blame," Shane said quietly. "Not anymore."

"Wish I believed that," Patrick whispered and he suddenly looked every one of his seventy-seven years. "But the mistakes I made are the point of this conversation."

"Meaning?"

"Meaning don't do what I did." He pulled his hands from his pockets and waved his arms to encompass the high-rise office, the awards and the incredible view from the bank of floor to ceiling windows behind his desk. "Right now, being in charge looks great. The challenge. The fun of beating the others."

Shane shrugged.

"I know you, son," Patrick said, stabbing his index finger at Shane. "I know you thrive on the competition, just like a true Elliott. But remember, winning doesn't mean a damn thing if you've got nothing but the victory to show for it."

Three

Rachel opened the freezer door for the third time in a half hour and stared at her nemesis. It sat there next to a stack of frozen dinners and mocked her silently.

Her own fault. She never should have bought it. But she'd had a weak moment right after work.

Well, actually, she'd been having plenty of weak moments lately. Every time she thought about quitting her job and walking away from her only connection to Shane Elliott.

"It's the right thing to do," she muttered as icy fog wafted from the freezer to caress her face.

Her hand tightened on the white plastic door handle and she squeezed as if gripping a lifeline. She had to quit. She knew it. She'd only been postponing the inevitable because she hadn't wanted to leave EPH until Shane had won the competition between him and his siblings.

"Well, that excuse is gone. You've helped *The Buzz* do so well in this last year that he's *bound* to win. What've you got left?" she asked herself, knowing damn well there wasn't an answer.

She shivered, and reached into the freezer, her fingers curling around a small carton covered in ice crystals. "Fine. I surrender. We both knew I would or I wouldn't have bought you in the first place."

When a knock sounded on her front door, she backed up instantly, leaving the carton where it was and slammed the freezer shut. She ran both hands over her wavy blond hair, released from the tidy French twist she kept it in while working. Then she automatically smoothed the gray skirt she still wore and shuffled out of the tiny galley kitchen in her pink fuzzy slippers. As she walked, she glanced at the pineapple shaped clock on the wall.

Eight o'clock.

Great.

Shane would be just sitting down to his first glass of champagne with Tawny the wonder girl. Glad she'd reminded herself of *that.* Oh, yeah, it was definitely time to quit her job.

She passed her overstuffed sofa on the way to the door and absently straightened a bright blue throw pillow. Rachel's gaze flicked quickly around her West Village apartment in approval. Only a one bedroom, it was plenty big enough for her. Plus, it was a family neighborhood, with a deli on one corner and a small grocery store on another.

In the five years she'd lived here, she'd transformed the old apartment into a cozy nest. She'd painted the walls a soft, French country lemon-yellow and done the trim in pale off-white. The furniture was large, overstuffed and covered in a floral fabric that made her feel as if she lived in a garden.

Natalie Cole sang to her from the stereo on the far wall and from downstairs, came the tempting scent of her neighbor Mrs. Florio's homemade lasagna. With any luck, Rachel thought, scuffing her slippers over the hardwood floor, she'd be getting a care basket of leftovers in the morning. Mrs. Florio, God bless her, thought Rachel was far too skinny to "catch a nice man" and took every opportunity to fatten her up.

Smiling to herself, Rachel looked through the security peephole and sucked in a gasp as she jumped back, startled.

Shane?

Here?

He knocked again.

She took another peek and watched as he leaned in toward the fisheye lens and grinned. "Rachel, come on. Open up."

Quickly she gave herself a once-over. Still in the yellow silk blouse and gray skirt she'd worn to work, she suddenly wished she was dressed in sequins and rhinestones and on her way out the door to meet…*anybody.*

"How do you know I'm here?" she demanded. "I could be out on a hot date." Sure. In an alternate universe.

"You're talking to me," he said, still grinning into the peephole. "So you're there. Now, you going to let me in or what?"

In the four years she'd worked for Shane he'd never once come to her apartment. So what in heaven would bring him here now? Did he somehow sense she was going to quit? Was he trying to undermine her decision?

"This is so not fair," she muttered as she quickly undid the chain, then twisted first one, then another dead bolt locks. Finally she turned the knob and opened the door.

Shane didn't wait for an invitation; he crowded past her into the living room, then turned around to look at her. In one hand, he held a bouquet of lilacs—Rachel's favorite flower—and in the other a huge bottle of champagne.

Stomach jittering, Rachel closed the door and leaned back against it. "What're you doing here, Shane?"

"This is a nice place," he said, glancing around at the apartment.

"Thanks."

"Wasn't easy to find," he added. "Had to go down to personnel and look up your records to get your address."

Her stomach did another wild twist and flip and she swallowed hard. "And why would you do that?"

"So I could bring you these," he said, handing her the lilacs.

The heavy, sweet perfume reached for her and Rachel just managed to keep from burying her nose in the blossoms and enjoying the thrill of Shane bringing her flowers. But there was something else going on here and she had to know what it was.

"Shane, why are you bringing me flowers?" she asked, silently congratulating herself on the steadiness of her voice. "Aren't you supposed to be at Une Nuit giving Tawny a bouquet of daisies?"

"Tawny!" He slapped the heel of his hand against his forehead. "*That's* her name. Why can't I remember that?"

"Good question," Rachel said. "Maybe because there are too many Tawnys, Bambis and Barbies in your life to keep them straight?"

He slanted her a look and then smiled and shrugged. "Maybe." Sweeping his gaze around the room again, he started for the kitchen, talking over his shoulder as he went. "Anyway, don't worry about what's her name. I called Stash. Told him I couldn't make it and to give…"

"Tawny," Rachel provided as she followed him into her kitchen.

"…right. Told him to give Tawny whatever she wanted on the house and to offer my apologies."

"So you stood her up."

"Had to," he said, setting the champagne bottle down onto the counter and shifting a look at the white cupboards. "Champagne glasses?"

Still clutching her lilacs, Rachel pointed with her free hand. "Just wineglasses, sorry."

He shrugged again. "That's fine." Then he opened the cupboard door, reached two glasses and set them on the counter.

This was too hard. Now that she'd seen him here, in her place, she'd never really be able to get him out again. She'd always be able to pull up the memory of him standing in her living room, rooting through her kitchen. Heck, she'd probably never be able to look through the peephole again without seeing his smiling face looking back at her.

"You shouldn't be here," she blurted, fingers tightening around the lilacs that must have cost him a small fortune.

Springtime flowers in the dead of winter? And she was sappy enough to really enjoy knowing that he'd remembered *her* favorite flowers even when he couldn't remember Tawny's.

His fingers on the wire cage of the bottle top, he paused to glance at her. His gaze swept her up and down, from her tousled hair to the tips of her furry slippers. Slowly a smile curved his mouth. "Why? You really do have a hot date?"

Straightening up a little, she said, "I was planning on spending the night with *two* guys, actually."

"Yeah? Who?"

Rachel sighed. It was pointless to pretend, since she wasn't exactly dressed for going clubbing. "Ben and Jerry."

Shane grinned as he started working on the champagne cork again. "This'll be better."

"I don't know," she said, moving past him to grab a cut glass vase from another cupboard. She glanced at him as she filled the vase with water. "It's *chocolate* ice cream."

"Not nearly good enough for the occasion."

"Which is?" she asked, stuffing the lilacs into the vase and giving them one last, lingering caress.

"We're celebrating." The cork popped, slamming into a cupboard before bouncing to the floor, and Shane held the bottle over the sink as champagne frothed and foamed out the neck. As he filled both of the heavy green glasses to the rim, he looked down at her, winked and teased, "Ask me what we're celebrating."

A jolt of excitement sizzled inside her. "What're we celebrating?"

"We did it, Rachel," he said, setting the bottle down and handing her one of the glasses. He picked up his own then clinked it against hers. "We won the contest. I'm the new CEO."

That single jolt of excitement burst into a fireworks display of pleasure that lit up her insides like the Fourth of July. "Shane, that's great."

It was. It really was. Even though it was now official and Rachel knew she'd be leaving, she was just so damn happy for him. He'd worked hard for this and really deserved it. That he was so pleased about it only went to show how much he'd changed in the last few years.

"I know," he said, taking her elbow and leading her out of the kitchen into the living room. He steered her onto the couch, said, "I'll be right back," and went back to the kitchen to retrieve the champagne.

He set the bottle down on the glass-topped coffee table, then sat down beside Rachel on the sofa. She watched him over the rim of her glass while she took a huge swallow. Bubbles filled her nose, her mouth and apparently, her mind.

Watching him, Rachel wanted to reach out and smooth back the lock of dark hair lying across his forehead. She curled her fingers around the stem of her glass to keep from doing just that. Instead she settled for looking at him. Shane had always been a good stare. The man was simply gorgeous.

Shining moss-green eyes, strong chin, wide smile and broad shoulders. He was the stuff that dreams were made of. Rachel should know. He filled her dreams almost nightly.

"You know," he was saying, "when my father broke the news to me a while ago, all I could think about was that you should have been there to hear it, too."

She took another gulp of champagne, hoping to ease the sudden dryness in her throat.

"You're the real reason I won, Rachel."

A happy little glow dazzled her insides, but she deliberately squashed it. "That's not true, Shane. You worked hard for this. You deserve it."

"Maybe," he said nodding, running the tip of his

index finger around the rim of his glass. "But even if it's true, I couldn't have done it without you."

"Oh, absolutely," she agreed smiling.

So much easier to keep this conversation light and teasing, as she always did. So much better for her equilibrium if she didn't start fantasizing about Shane throwing himself at her feet, proclaiming his love and begging her to marry him.

Oh for heaven's sake.

She took another big drink of champagne and didn't complain when Shane reached for the bottle and topped off her glass and then his own.

"We'll be moving into my father's office at the first of the year."

You will, she thought silently, wishing she could stay. Wishing she could be a part of his life. But it was just getting too painful.

"I'm guessing you'll want to redecorate," she said wryly.

"Oh, yeah." His grin was devastating. All the more so since he seemed to be oblivious to the power he wielded. "I can't stand the antique thing, but the glass and chrome look doesn't seem right for up there, either."

"I guess not," she said, as the music playing shifted from a drum pounding dance rhythm to something slow and sultry.

"This means a big raise," Shane said, leaning back into the sofa cushion. "For both of us."

"Uh-huh." A raise would have been nice.

"And a bonus," he said, "if you can locate our

mysterious columnist and convince her to keep writing for *The Buzz*."

"Shane—"

"I know," he interrupted, "we haven't been able to find her, but she's out there somewhere, Rachel."

"And doesn't want to be found." Oh, she really didn't want to be found.

"Yeah, but I've been thinking," he said, refilling their glasses again.

Rachel looked at the bubbles in her wineglass and told herself to stop drinking it so quickly. Already, her mind was a little fuzzy and her vision blurred just a little bit. Should have eaten that ice cream, she told herself.

She shook her head and told herself to pay attention as Shane kept talking.

"Tess said she's quitting her job. So I'm thinking, what if we just hire her to work for us?"

"She does," Rachel argued and wondered why her tongue suddenly felt a little thick. "She writes a column for *The Buzz*."

"Yeah, but if we made her a *staff* writer, she could call her own shots. Do advice, gossip, whatever." He jumped to his feet as if unable to sit still beneath the onslaught of too many ideas. "The readers love her, Rachel. She's funny and smart and that comes across in her column."

She almost said thank you. Catching herself just in time, Rachel frowned at her champagne and leaned forward to carefully set her glass on the coffee table. A buzz was good. Drunk was not.

"Why is this so important to you, Shane?"

He turned around to look at her. Taking a long gulp of his wine, he shook his head. "Not sure. All I know is she's good and I'm not going to let her slip away."

"I don't think you have much choice."

He smiled at her and something warm and liquid slid through her veins, leaving a trail of fire that seemed to be burning right through her skin.

Oh, boy.

"That's where you're wrong. You're my secret weapon, Rachel."

"Me?"

"You've got more contacts in the city than the mayor. You can find out who Tess is and where we can find her."

"Oh, I don't think so."

Setting his glass down on the table, Shane reached for her and pulled her to her feet. She swayed a little, but he steadied her fast.

"Rachel, you can't quit on me now."

Quit? How'd he know she was going to quit? She stared up at him and, just for a minute or two, lost herself in the green of his eyes. "Did you know," she whispered, "you have tiny gold flakes in your eyes?"

The smile faded from his face and his hands on her arms gentled, his thumbs rubbing against her silk blouse. "I do?"

"Yes," she said, leaning in even closer, tipping her head back to keep her gaze locked with his. "I never really noticed before, but…"

"Your eyes are green, too," he said, his voice

almost lost under the slow pulse of the music. "Soft green. Like summer grass."

Her pulse quickened, her heartbeat jangled wildly and a swirl of something hot and needy settled in the pit of her stomach. And Rachel was loving every minute of it.

His hands slid across her back and dropped to her waist. She felt the heat of his touch right through the fabric of her blouse and she wondered absently if his handprints were branded on her skin.

She hoped so.

"Rachel," he whispered, his hands moving on her back again in long, languorous strokes that fanned the fire simmering inside her into hungry flames. He took a breath, held it as his gaze moved over her face as if he'd never seen her before. As if she were the most beautiful thing on the planet. Then he released that pent-up breath and said, "I'd better—"

Go.

He was going to leave.

Already he was releasing her, taking a small step back, putting a small slice of safety between them. And suddenly Rachel knew she couldn't let this moment pass. Let him leave without at least showing him once just how she felt.

"—kiss you," she said, finishing his sentence the way she wanted it to be. She went up on her toes, slid her arms around his neck and tipped her head to one side. He watched her, not moving. She felt the tension in his hands. She was pretty sure time itself stood still for one amazing moment.

Then she laid her mouth over his and put everything she had into the kiss she'd been daydreaming about for a solid year.

Four

For a fraction of a second, Shane was too surprised to react.

He caught up quick.

Rachel's lips were warm and soft and the taste of champagne clung to them, giving him more of a rush than drinking the expensive wine itself had. He pulled her tighter, closer, wrapping his arms around her and squeezing as he devoured her mouth.

Random thoughts flashed through his mind like fireflies winking on and off on a hot summer night.

Rachel.

He was kissing Rachel.

And it felt good.

Right.

Her mouth opened under his tender assault and his tongue swept inside to taste her more deeply. To feel her heat, to claim…something.

Something he couldn't name but knew was within his reach. Something that he'd never thought to find.

Fin had long teased him about the right woman being there under his nose for four years, but he'd never really considered that she might be correct. His twin had hinted that Rachel Adler could, with a little effort on his part, be much more to him than a fabulous assistant.

But he hadn't listened. Hadn't really believed that Rachel and he would be able to…connect so completely. So amazingly.

Her hands slid up his back and he wished to heaven he'd taken his suit jacket off when he arrived. He wanted to feel her small, capable hands with their short, neat nails on his skin.

That thought jolted through him with the impact of a crashing meteor.

Then a ball of fire settled in the pit of his stomach and stretched out tentacles to every corner of his body. Heat radiated from him and fed the raw, raging hunger clawing at his insides.

He tore his mouth from hers and ran his lips down the length of her neck. "Sweet. So sweet."

"Shane." His name, on a sigh of sound that rushed through him with the force of a category 5 hurricane.

Her hands tangled at the back of his neck, fingers twining through his hair, nails scraping his skin.

Sensation boiled within and Shane had to fight for air.

He'd never known such an overwhelming desire. Such a demand from his body.

Such all consuming *need.*

He slipped his hands beneath the tail of her silk shirt and smoothed his palms over her back. Her skin was more tantalizing than the silk. Smoother, softer. He sucked in air like a dying man and licked the pulse point at the base of her throat.

She gasped and tipped her head to one side, silently inviting more of his attention. He gave it to her. As his hands stroked her back, he nibbled at her throat and covered that pounding pulse point until he could taste her need for him throbbing with every beat of her heart.

"Rachel," he murmured against her skin. "I'm not sure what's going on here, but I want you."

"Oh good," she said, sighing again and leaning into him more completely. "That's very good. I want you, too. Now, okay? Does now work for you?"

He smiled and lifted his head to look down into her passion-glazed eyes. His smile faded in a new burst of hunger. "Yeah, now works for me in a big way."

He looked around the room, as if expecting a bed to magically appear. If it didn't, he was thinking the couch would do. Plenty long enough. And if she didn't like the couch, then the floor. Or standing up against a wall.

Something.

Soon.

He had to have her.

Had to bury himself inside her and feel her heat taking him in. Had to watch her eyes blur and feel her breath catch. Had to see a climax shatter the cool green of her eyes.

"Bedroom," she said, lifting one hand to point. "Through there."

"Right." He didn't waste time. Couldn't. Sweeping her up into his arms, he crossed the room in a few long strides and kicked the partially ajar door wide-open.

A double bed with four heavy posts sat against one wall, its mattress covered by a floral quilt. The curtains were open and through the lacy sheers, a streetlight shone from outside, illuminating the softly falling snowflakes drifting past the glass.

They were three stories up. No one was going to be peeking in at them, so Shane left the curtains open to the pale wash of light. He wanted to see her.

Wanted to watch her.

He carried her across the room and set her on her feet. She staggered slightly and Shane smiled. He knew how she felt.

Everything was just a little off center.

"You're not changing your mind, are you?" she asked.

"Not a chance," he whispered and reached for the top button of her blouse. In less than a few seconds he had them all undone and was pushing the silk down her arms to let it fall onto the floor.

"That's good," she said, swallowing hard and nodding. "Really good."

Shane nodded back at her. "How about you? We can still stop."

"Are you kidding?" she asked and stepped into the circle of his arms, wrapping her own arms around his neck and hanging on. She looked up into his eyes and said, "No one leaves this room until we're absolutely through with each other."

He gave her a quick grin. This was the Rachel he knew and admired. Sure of herself. Confident. "I learned a long time ago that it pays to listen to my assistant."

Then he kissed her again and quickly worked the hooks at the back of her bra. The fragile lace parted and she twisted in his arms, freeing herself while simultaneously pushing his jacket off his shoulders.

Shane felt the same urgency pounding inside him and worked with her. In a couple of minutes, they were both naked and tumbling onto the mattress. The quilt was cold against his skin and the fabric felt old and soft. The antique bed creaked and groaned under their combined weight, but neither of them noticed.

In the wash of light streaming through the windows, Shane looked his fill of her. Full breasts, narrow waist and rounded hips—she was built with curves in all the right places, as, in his opinion, all women should be. He ran his hands over those curves, tracing every line with his fingertips until she was writhing beneath him, her breath coming fast and furious.

As her need peaked, so did his. He felt every one of her thundering heartbeats as if it were his own. He touched her and she shivered. He stroked her and she sighed. She lifted one hand to drag her nails across his chest and he felt each gentle scrape as if it were a flaming arrow.

"Yes, yes," she whispered, "you feel so good, Shane." She turned into him, parting her legs for his questing fingers.

His heartbeat jumped, his breath caught. He slid one hand down, down across her rib cage, over her abdomen and past the juncture of her thighs. She jerked in his arms and tried to close her legs.

"Rachel?"

"I'm too on the edge. It's coming. And I don't want it to," she breathed shakily. "I want this to last. I don't want it over so fast."

"It's not over," he assured her, his voice tight, scratching past the knot of need lodged in his throat. "We have all night. Now let me take you."

She clutched at his shoulders as his fingers dipped lower to find her depths. She was hot, damp, ready for his touch. He watched her as he slid his hand lower, caressing her intimate folds.

She gasped and stiffened in his arms at that first molten contact. "Shane!"

Her climax hit her hard, shaking her from head to toe. She tipped her head back into the mattress, bit her bottom lip and, keeping a death grip on his shoulders, shuddered as her body erupted from within.

More aroused than he'd ever been in his life, Shane watched her as she rode the crest of pleasure, shaking, trembling in his grasp, her fingers clutching at him. Mouth dry, pulse hammering, he bent his head and took her mouth as she gasped for air. He wanted to feel that again. Feel her body exploding for him, *because* of him. He wanted to hear her gasp and scream his name.

Her body still shuddering, he took her up again, pushing her high and fast. Sliding first one then two fingers inside her as his thumb stroked the very core of her, he stroked her inside and out.

Rachel dragged in air, knowing it wasn't enough. She might never get enough air again. Her brain was melting, but that was probably because her body was on fire.

The first orgasm had hardly finished shimmering through her when Shane had her on the climb toward number two. And now that she knew how good it was, she couldn't wait for it to happen again. Her body hummed and sizzled. Her blood felt as if it were boiling. Her limbs were weak and energized all at once.

She twisted up closer to him, loving the feel of his skin against hers. The soft curls of dark hair on his chest felt like silk, and the muscles beneath his skin felt like steel. His body was hard and strong and, right at the moment, as necessary to her as the breathing that just wasn't working quite right.

Her mind numbed out, short-circuited from the

onslaught of sensations rocketing through it. She couldn't think, could barely see, and it didn't seem to matter. All that mattered was that he not stop touching her.

His hands moved on her and she opened her legs wider, loving the feel of him on her, *in* her.

He took her mouth again in another kiss and she knew that breathing was no longer an option. But who needed air when she had Shane? His tongue mated with hers in an erotic dance that sent shock waves of need and desire sliding through her system.

His breath brushed her cheek and she moved toward him, somehow trying to burrow into him. She hooked her left leg over his hip and groaned when his fingers dipped deeper inside her.

"I've gotta be in you," he whispered, tearing his mouth from hers to bury his face in the curve of her neck. His whiskers scratched her skin as he licked and tasted his way across her throat and down to her collarbone.

"Oh, yeah, inside me. That's good. That sounds good to me, too."

"Protection," he muttered thickly, dipping his head to bite her neck.

His teeth stroked her fevered skin even as that one word he'd said sailed through her brain and came to a dead stop.

"Protection. Yeah. Okay." And her without a single condom in the house. She couldn't let him leave. Couldn't *not* feel his body within hers. She had to have him. *Now.* Struggling to breathe and think and speak at the same time, Rachel finally found the words she needed. "I'm on the pill. I'm good if you're—"

"Clean as a whistle," he assured her.

"Me, too. Good for us."

"Oh, yeah, excellent for us," he whispered, moving over her, settling himself between her updrawn thighs. "Best news I've ever heard."

She nodded. "Right there with you."

And then there was no more talking. This was too important for talk. Too important for thought.

Too damn important period.

His body pushed into hers and Rachel's breath caught. She arched up, meeting him, opening for him, welcoming him in deeper, harder. He was so big. So hard.

So wonderful.

He rocked his hips against hers, filling her, engulfing her with sensation. Then he took her hands and, capturing them in his, held them down at either side of her head. She tried to move and couldn't. Then she realized she didn't care about moving. She only wanted to feel.

He stared down into her eyes as he withdrew and advanced, his body lighting hers up like a fireworks show.

Every hard, solid inch of him filled her and when he pulled free of her body only to slide himself home again, Rachel groaned. This was all she'd ever dreamed of, wanted, and more.

As Shane's body drove hers toward completion, she realized that she never could have imagined this. Nothing in her experience—all right, her experience was pretty limited—could have prepared her for this. For the clamoring feelings, the mind-shattering explosions, the frantic, demanding need.

He looked down at her and she stared up into eyes that were green and gold and dark with passion. His generous mouth tight, his jaw locked, he stared into her eyes as if he couldn't have looked away if his life depended on it.

Music poured into the room from the stereo in the living room; the quilt beneath her felt cool and soft. And in the pale light, Rachel burned this image of Shane on her mind so that she would always have it with her.

He kept a tight grip on her hands, pinning her to the bed. Her hips rose and fell with him to the rhythm he set, and when electric sparks began in her bloodstream, she raced with him toward the release she knew was waiting just out of reach.

"Shane?" she called his name aloud. Had to say it. Had to hear it. Had to convince herself that this was real and not just another of her lonely dreams.

"Come for me," he said, his voice a rumble in the dimly lit room. "Come for me again. And then again."

With a shriek of bone-deep ecstasy, she did. Clinging to him as her body exploded into a fiery burst of sparks and color, she was only dimly aware when he called her name and followed her into the void.

A kaleidoscope of colors was still revolving behind her closed eyes when Rachel felt Shane roll off of her and to the edge of the bed. "What?"

She forced her eyes open and looked at him. Just one look was enough to make her body start humming again, ready for another go. Apparently, though, Shane was finished.

"You're *leaving?*"

He looked at her and gave her a grin that weakened her knees enough to make her grateful she was lying down.

"Just going to the living room. For the champagne."

"Ah. Good idea."

"Yeah," he said, leaning down to plant a quick kiss on her mouth. "Seems I'm just full of good ideas tonight."

She watched him leave the room and couldn't complain about the view. He even had a nice butt. But a second later, Rachel closed her eyes again and shifted lazily on the quilt her grandmother had made more than fifty years before. She winced at that thought and rolled off the bed. Quickly she pulled the quilt back and draped it over the foot of the bed, then lay down again on the clean, lavender-scented sheets.

Every inch of her body felt used up and happy.

But just as she acknowledged that fact, her brain started clicking along, demanding to know what she was going to do next. How could she sleep with her boss? How tacky was that? And how could she ever look at him at the office again without imagining that great butt?

Stop it. She didn't want to think.

Not tonight.

Heaven knew there'd be plenty of time for thinking and torturing herself later. For the moment, she only wanted to enjoy what she was feeling.

Icy cold trickled onto her breasts and her eyes flew open.

She looked up, directly into Shane's eyes and her heart thudded in her chest. "What're you…"

He drizzled a little more champagne onto her breasts, then set the bottle down onto the nightstand beside the bed. Climbing in beside her, he said only, "I was thirsty."

Then he bent his head to take first one of her nipples, then the other, into his mouth. His tongue twirled around and around the rigid, sensitive peaks and Rachel groaned as he suckled her. Her fingers curled into the sheet beneath her and she held on tight as her world rocked crazily from side to side.

He lapped at her, nibbled her flesh with the edges of his teeth and then suckled her again. She felt each drawing tug of his mouth straight to the heart of her.

Her body lit up again and when he lifted his head, she wanted to weep for the loss of his mouth. She drew in a deep gulp of air and blew it out again in a rush.

"Still thirsty," he quipped and grabbed the bottle. Carefully, he poured the frothy wine atop her breasts, down her rib cage and let it pool in her belly button.

Rachel shivered, but not because the champagne

was so cold. No, she was only surprised it didn't boil on contact with her skin. "Shane..."

"And a sip for you," he said, lifting her head from the bed and holding her as he tipped the mouth of the bottle to her lips. She took a long drink, easing the dryness in her mouth before she raised up and kissed him. She tasted him, the wine and passion.

And she wanted more.

"Are you ready?" he asked, easing her down and setting the bottle back on the table.

"Oh, I think so," she said, reaching for him.

He shook his head, caught her hands in his and said, "Then find something to hold onto."

He lowered his head to her breasts again and Rachel took his advice. Reaching back, she grabbed hold of the headboard and clung to it like a life rope tossed into a stormy sea. He sucked at her nipples, then moved down, licking the champagne off her skin as he went. Across her ribs, down over her abdomen and into the tiny pool of wine in her belly button.

She sucked in air, groaned out his name and held on even tighter. Her skin was on fire. Heat coiled inside and threatened to burst free. She felt every single nerve ending alive and hopping and oh, she hoped it never stopped.

He shifted position, moving to kneel between her legs, and Rachel smiled, eager for him to enter her again. Eager to feel the race to completion crowding in on her one more time.

But he had another surprise for her. Scooping his

hands beneath her bottom, he lifted her hips off the bed and smiled at her.

Her stomach did a quick somersault.

"Shane—"

"Hang on tight, Rachel," he whispered deeply. "This ride's about to get bumpy."

Five

His mouth covered her and Rachel groaned, his name sliding from her throat on a whisper of wonder. She watched him take her, couldn't look away. She concentrated on the feel of his hands on her behind, the lush sensation of his mouth, the hush of his breath.

Outside, the wind tossed snow against the frosted windowpanes. But inside, she was half surprised not to see steam rising from the bed.

Again and again, his lips and tongue worked her flesh, firing her blood, fuzzing her brain. She couldn't think. Couldn't remember *ever* thinking.

She was simply a mass of sensation. Her nerves stretched to the breaking point and hovered there as the tension in her body built and screamed through her, demanding release. Demanding satisfaction. Demanding his body inside hers.

Now.

"Shane," she managed to croak despite the tightness in her throat. "I want—I need you in me. Please."

He set her down and moved to cover her. "I need that, too," he whispered and wrapping his arms around her waist, he held onto her as he rolled onto his back.

And Rachel was straddling him, looking down into his eyes, feeling herself drowning in a sea of gold-flecked green.

She moved on him and Shane bit back a groan. In the lamplight pooling in through the windows, she looked like a goddess. Her honey-blond hair loose and waving about her shoulders, her breasts high and full, a knowing smile on her luscious mouth.

Something beyond lust, beyond desire quickened inside him. But it was forgotten in a new rush of need as she moved on him again. Swiveling her hips, she took him deep inside her body and sighed with satisfaction as she set a slow, steady rhythm between them.

He reached up, cupping her breasts and tweaking her nipples with his thumbs and forefingers. She sighed and that soft sound filled him with fire. He dropped his hands to her hips and guided her on him, helping her move.

Pushing himself higher and deeper inside her, he felt the first shuddering ripples of her climax wash through her. He saw her eyes glaze over, watched as her head fell back, and when she called his name,

Shane's body erupted and he jumped into oblivion, holding her close as he fell.

Rachel woke up a couple of hours later. She opened her eyes and found herself staring at the floor. Clinging to the edge of the mattress, she was cold and realized that not only had Shane hogged the bed, he'd also stolen all the blankets.

A sign?

Sliding off the bed, she hurried to the closet, threw it open and grabbed her robe. With the thick, dark green terry cloth wrapped around her, she tied the belt at her waist and looked at Shane, sprawled across her mattress. Torn between the glow of having been well loved and already worrying about how in the hell she would ever be able to look him in the eye again, Rachel chewed at her bottom lip. Her mind raced with possibilities and consequences.

None of them pleasant.

She wasn't an idiot.

She knew darn well that the hours they'd spent together in her bed wouldn't mean to Shane what it had to her.

Sure, they'd made something magical between the two of them, but he wasn't in love with her. She knew that.

What she didn't know was why he'd—

Stop.

Rachel shut her brain off, refusing to continue wandering down the twisted paths her mind kept showing her. It was too late to turn back the clock and prevent this night from happening, even if she wanted to. Which, to be honest, she didn't.

Turning her back on Shane, she slipped from the bedroom and walked quietly through the darkness. She paused in the living room long enough to turn off the stereo, then continued on to the kitchen, moving through a silence so loud it was deafening.

There, she moved around the familiar space, not needing a light. She filled the coffeepot with water, set it back on the hot plate and filled the basket with a few scoops of dark, rich Colombian coffee grounds. She hit the button and stood in the shadows as the coffeemaker hissed and gurgled, scenting the air with an aroma that was both comforting and familiar.

She stared out the window and nearly hypnotized herself watching snow drifting past the glass. Her body still hummed with satisfaction and yet...she couldn't settle. Couldn't enjoy even the memories of what she and Shane had shared. Because she knew that with the morning light, everything between them would be changed.

Forever.

What she *didn't* know was what to do about it.

Rubbing her hands up and down her arms against a chill she felt right down to her bones, she walked back to the bedroom, opened the door quietly and stood on the threshold. He was still sleeping, so Rachel indulged herself and watched him unnoticed as he slept.

Something inside her turned over and she realized that sleeping with him had only intensified her feelings. And she wondered what in the heck she was supposed to do now.

How could she look at him again, knowing what it was like to be in his arms, and pretend she didn't want it to happen again?

How could she face him at work and *not* remember his kiss, his body wrapped around hers?

"You're watching me."

His voice rumbled from the shadows and she jumped. "Didn't know you were awake."

He rose up and braced himself on his elbows. The quilt covering him slid down his broad, naked chest and puddled at his hips. She couldn't see his eyes in the dark, but she felt his gaze as surely as if he'd reached out to touch her.

Oh, she was in such deep trouble.

"I smelled the coffee."

Of course he did. He hadn't been reacting to some secret sense telling him she was nearby. They weren't *connected* on some higher emotional plane, for Pete's sake.

She swallowed regret and grimaced at the bitter taste. "It's ready if you want some."

"Sounds good."

Well, isn't this nice and stiff, she thought. Any more polite and there'd be icicles hanging in the air between them. But she didn't say that. What would be the point? She only nodded and left, knowing he'd get up and follow her.

It took him a few minutes and when he walked into the now brightly lit kitchen, he was dressed, his suit coat slung across one shoulder hooked on his index finger. He laid the jacket down over the back of a chair, then took the coffee mug she offered him.

"Thanks."

"You're welcome." How very dignified they were, when only a couple of hours ago, they'd been all over each other.

"It's good," he said after taking a sip.

Rachel tugged at the collar of her robe, feeling at a real disadvantage with him in his suit and her…well, naked under a layer of terry cloth. To occupy herself, she reached for her own coffee cup and folded both hands around it. Taking a long sip, she let the heat shoot through her before she spoke again.

Then, keeping her voice light despite the ball of lead settled in the pit of her stomach, she said, "So when does everyone else get to hear the news about your big win at EPH?"

He studied the surface of his coffee. "My father's going to officially announce it at the New Year's party."

"But word will get out to the family long before then."

"Probably," he agreed, a half smile on his face.

"You're looking forward to your brothers and sister finding out."

"Of course. And you should, too."

She leaned back against the edge of the counter. "Why's that?"

"Because we're a team, Rachel," he blurted, then let his voice trail off and his gaze drift back to his coffee.

Awkwardness rose up and sat between them like an ugly troll waiting to be recognized.

So Rachel did.

"We're not a team, Shane. I work for you."

His gaze snapped to hers. "Yeah, but—"

She set her coffee down on the countertop and stuffed both hands into the pockets of her robe. Her bare toes curled on the cold floor. "What happened between us tonight—"

"Was a mistake, I know," he said and Rachel's jaw dropped.

"Well, that was honest."

He set his coffee down on the small table, pushed his hands into his slacks pockets and started pacing. A few steps to the counter, then a few steps back again.

"It was my fault," he said, his voice gruff, laced with an emotion she couldn't identify. "And it shouldn't have happened. Damn it, Rachel, you *work* for me—"

"That's right," she said firmly, fighting back the quaver wanting to sound in her voice. "I *work* for you—but I make my own decisions. And last night was as much about *my* choices as yours."

He blew out a breath. "Fine. We both decided. But I should have been the one to back off."

A choked laugh shot from her throat. "Oh, yes. The big strong man should have found a way to save the little woman from herself. Is that it?"

His features tightened up and the muscle in his jaw twitched. "Damn it, that's not what I meant."

"I'm not so sure." Heck, she wasn't sure of anything at the moment. All she knew for a fact was she wanted him out of her house before she did something really stupid like cry.

Oh, wouldn't that be the cherry on top? Sleep with your boss then cry about it in front of him. Hey, atta girl Rachel, she told herself. Keep doing dumb stuff.

God, this conversation was even harder than she'd thought it would be when she was simply dreading it.

He glanced at his wristwatch, then to her. "Maybe we shouldn't try to talk about this now."

She nodded stiffly. "Maybe not."

"I should probably go."

"Good idea." Go already, she screamed inwardly. Hurry it up before the tears start.

God, she felt like an idiot.

But she'd brought this on herself. She was the one who kissed *him.* Heck, after that, of course he had to have sex with her. Turning her down would have been embarrassing. How much kinder to just sleep with the poor little lonely assistant.

A pity romp.

Great.

What every girl dreams of.

He picked up his jacket and shrugged into it. Straightening the collar and lapels, he looked at her and oh God, she saw concern in his eyes.

Concern. So close to sympathy.

To pity.

"I'll see you at work later?"

She lifted her chin, and forced herself to speak

past the knot in her throat. "Sure. I may be a little late because—"

"Doesn't matter," he interrupted. "Take your time. In fact, take the morning off. Come in this afternoon."

He was in no hurry to face her at work, was he? "Fine. I'll see you later."

He nodded and looked for a second as if he wanted to say something more. Thankfully he thought better of it and walked away. When he left the apartment, he closed the door quietly behind him. And Rachel was alone.

Again.

Shane tried to keep his mind on the job, but it wasn't easy. For one thing, every time he passed Rachel's empty desk, he remembered why she wasn't there.

Of course, if she *had* been there, it would have been even harder to walk past her desk. What an idiot he was. What had he been thinking?

He hadn't been thinking at all. Just reacting. To some really incredible feelings. To the press of Rachel's mouth to his. To the rush of holding her in his arms. He muttered an oath, pushed one hand through his hair and told himself to stop remembering. To stop reliving those hours with her.

He might as well take a vow to not breathe.

Restless, Shane pushed away from his desk and turned to stare out the windows. Snow was still falling, with more predicted. On the street far below him, people were rushing down sidewalks, oblivious to the cold. Twinkling lights lined the storefronts and he imagined the street corner Santas were doing a booming business.

It was the end of a long year. His family was closer than they'd ever been and he'd earned the CEO position at the company. By rights, he should be celebrating right now. Instead he felt as though he'd lost something important.

"Crisis! Crisis!"

Shane spun around to face Jonathon Taylor as he gave a perfunctory knock and hustled into the office. "What's wrong?"

"Oh, only the end of my Fourth of July spectacular, that's all." Jonathon lifted both hands dramatically into the air before letting them fall to his sides again.

Good. Business. A chance to concentrate on something besides Rachel. Folding his arms across his chest, Shane watched as the other man paced frenetically around the office. "What happened?"

"My queen," Jonathon moaned theatrically, "my star of the issue—Leticia Baldwin—"

"Ah…" Shane walked back to his desk and sat down. Letty Baldwin, the latest of America's sweethearts. A young actress with talent as well as beauty. "She won't do the article?"

"Oh, she'll do it," Jonathon pouted as he dropped into the chair opposite Shane's desk. "But she's going to be seven months pregnant when it's time to do the photo shoot. Can't exactly use the red, white and blue bikini theme I had in mind. This is just a disaster, Shane. She was my centerpiece. My star. My—"

"—queen, yeah I get it."

He slumped lower in his chair, his spine becoming an overcooked noodle. "I'm shattered."

Shane laughed.

Jonathon glowered at him. "I'm so happy to amuse you."

"Sorry," Shane said, lifting both hands to appease his friend. "It's just that I really needed this little crisis of yours, that's all."

"At least one of us is happy."

"Jon," Shane said, leaning back in his chair, "does Letty Baldwin still want to do the issue?"

"Oh, definitely. Her agent's convinced her that it would be good exposure. And it would, of course."

"Then do it now."

"What?"

"The photo shoot," Shane said slowly, patiently. "Set it up with Ferria and Letty's people. Do the shoot now and just sit on the pictures until the issue's ready to go to press."

Jonathon's features smoothed out as he thought about it. "We could, couldn't we?"

"As long as she agrees, I don't see why not."

"Sandy will throw a fit," Jonathon mused, and seemed to enjoy the idea. "She's already shrieking over the expenses for this quarter."

"I'll handle Sandy," Shane assured him, making a mental note to call his managing editor and smooth over any ruffled feathers.

"Brilliant," Jonathon shouted and bounded from his chair, rubbing his palms together. "This, my king, is why you're in charge."

As Jonathon left, Shane could only wish that all of his problems were so easily solved.

Six

Rachel carried a cup of coffee into Shane's office and braced herself before meeting his gaze. She needn't have worried. After stalling around for three hours, she'd finally come into work, only to be so busy she hadn't had to face Shane all afternoon.

Until now.

Every day at four-thirty, he had a cup of coffee while going over the day's reports, bringing himself up to speed on the different divisions and setting up appointments for the following day. It was a routine. One she'd long since become familiar with.

In fact, over the last few years, she'd come to enjoy this last half hour of the workday. It gave her a chance to relax with a man she both loved *and* liked. Of course, today there'd be no relaxing.

She felt as though every nerve in her body was strung tight and plugged into an electrical outlet.

He looked up as she entered and gave her a distracted smile. "Come on in, Rachel."

She carried the cup of coffee to him and set it down on his desk. Tension arced between them with all the dazzling light and power of a lightning strike. She could almost hear the sizzle in the air.

"How are you?"

"I'm fine, Shane," she said, lying through her teeth. But damned if she'd slink around the office. "And you?"

He reached for the coffee cup, but instead of picking it up, he trailed the tips of his long fingers over the curved handle. Rachel's gaze locked on the movement, and in an instant, her body lit up as she remembered the feel of those fingers on her skin.

Okay, this was going to be a touch more difficult than she'd thought.

"Worried," he said finally and she shifted her gaze to his.

"About…?"

He scowled at her. "About *us,* Rachel. About our working relationship."

She felt a warm flush of embarrassment move through her and she could only hope it wasn't blazing on her face. This was so not fair. She'd dreamed about Shane for over a year, had imagined what a night with him would be like. And now those dreams had become nightmares.

All she had left was her pride and she was going to cling to it with everything she had. "Our working relationship doesn't have to change at all, Shane," she said and hoped to heaven she sounded more sure than she felt.

"Is that right?" He stood up, pushed the edges of his suit jacket back and shoved both hands into his slacks pockets. "So, everything is normal."

"That's right."

"Then why haven't you ragged on me once about work?"

"Excuse me?"

"Normally you'd have come in here carrying that memo pad that's practically stapled to your hand," he pointed out. "And you'd be reading me the list of meetings to go to, warning me about which ones I couldn't duck. Any other day, you'd be standing there telling me who to call, when to do it and what to say."

Rachel sniffed, a little irritated that he knew her so well. But then, they were a team, weren't they? A well-oiled machine. It wasn't *his* fault that she'd fallen in love with him and changed everything. "I'm so very sorry. I had no idea I was that bossy."

He pulled one hand free of his pockets and waved at her. "Bull. Of course you did." He came around the edge of his desk and started toward her. But he stopped a few steps short, as if he couldn't quite trust himself to get too close.

Oh, you're dreaming girl, she told herself. It

was probably more like he was afraid his too aggressive assistant would jump his bones again if he wandered too near.

God help her, he was probably right.

"But that's why we've always worked together so well," he was saying and Rachel shut down her brain and opened her ears. "You keep me focused on the job and I give you somebody to nag."

"Very nice," she muttered.

"And now it's ruined," he snapped.

"Maybe that's for the best."

"Like hell it is," Shane said grimly. "How the hell can I get anything done when I can damn well *feel* the tension between us?"

Okay, she'd made up her mind earlier to be aloof. Distant. To do what she could to pretend that last night had never happened. But now that Shane had pried the lid off this particular can of worms, why should she try to jam the lid back on?

"You're not the only one, you know. Forgive me," she said, "for being just a little on edge. It's not every day I have to face my boss after he's seen me naked."

Shane winced. "I could say the same."

"Yeah," she agreed, "but from my perspective, this is just a little bit harder."

"How's that?"

She laughed shortly and felt the sound scrape against her throat. "This is a cliché for God's sake. Employers have been diddling with their secretaries/assistants for generations!"

"Diddling?"

"Don't you dare smile at me," she shot back. "Diddling is a perfectly good word."

"You're right," he said and took one cautious step closer. "But don't you lump me in with some sleazy guy who makes a habit of sleeping with his secretary."

"Assistant."

"Fine. Assistant." He shoved one hand through his hair and Rachel remembered how soft his thick, dark brown hair was. How it felt streaming through her fingers. She swallowed hard.

"My point," he continued, his voice hardly more than a growl, "is that what happened between us shouldn't have happened at all."

"Yes," she said tightly, "I believe you covered that this morning with the whole 'mistake' thing."

"Well, wasn't it?"

Her hands at her sides, she curled her fingers into her palms and squeezed until she felt the indentation of every nail digging into her skin. *Mistake?* No doubt. Did she regret it? She certainly should. But she couldn't honestly say she did.

She'd wanted him for so long how could she possibly regret having him? Even if it meant having to deal with the messy repercussions.

Watching his face, trying to read the maelstrom of emotion in his eyes, Rachel said, "Of course it was."

Was that disappointment flashing across his eyes? If it was, it was gone almost immediately.

He nodded, blew out a breath and said quietly, "At least we agree on that."

"Yay us."

A half smile quirked the corner of his mouth then disappeared again. "The question is, can we work past it? Can we just forget about what happened and go back to the way things were?"

"I don't know," she said honestly after a long, thoughtful pause. "I'd like to think so."

A small thread of panic jolted through Shane as he watched her. He'd called their time together a mistake. But he didn't regret it. How could he? He'd never experienced anything like what he'd found with Rachel.

He'd been thinking of nothing *but* her for hours. And now that she was standing there in front of him it took every ounce of self-control he possessed to keep from grabbing her and kissing her until neither of them was able to think.

But that wouldn't solve a damn thing. It would in fact, only make a weird situation even more uncomfortable.

"Rachel, I don't want to lose what we have. Our friendship."

"I think that ship has sailed, Shane." Her mouth curved sadly.

"I don't accept that."

Her green eyes filled with tears and he held his breath, hoping to hell they wouldn't fall. He was a dead man if she started crying. Nothing in this world could bring a man to his knees faster than a strong woman's tears.

As if she heard his panicked thoughts, she blinked quickly, furiously, and kept her tears at bay.

"You have to, Shane," she said, with a slow shake of her head. "If we hope to salvage this working relationship, we both have to accept the facts. We're not friends. We're not lovers. To be honest, I'm not sure what we are anymore."

After work, Shane was too irritable to go home alone and not in a good enough mood to call a friend. That last conversation with Rachel kept rewinding and playing in his mind and he couldn't quite seem to settle with it. Things were different between them now and he didn't have a clue what to do about it.

It had been a long time since he'd let his groin do his thinking for him.

Now he remembered *why.*

If he hadn't given in to his own desires the night before, everything in his world would be running great. He'd won the competition in the family, *The Buzz* was gaining strength every damn day and he'd finally realized that he was doing *exactly* what he should be doing.

He stepped out of the EPH building into a face full of wind-driven snow. Shrugging deeper into his overcoat, he squinted into the wind and glanced around. The sidewalks were crowded, as usual. Manhattan streets were never quiet. Cabs carried customers, buses belched along the street and a police squad car, lights flashing, siren whining, fought to get through the congestion.

He loved it.

Loved the noise, the hustle, the rush of life that pulsed in the city like a heartbeat. Stepping out onto the sidewalk, he fell into step with the crush of people instantly surrounding him. You had to keep up when walking these sidewalks. Move too slowly and the crowd would knock you down and kick your body to the curb, all without losing step.

Smiling to himself, he realized he was in the perfect frame of mind for walking in Manhattan.

He wasn't sure where he was going, he just knew he didn't want to go home. God knew there were plenty of women he could call for company, but that thought left him a lot colder than the melting snow sliding beneath his coat collar.

Hands in his pockets, he let his gaze drift while his mind raced. Strings of twinkling lights lined the front windows of the shops he passed, and the combined scents of hot chocolate, steaming coffee and hot dogs poured from a street vendor's cart. He came to the end of the block and while he stood waiting for the light to change, he glanced in the front window of Hannigan's.

A bar that was too upscale to be called a tavern, but too down to earth to be classified a club, Hannigan's offered cold beers and friendly conversation. Sounded a hell of a lot better than going home alone.

Shane marched to the door, pulled it open and was slapped with a blast of warmth, coated with laughter and the jangling beat of Irish folk music.

He shrugged out of his coat, hung it on the rack by the door, then made his way through the tangled maze of tables and chairs.

The hardwood floors were gleaming, a fire danced in the stone hearth on the far wall and behind the polished mahogany bar, a gigantic mirror reflected the faces of the patrons.

Shane pushed through the crowd, made his way to the bar and leaned both elbows on the shining top. When the bartender worked his way down to him, he said quickly, "Guinness."

In a few minutes, the practiced barman was sliding over a perfectly built drink, with a thick layer of cream colored foam atop dark, rich beer. Shane picked up the glass, took a sip and turned to look at the crowded room. His gaze slid across a few familiar faces; after all, everyone who worked in the neighborhood ended up in here at one time or another.

At a booth in the back sat a man more familiar than the rest. Shane headed that way, deftly avoiding a waitress with a laden tray. He tapped on the tabletop, waited for his nephew to look up at him in welcome, then slid into the booth opposite him.

Gannon Elliott was a big man, with black hair, sharp green eyes, and in the last year or so, a ready smile. At thirty-three, Gannon was only five years younger than Shane. The two had grown up more like brothers, though Gannon was his nephew, the son of Michael, Shane's oldest brother.

"Didn't expect to see you in here, Gannon."

The other man shrugged. "Erika wanted to do some Christmas shopping," he said, sliding his half full glass of beer back and forth on the tabletop. "Hannigan's sounded like a better idea to me."

"Christmas shopping." Shane slumped back against the red leather booth. "Haven't started that yet."

"My suggestion?" Gannon quipped, lifting his glass for a long drink. "Get married. Turns out women *like* shopping."

Shane smiled, both at the ridiculous notion of getting married and at the change in his nephew. Only a year ago, Gannon would still have been at work, staying late into the night. More like his grandfather Patrick than any of Patrick's kids were, Gannon had lived and breathed the family business.

Until Erika.

"What about you? Why are you sitting here having a drink with me?" Gannon took another swallow of his beer. "Why aren't you out with that Hollywood girl…what's her name, Amber or Brownie or something?"

Shane frowned, thinking about the woman he was supposed to have had dinner with the night before. He *still* couldn't think of her damn name. But if he'd only met her as planned, none of that mess with Rachel would have happened and he wouldn't now be sitting in the middle of a mess.

"What is that woman's name?" he muttered. "Never mind. Anyway, I wasn't in the mood."

Gannon laughed. "*You?* Not in the mood for a gorgeous woman? You feeling all right?"

"Funny." He took a sip of Guinness and savored the taste.

"Didn't mean it to be funny," Gannon said, studying him now through shrewd green eyes. "Something going on? You should be happy as hell. Heard you won the CEO position."

Shane's gaze snapped to him. "Who told?"

Someone at the bar laughed loudly and the music changed, drifting from a ballad in Gaelic to a jittering rhythm that even had Shane's toes tapping in time.

"Hell," Gannon laughed, "who *doesn't* know? Everyone in the company pretty much had it figured out a few months back. When those third-quarter profit statements came in, it was clear no one was going to be able to catch you."

Pride rippled through Shane, but it didn't do a damn thing to ease the knot of something else tightening in his chest. "Thanks. It was a team effort, though. We *all* made it happen. Everyone at *The Buzz* worked their asses off."

"Which begs the question again," his nephew said. "You should be happier than hell right now. Why aren't you?"

"Long story."

"Do I look busy?"

Shane chuckled. "No, you don't." He nodded, paused for another sip of beer, then said, "Okay, but before we get into the sad, sad story of my life… How's your mom doing?"

Gannon's mother, Shane's sister-in-law Karen,

had been battling breast cancer for the last year. And after a double mastectomy and a debilitating round of chemotherapy, the family was hopeful that she'd beaten the cancer.

Gannon blew out a breath and smiled. "She's doing good. Great, in fact." He signaled the waitress by holding up his empty beer glass, then shifted his gaze back to Shane. "Dad's at her side round the clock. It's pretty amazing to see, really. They've…rediscovered each other, I guess you'd say. And even with the cancer threat hanging over us all, they're so damn happy, it's ridiculous."

"I'm glad."

"Yeah," Gannon said wistfully, "me, too." When the waitress brought him a refill and took away his empty glass, Gannon turned his gaze on Shane. "So, now that we've covered Mom, what's going on with you?"

Shane really didn't want to get into it with his nephew. But who the hell else would understand? Gannon and his wife, Erika, had started out working together—and had an affair. It had all blown up in their faces of course, but they'd finally found their way back to each other and now seemed happy as clams.

Whatever the hell *that* meant.

"Before I get into that," he said, easing into an uncomfortable conversation, "when you and Erika first started your…"

"Affair?"

"Okay." Shane nodded. "Was it hard to work together? Was it…clumsy? Awkward?"

Gannon scraped one hand across his face. "It

wasn't simple," he finally said. "But we both knew what we were doing. We both *chose* to have the affair. Even though it ended badly."

"So you didn't have trouble working together once you'd had sex?"

"If you mean could I keep from imagining her naked, then no. But we managed. For a while." He frowned to himself.

Shane knew what he was thinking about. Gannon was one of the most private men Shane had ever known. The idea of people gossiping about him was anathema to him. The minute talk had started up in the company about his affair with Erika, he'd called it off. Erika had quit soon after and it hadn't been easy for Gannon to talk her into coming back once the Elliott family competition had started last January.

It hadn't been easy, but Gannon had finally realized just what Erika meant to him. And now they were married, and already a week overdue to become parents for the first time. "How's Erika holding up?"

"*She's* doing great," Gannon admitted. "I'm the one who jumps every time she makes a sound. But the doctor said if she hasn't delivered by next Monday, he'll induce. Thank God."

"That's good. Good." Shane nodded, then said under his breath, "I think I've done something really stupid."

"Rachel?"

"Is that a good guess or is there already talk?"

"No talk." Gannon took a drink. "It's just that Fin used to tell me all the time about how perfect Rachel was for you only you were too dumb to see it."

"Ah," Shane mused, "good to be loved by your family."

"Hey, we love you even when you're stupid."

"Small consolation."

"So," Gannon continued, "I'm guessing that things are not really rolling right along now that the situation with Rachel's…changed."

"You could say that." He shook his head and stared up at the pierced tin ceiling. "Hell, Gannon, I don't even know what to say to her anymore. I keep thinking about last night and—" He shut up fast, but it was pointless, since his nephew already understood exactly what Shane was feeling. Been there, done that.

"Don't use me for a template, Shane," Gannon said tightly. "I almost lost Erika, so I'm sure as hell not the one to give you advice."

Shane took a long, deep drink of his beer, then set the glass down again carefully. "Yeah, but you *loved* Erika. Even when you were being an idiot, you loved her."

"You don't love Rachel?"

Love?

He'd never really thought about love. Always been too busy just having a good time. But in his bones, he knew damn well that Rachel was different. She wasn't just another woman in a long string of unremarkable relationships.

But love?

Shane sighed and signaled the waitress. “Damned if I know.”

Seven

Ben & Jerry's was a sad substitute for sex with Shane.

But, since it was all Rachel had, she indulged. Curled up on the couch, with the TV muted and showing some old black-and-white movie, she dug her spoon into the chocolate chunk ice cream. One bite after another slid down her throat despite the huge knot lodged there.

"Idiot," she muttered, pausing to lick her spoon. If she had any spine at all, she'd be out tonight, doing some Christmas shopping. Getting on with her life. Forgetting about Shane.

Apparently, though, her spine was pretty much a wet noodle.

She glanced around the room, sighing. But for the

three Hollyberry scented candles burning in a twisted metal candelabrum on top of the entertainment center, there were absolutely no decorations up. This just wasn't like her.

Ordinarily Rachel was a real Christmas nut. Nothing she liked better than dragging out all of the boxes filled with her Christmas goodies. Stuffed animals, three crèches, hand knit stockings she'd made during her knitting phase, silk garland and the wreath she'd made the Christmas before.

But no. She couldn't get her mind off her troubles long enough to care about the most magical season of the year.

"Just pitiful," she murmured and dipped her spoon back into the carton for another chunk of chocolate.

When the phone rang, she ignored caller ID and all but lunged for it, desperate to hear a voice other than her own. That feeling lasted less than ten seconds.

"Honey," her mother cooed in a voice pitched to carry over fifty thousand screaming fans in Yankee Stadium. "I'm so glad you're home!"

"Hi, Mom." Rachel swallowed fast and instantly took another bite of chocolate. She loved her mother, she really did. But every year about this time, Celeste Adler started in on the "you're not getting any younger" speech. Her mother was bound and determined to get her older daughter married and "settled." Rachel's younger sister, Rita, had been married two years and the "perfect" daughter was already pregnant. With twins.

So basically, even if Rachel got pregnant right this minute, Rita would still outdo her.

Pregnant.

For just an instant, she allowed herself a brief, tantalizing dream. One night with Shane and a baby to remember it by. Wouldn't that have been something? She sighed and took another bite of ice cream. No way. Her birth control pills were way too effective. Other women might have an accident, but Rachel wouldn't. Even her body was a rule follower.

"Rita had an ultrasound this morning and she let me come in with her and ohmygoodness—" that last was crammed into one breathless word "—it was the most exciting thing ever. You know, Rita's husband Jack is just the most wonderful man."

Rachel rolled her eyes. Jack would never be simply *Jack.* His full name from now unto eternity would be *Rita's Husband Jack.* Poor man. But then, she told herself as she crunched quietly on an extra big chunk of chocolate, no one had held a gun to his head. He'd dated Rita for two years. He knew exactly the kind of whacko family he was marrying into.

Not whacko in a bad way of course. She loved them all. But did she really need to hear a speech every year about how she was all alone? Thanks, no.

"He gave me a big hug and called me Grandma right there in the doctor's office, isn't that the sweetest thing?"

Suck-up, she thought, but said only, "Yep. Jack's a keeper."

"Oh my yes, and I just cried and cried. I'm so emotional about my girls, you know."

Rachel's spoon scraped the bottom of the carton and she frowned. Darn it. Only a couple bites left. She should have been more prepared. She knew darn well that her mother called every Wednesday night without fail. She should have stocked extra ice cream.

"I know, Mom."

"And Rita's thinking of naming one of the babies after me, if one is a girl, that is."

Great. Just what the world needed. Another Celeste.

"That's nice." Rachel tucked the phone between her neck and her shoulder and shifted a look at the television screen. *It's a Wonderful Life* was playing. Of course it was. It had become almost more of a tradition than Midnight Mass.

While her mother talked, Rachel concentrated on George Bailey's trials and tribulations. As he stood at the top of the bridge looking into the icy river, Rachel completely understood why he was considering the leap.

"So, honey, anything new to tell me?"

Rachel froze, silently thanking God that her mother was safely tucked up in her house in Connecticut. If Celeste was looking right at her, she could use her motherly psychic powers and know exactly what her daughter had been up to.

That was one humiliation she didn't have to suffer through, anyway.

"Nope," she said after way too long a pause, "same ol', same ol'..."

"Uh-huh, that's nice, dear. Did I tell you that Margie Fontenot's grandson Will is coming to town for Christmas this year?"

Oh God. She knew what was coming. Another fix-up. Frantically Rachel scraped at the ice cream carton, hoping for more chocolate—which she now so desperately needed. "Really?"

"Oh, yes," her mother continued excitedly, "he's a *doctor,* you know."

Oh man, Celeste's Holy Grail.

Hook a doctor for poor Rachel.

"That's nice," she said ambiguously, scrambling off the couch, clutching the empty ice-cream carton and spoon. Hustling into the kitchen, she tossed the carton into the trash, the spoon into the sink, then turned to the pantry. While her mother oohed and aahed over Margie's fabulous grandson, Rachel scrounged for cookies. Preferably *chocolate* cookies.

She settled for a stale Pop-Tart.

Taking a bite, she leaned against the counter and closed her eyes. Only have to hang on a few more minutes, she assured herself. Celeste's calls never went longer than ten minutes. Long distance charges, *donchaknow.*

"Anyway, honey," her mother said, then muttered, "oh Frank, go watch TV. Rachel knows I'm only trying to help." When she came back again, she said, "Your daddy says hello, honey."

Rachel smiled in spite of everything. God bless her father. Always trying to reel his wife in when her latest matchmaking attempt kicked in. "Hi back."

"She says hello. Yes," Celeste added, emphasizing the word with impatience, "I'll tell her to check her door locks."

Rachel grinned and chewed a rock-hard, cold toaster pastry. Her mom was only interested in romance or the promise of one. Her father, on the other hand, installed a new lock on Rachel's door every time they came to the city. Pretty soon she was going to have to buy an extra door to accommodate them all.

"Check your locks."

"Already done."

"Thank heaven." Celeste lowered her booming voice and Rachel knew it was because she was trying to avoid having her husband overhear. "Anyway, honey, we're giving a little party the weekend before Christmas this year. Nothing special. Just a few friends."

"Like Margie?" Rachel guessed, barely containing the helpless snarl as she tore off another chunk of dry Pop-Tart.

"Of course, honey, you know how fond I am of Margie," her mother went on, picking up speed as she finally reached her destination. "And of course, since Will is here in town visiting, he'll be attending, too. Won't that be nice? I just *know* you two will have so much in common."

Rachel sighed. "Where's he live?"

"Phoenix, I believe."

Well sure, Rachel thought. She lived in Manhattan and worked at a magazine. Will was a doctor living in Phoenix. So much in common it was uncanny. Almost eerie. Must be Kismet.

God, the pity just kept on coming. It was her own fault, though. If she hadn't spent so much time thinking about Shane, maybe she could have met someone else by now. Someone she actually might have a future with. She took another bite.

"Mom…"

"Now, don't you get your back up, young lady," her mother said, clearly hoping to disarm Rachel before she could get a head of steam going. "It's Christmas. It's a time for having friends and family together and we're *going* to be together. Understood?"

Rachel's chin hit her chest.

If she were George Bailey at this moment, she'd be jumping off that bridge. And if stupid Clarence saved her sorry butt, she'd just have to kill him.

But as much as she might like to refuse her mother's invitation, they both knew she wouldn't. She'd never missed Christmas with her family and she wasn't going to start now. "Understood, Mom. I'll be there."

"That's my girl," Celeste cooed again, gracious in victory. "So, would you like me to e-mail you a picture of the twins in utero?"

"Sure," she said. "Why not?"

After all, once those twins were born, they were going to take a lot of heat off of Rachel.

"I'll do that right away, honey. But first I have to call your sister and make sure she's all right."

"But you just saw her this morning." Rachel

frowned at the magnetized grocery list stuck to the refrigerator. Picking up a pen, she scrawled CHOCOLATE in capital letters and underlined it half a dozen times just for emphasis.

"Pregnant women need taking care of," her mother assured her.

"Okey dokey, then," Rachel said with a sigh. "Say hi to Rita for me."

"I will. Now good night, honey, and your dad just said for you to check your locks again. We love you!"

With those final words ringing in her ear, Rachel heard her mother hang up and then listened aimlessly to the dial tone humming frenetically. She loved her mother, but after one of these phone calls, Rachel always felt a little disappointed in her own life.

Or rather, her *lack* of a life.

Christmas time and the only romance in her future was a setup fixed by her *mother.*

Stabbing the power button, she turned the phone off and carried it and what was left of her stale treat into the living room. Once there, she curled up on the couch again and turned up the volume on the movie.

And if a few tears escaped and rolled silently down her cheeks, who but she would know about it?

Shane stood outside Rachel's apartment door and asked himself again what the hell he was doing there. He should have just gone home after leaving

Gannon in the bar. But instead, he'd found himself heading for Rachel's.

Which said exactly what?

That he was still uncomfortable with the way they'd left things at the office? That he still felt like a sleazy boss for having sex with his assistant? That he simply wanted to see her again?

Yes, to all of the above.

It wasn't a good idea, though, and he knew it.

And even as that thought shot through his brain, he lifted his hand and knocked on her door.

"Shane?" Her voice was muffled. "What're you doing here?"

He glanced up and down the hallway, then directly into the peephole he knew she was watching him through. "I wanted to talk to you, Rachel."

"About what?"

He didn't hear any locks turning and she sure wasn't opening the door.

"Do you think I could come inside?"

"Why?"

He blew out a breath, leaned into the peephole and said, "Because I don't want to have this conversation in the hallway."

"Fine."

At last, he heard the distinctive sounds of a chain being dragged off and several dead bolts clacking. When she opened the door, he stepped inside before she could change her mind.

"What do you want, Shane?"

He glanced quickly around the room, took a sniff

of Christmas-scented air, then turned his gaze on her. Her blond hair was loose, waving over her shoulders. She wore a white cut-off T-shirt and pale green sweatpants that hung low on her hips, baring several inches of flat, toned belly. She was barefoot and her toes were painted a dark, sexy red.

A blast of heat and need shot through him, rocking him to his bones.

She still had the door open, one hand gripping the knob as if for support. Her wary gaze was locked on him and Shane nearly regretted coming over here. Nearly.

"Afraid to close the door?" he teased. "Worried about what might happen?"

She slammed it shut. "No."

Turning her back on him, she walked to her sofa, sat down in one corner of it and drew her knees to her chest. Focusing her attention on the television set, she proceeded to ignore him. Completely.

What kind of twisted guy was he that he was enjoying this?

He took a seat on the sofa, too, but watched her instead of the TV. "I just thought we should talk."

"Ah," she said, not taking her eyes off the old movie on the television, "because it went so well earlier today."

"No, because it didn't."

She sighed, tightened her arms around her updrawn legs and said, "Shane, there's absolutely nothing left to say, you know?"

"We can't just leave it like this, Rachel."

Finally she shifted a look at him and he saw her eyes, green and soft, and felt a ripple of something warm move through him.

"I know," she said quietly. "I've been thinking about it all night."

Shane's insides fisted. He had a feeling he wasn't going to like what was coming next. The expression on her face warned him that whatever she was thinking, it wasn't pleasant. Still, he'd never been a coward. "And what did you come up with?"

"There's really only one thing to do."

"Yeah?" Wary now, he kept his gaze fixed on hers and saw regret flash quickly across the surface of her eyes. He braced himself and even then, he wasn't prepared for what she said next.

"I'm turning in my two weeks notice."

Eight

"What?"

It did Rachel's heart good to see how shocked he was by her resignation. But it didn't change anything. In the last couple of hours, she'd done a lot of thinking.

She'd sat through George Bailey's problems, watched the resolution and cried when Clarence got his wings. But somewhere during her movie marathon, she'd come to grips with what she knew she had to do.

Her heart ached, but there was simply no other reasonable option. If she stayed at *The Buzz,* working with Shane, she'd never be able to move on with her life. She'd always be in love with him. No other man would be able to compare to him, so she'd end up alone and watching old Christmas movies in the dark by herself.

So as painful as this was, there really wasn't any choice.

"What're you talking about?" Shane demanded, jumping to his feet and glaring down at her. "You can't quit."

"I just did." She met his gaze squarely and hoped he couldn't read on her face the misery she was feeling.

"This is your solution? Running away?"

"I'm not running, I'm sitting."

"If that's a joke, I'm not smiling."

"Neither am I," she said, unfolding her legs and pushing off the couch. Starting to feel just a little bit cornered, she made a move to walk into the kitchen, but Shane's hand on her upper arm stopped her in her tracks. She stared down at his hand for a long couple of seconds before lifting her gaze to his.

He let her go, jammed his hands into his pockets and muttered, "You can't quit on me, Rachel. Not because—"

"You can't even say it," she said with a slow shake of her head. "Because we had *sex,* Shane. And I think it's a pretty good reason to quit."

"I don't." He pulled his hands free of his pockets, scooped them both through his hair, then let them fall to his sides. "Damn it, we're a team. We work great together. You really want to throw away four good years because of one night?"

No. What she *wanted* was to have more than one

night, but she couldn't very well tell him that, now could she? Just as she couldn't tell him that it would be impossible for her to pretend indifference to him now that she knew what it was like to be in his arms. How could she arrange his dates with other women when her own heart would be breaking?

"No." One word, firmly spoken. "You don't need me, Shane. You won the competition. You're the head honcho now."

"Which means I'll need you even more."

"No, it doesn't. You're just *used* to having me there. You'll survive." She wasn't entirely sure she would, but that was her problem.

"Don't do this, Rachel."

"I have to."

"I won't accept your resignation."

She smiled. At the core of him, Shane Elliott would always have a healthy ego. "That won't stop me."

"What will?"

"Nothing."

He stepped in close. So close that the scent of his cologne reached for her, dragging her in closer for a deeper breath. She closed her eyes. If she looked up into those green eyes of his, she'd be lost. If she saw his mouth only inches from hers, she wouldn't be able to resist taking another taste of him.

His hands dropped onto her shoulders and she felt the heat of his touch slide deep within her.

"I won't stop trying to change your mind," he warned, his voice deep, ragged.

"I know that."

His hands tightened on her. "Look at me."

"I'd rather not," she admitted.

He sighed. "I came over here tonight to— I don't know. Apologize for last night?"

She winced.

He stroked one hand over her hair, his fingers sliding through the silky strands. "But now that I'm here with you again, an apology is the last thing on my mind."

"Shane—"

"Open your eyes, Rachel."

She did and instantly felt swamped by the emotions churning in his gaze. Her stomach dipped and rolled, her heartbeat jumped into a fast gallop and a curl of something warm and delicious settled low inside her. "Shane, this isn't a good idea."

"Probably not," he allowed, lowering his head infinitesimally.

She licked her lips, heard her blood humming in her veins and knew without a doubt that if she let him kiss her, she was only asking for more trouble. Being with him again would only make their inevitable parting that much harder.

And yet…

She'd wanted more than one night with him. This was her chance. This was her chance to have *him* seduce *her*. The night before had been her idea. Tonight, Shane was the one taking charge. Showing her how much he wanted her.

And if she couldn't have his love, then tonight, she'd settle for being wanted.

He kissed her and Rachel leaned into him, giving herself over to the glory of his mouth on hers. To the solid strength of him towering over her. To the feel of his hands sliding down her back and beneath the waistband of her pale green sweats.

His big hands cupped her bottom and pulled her tight against him. So tight that she felt his erection, hard and thick, pressed into her abdomen. Swirls of longing, of need swept through her like the ripples on a pond after a stone's been thrown in. Over and over again, sensations crested, fell and rose again.

She moaned and twisted her hips against his. In response, he pulled her even more tightly to him, grinding his mouth against hers. His tongue claimed her, mating with her own in a wild, frenetic dance of desire that pulsed in the air around them both.

Rachel's fingers dug into his shoulders and she held on for all she was worth. Her knees wobbled and the world tipped slightly off-center. But she didn't care. Nothing was more important than the feeling of Shane's arms around her, his body pressed to hers.

Laboring for air, Shane broke the kiss, stared down into her eyes and gave her butt a squeeze. "Yes?" he asked, his voice broken with need.

"Oh, yes," she said and leaped at him, wrapping her legs around his hips and hanging on as he started for her bedroom.

One corner of her brain couldn't believe she was

doing this again. Compounding one mistake with another exactly like it couldn't be the right thing to do. But then again, if she was quitting her job anyway, she might as well make the most of the time she had with the man she loved.

Reaching down between their bodies, she slid one hand down to the zipper of his slacks and when she pulled it down, he sucked in air like a dying man trying for one last gasp. Her fingers curled around the hard, thick length of him and he tucked his face into the curve of her neck. His teeth and tongue worked at her flesh as if the very taste of her meant life itself.

Rachel saw stars exploding behind her eyes. Every square inch of her body felt alive with sensation and almost too sensitized. And she wanted more.

Now.

"Can't wait," he muttered thickly and stopped just outside her bedroom door. He set her on her feet, dragged her clothes off and tossed them to one side, then lifted her again.

"No waiting," she agreed, wrapping her bare legs around his waist and hanging on.

He turned quickly, braced her back against the wall and when she rose up slightly in his arms, Shane pushed his body hard into hers. Rachel groaned as he filled her. Her body stretched to its limits to accommodate him, she bore down hard, taking him even deeper inside.

Bracing one hand on the wall to her side and one

hand on his shoulder, Rachel helped all she could, but Shane didn't need assistance. He took her weight and held her easily, lifting her up and down on his length until they were both tortured with a burning, fiery need that sizzled between them.

Again and again, he withdrew only to plunge into her depths one more time. His breathing was ragged, his eyes glazed. Rachel's heart pounded until it was nothing but a deafening roar in her own ears.

Shane couldn't think. Could hardly see. All he could do was feel. And what he was feeling was even more intense than anything he'd experienced the night before.

Most of the day, he'd tried to convince himself that the night with Rachel hadn't been as amazing as he remembered it. Now he knew that for the sad lie it was.

Rachel took him to places he'd never imagined. Made him feel things he'd thought himself incapable of. Made him want more.

Her body surrounded him, her mouth opened on a sigh and her eyes closed as the first wild, frantic pumping release jolted through her. He watched pleasure claim her for as long as he could and then finally, he allowed himself to follow after her.

She hung limp in his arms and Shane was grateful for the wall at her back. Otherwise, they'd both be lying in a puddle on the floor.

"You okay?" he whispered.

She chuckled. "I'll let you know when I get feeling back in my legs."

He smiled. "I hear that."

"Shane—"

He dropped his head to her shoulder. "Let's not start the 'mistake' talk again."

"Why not?" she asked quietly. "Seems appropriate."

He lifted his head and looked down into her eyes again. Strange, he'd never really noticed what a beautiful shade of green her eyes were before last night. And now he couldn't seem to tear his gaze away.

"I didn't come over here tonight to do this."

"I know that," she said and shifted position slightly.

That small movement was enough to wake his body up and stir fresh desire. He hissed in a breath and tightened his hold on her. "But I'm not sorry we did it."

She leaned her head back against the wall and inhaled sharply as he pushed his hardening body into her again, setting off a fireworks display of sensation. "No," she admitted, "I guess I'm not, either."

"Glad to hear that," he said tightly, pushing them away from the wall and starting for the bedroom again. "Because I don't think we're finished."

She shivered and lowered herself onto his length as hard as she could. "I think you're right."

He walked right up to the bed, reached down and dragged the quilt back, then fell onto the mattress, still fully clothed and deep within her body.

Rachel laughed and he noticed a tiny dimple in her right cheek. He'd never noticed that before, either.

"Maybe you should get undressed first," she said, then gasped when he rocked his hips against hers.

"After," he muttered and rolled to his back, taking her atop him where he could watch her. "I'm not stopping now."

"Good idea." Smiling, she reached for the hem of her little T-shirt and whipped it up and off, tossing it into the shadows of the small room. Then, watching him, she covered her breasts with his hands and twisted her hips on him, creating an unbelievable friction that stole his breath.

Riding him, she took him places he'd never thought to go and couldn't wait to visit again. The bed beneath him was soft and smelled of lavender. The woman above him was amazing and her scent was soap, shampoo and woman.

Like a man possessed he guided her hips, steering her into a mind-numbing rhythm. She was the only thing in the world he could see. Feel. And all too soon, an explosion burst up between them, leaving his body shattered, his bones shaken and his heart quivering.

Two hours later, they were naked, lying in a pool of white, thrown through the windows from the streetlights outside. Rachel stared at the ceiling and listened to Shane's ragged breathing.

Her own heartbeat was racing and her body was still sizzling when she acknowledged that once again, she'd been an idiot. But how could she possibly have turned him down, when all she'd been able to think about since the night before was being with him again?

Despite how wonderful her body felt, her heart

was aching. By giving in to the urge to be with him, she was only setting herself up for more pain.

This had to stop.

"You're thinking," he murmured.

"Aren't you?" she countered.

"No." He turned his head on the pillow to look at her. Reaching out, he skimmed one hand across her bare belly and Rachel shivered. "When I'm with you I don't want to think. Don't want you to, either."

She sighed now. "*Not* thinking is what got us here in the first place."

"Exactly."

Eyes closed, she savored his touch for a second or two, indulging herself. Oh, she wanted him to take her again. Wanted to take *him* again. And because she wanted it so badly, she rolled out from under his touch and slid off the bed.

Now that her blood wasn't on fire, she could think more clearly. And though it broke her heart to admit it even to herself, she knew that being wanted would never be enough for her.

She wanted love.

She wanted family.

And she would never get that from Shane.

He blew out a frustrated breath and pushed himself up onto one elbow. "Rachel—"

"Shane, this just can't keep happening," she said, turning to find her clothes, then snatch them up off the floor. In the pale wash of light, she pulled her T-shirt on, then struggled into her sweats, hopping first on one foot, then the other. When she was finished, she picked up Shane's clothes, too, and tossed them at him.

He grabbed at them then dropped the pile onto the bed beside him. "You know, maybe there's a reason we keep ending up here."

Impatient with both herself and him, she huffed out a breath and shook her hair back from her face. "Oh, there's a reason all right. Neither one of us can be trusted."

He gave her a weary laugh. "You may have a point."

A stab of something cold and lonely poked at her insides but Rachel fought to ignore it. She wouldn't let him see what his simple statement had done to her. Instead she said, "This is why I had to quit, Shane. Why I *still* have to."

Muttering darkly, he rolled off the bed and stood up to get dressed. As he stepped into his clothes, he argued with her. "What we've had with each other has nothing to do with work."

"Of course it does." She planted her hands on her hips, lifted her chin and continued. "You know how it was today. We could hardly talk to each other."

"Didn't seem to have any trouble tonight."

"That—" she waved her hand at the bed "—is *not* talking."

He tossed his suit coat onto the rumpled mattress. "Rachel, you're making too big a deal out of this."

"And maybe you're taking it too lightly."

Shane pushed one hand through his hair and yanked while he went at it. The pain shooting through his skull was a small, but welcome distraction from the woman making him nuts. "What do you want me to say?"

So much, she thought, but didn't say. Oh, she wanted it all. She wanted him making love with her and *being* in love with her. But since she couldn't have one, she wouldn't have the other.

In the moonlight, his green eyes flashed with annoyance and something else she couldn't quite identify. Maybe it was just as well.

If nothing else, she at least knew that her decision to quit her job and move on had been a good one. Now all she needed was the courage to go ahead with the plan. Somehow, somewhere, she found the strength to straighten her spine.

"I want you to say you accept my resignation," she whispered.

He grabbed his jacket and shrugged into it. Tugging at the lapels until it hung right, he just stared at her for a long moment. Rachel held her breath and counted the seconds as they ticked past as steadily as a heartbeat.

Finally, though, Shane nodded. "If it's what you want."

Want? No.

Need? Yes.

"It is. Thanks."

"Right." He nodded, looked uneasily around the room, then focused his gaze on her again. "I'd better go. I'll see you at the office tomorrow?"

"I'll be there."

* * *

Long after Shane was gone, Rachel sat at her computer. Her fingers flew over the keys, as her eyes blurred with tears she refused to shed.

One last Tess Tells All column.

One more time, she'd write down her feelings for her boss. One more time, she'd pour out her heart and mask it with humor. And one more time, she'd watch Shane read it, chuckle at Tess's cleverness and never see himself in the words.

Nine

A few days later, Rachel was wishing she'd just quit her job outright.

Working with Shane and maintaining a stoic, distant attitude was harder than it sounded. He was polite, courteous and completely unreachable. She should have been glad that he was apparently as determined as she to not let their own desires erupt again.

Instead she was only irritated.

Wasn't this hard on him at all?

Shaking her head, she scrolled down the list of RSVP responses to the annual Elliott Christmas Charity Ball. Making notations on who had and hadn't responded yet, Rachel lost herself in the work. It was the one thing she could depend on now. And if this year's ball was going to be the last one she arranged, then by heaven, it was going to be the very best one anyone had ever seen.

Every year, EPH sponsored a charity extravaganza, raising money for women's shelters and children's hospitals in the city. And for the last four years, Rachel had been integral to the planning and execution of the ball. She kept track of invitations, caterers, musicians, decorations. She arranged for Santa to appear at the party for the children who would be attending and she made sure that Santa had exactly the right present for every child.

This was one job she was really going to miss when she left the company.

"Hey," Christina said. "Earth to Rachel."

She blinked and looked up at her friend. Christina's silver-framed glasses were riding low on her nose and her bright blue eyes were fixed on Rachel.

"I'm sorry. What?"

"Honey," Christina said, lowering her voice and bending down to lean both hands on Rachel's desk, "you have something you want to tell me?"

"What do you mean?"

The older woman took a quick look around, assuring herself that no one was close enough to overhear. Still, she lowered her voice another notch. "A new Tess Tells All column just left Production for the boss's office."

"Really?" Rachel tried to look surprised. "I thought that last column was it for her."

"Apparently she had one more in her," Christina said, narrowing her eyes thoughtfully, "and it was a beauty."

Rachel lowered her gaze, picked up a stack of files and busily straightened them as if clean edges meant her life. "Why're you telling me?"

"Nice try," her friend countered. "But you forget. I've got years of experience dealing with kids trying to hide things from me."

"Christina…"

"You're Tess."

"Shh!" Rachel looked around now and when she was sure they were alone, she stood up, motioned to Christina and headed for the break room. Her friend was just a step or two behind her and when they entered the empty room, Christina shut the door and leaned back against it.

"It's true."

Rachel grumbled a little as she automatically straightened the counter before grabbing a coffee cup and pouring herself some. "Yes. It's true. Happy?"

"Delirious. I've had my suspicions for a while now, but this column just confirmed it." Locking the door, she walked toward her friend, got herself some coffee and while she dumped several heaping teaspoons of sugar into the brew, she said, "I can't believe you didn't tell me."

"I couldn't tell anyone."

"I'm not just anyone."

"True," Rachel said, taking a sip of coffee. "And I wanted to tell you about me being Tess but—"

"Oh," Christina said waving one hand at her, "who cares about the Tess thing? I want to know why you didn't tell me you slept with Shane."

"Oh God." Dragging a chair out, Rachel fell into it and set her cup on the table.

"Talk, sweetie. I want details."

"No details. Please. I'm trying to forget them myself."

"Damn. That bad?"

Rachel laughed at the disappointment on her friend's face. "Hardly. That *good.*"

"Ooh. So why the long face?"

"Because everything's changed now."

"That's good," Christina said, then frowned. "Isn't it?"

"I quit my job."

"No, you did not."

"I had to," Rachel said, cradling her coffee cup between her palms, savoring the heat radiating through her. "I can't work with him now. It's just too hard."

"That's bull and you know it." Christina sighed and leaned back in her chair. "Quitting solves nothing."

"It gets me away from him."

"Honey, you'll *never* be able to get away from him. You'll keep on loving him even if you wander off to Timbuktu."

"Well, there's a happy thought," Rachel muttered. "Anyway, my resignation is in and so are a few applications I've managed to drop off on my lunch hour the last couple of days. There are lots of magazines here in the city," she continued, wanting to steer their talk away from Shane. "So it's not like I'll never see you again or anything."

"Damn straight on that," Christina said, giving her a tight smile. "But here's a question for you. What do you think Shane's going to say when he sees this column?"

Rachel laughed miserably, picked up her coffee and took a sip. "He's read dozens of 'em so far and hasn't recognized himself. Why should this time be any different?"

Christina picked up her own coffee cup and smiled at Rachel over the rim. "Oh, didn't I mention that part? You screwed up in this one. You actually referred to Tess's mystery boss as *Shane.*"

Rachel's cup fell from suddenly nerveless fingers and hit the tabletop with enough force to send waves of hot coffee washing over both women.

Shane had been fielding phone calls all morning. From agents of minor celebrities hoping to make a splash in *The Buzz,* to heads of major corporations wanting to talk product placement. Normally he would have fobbed off most of those calls to the proper departments.

But for the last few days, he'd been doing everything he could to keep busy. Even if it meant getting back into the trenches. The plan was to keep himself so preoccupied he wouldn't have time to think about Rachel.

It wasn't working.

She was always there, right at the edges of his mind, waiting for a quiet moment to pop in and torture him. Damn it, he'd managed to work with Rachel—closely—for four long years. In all that time, he'd never looked at her as he would any other wildly attractive woman.

She'd just been there. Like an extension of himself. Part of his office, his work world. And in the last year, since his father had kicked off this ridiculous competition, she'd been the one to give him a kick in the can when he needed it. Hell, she was just as responsible as he for *The Buzz* winning the competition. Maybe more so. Because Rachel was always on top of things. She'd kept his life running smoothly for four years and he'd never even noticed her beyond being grateful for the help.

How the *hell* could he have been so blind?

How could he not have noticed her eyes, her mouth, her sense of humor, her legs, her agile mind, her breasts, her loyalty, her behind?

And why was he noticing all of that *now?*

Muttering darkly, he stalked across his office when the phone started ringing again. But this time, instead of answering, he let it ring and walked to the bank of windows behind his desk.

When the phone stopped ringing, he smiled grimly only to turn and frown at the quick knock on the door. Before he could call out for whoever it was to leave, the door swung open and Rachel was there.

Her blond hair was pulled back and twisted into

some sort of elegant braid she usually did. But now he'd seen it hanging loose and waving around her face and that was how he pictured her. In his mind's eye her plain, pale green business suit was replaced by a skimpy T-shirt and a pair of green sweats.

Oh man, he was in deep trouble here.

"You okay?" she asked, frowning at him.

"Fine." Or at least, he would be if he could shut off his brain. "What is it?"

Before she could answer, another woman sailed past Rachel into his office and demanded, "What makes you so crabby, I'd like to know?"

"Mom," he said and felt a smile warm his face.

Maeve Elliott was a tiny woman physically, but her personality made her seem larger than life. She'd married Shane's father when she was a nineteen-year-old seamstress in Ireland. And, though Shane could take exception to the way Patrick had ignored his children from time to time, the old man had always treated his wife as if she were the most priceless treasure on the planet. Which, Shane admitted silently, she was.

He came around the desk, enfolded her in a quick, tight hug, then stepped back to look at her. Impeccable as always, she wore a Chanel suit of icy-blue and her nearly all-white hair was swept up into an intricate knot on top of her head.

"So," she said, eyeing her son, "my question stands. Why so crabby, Shane?"

He frowned and shifted a look at Rachel, still standing in the doorway. "Just...busy."

"Then I won't keep you long," his mother said, half turning to motion Rachel into the office. "I just wanted to stop and tell you the news!"

Rachel came closer and Shane swore he caught a whiff of her scent. Just enough to tantalize. To tweak his memory of their last night together. To remind him there wouldn't be any other nights like it.

He bit back a scowl and focused on his mother, practically vibrating with energy. "What is it?" he teased. "Win the Mrs. America pageant, did you?"

"Ah, you were always the smooth one," she said, laughing. "No, no. Much better news. Our Erika's had her baby. A beautiful little girl she is, too. I'm a grandmother!"

"That's terrific," Shane said, meaning every word.

"Wonderful," Rachel added, smiling. "How's the new mom doing?"

Maeve smiled even wider. "Erika's doing just fine. It's Gannon who's having the breakdown. Poor love. Apparently being a witness to his wife's labor has left him flattened."

"Did he faint?" Shane asked, hoping for some good ammunition to tease Gannon with in the future.

"Of course not," Maeve said with a sniff. "It's just very hard seeing someone you love in pain."

"Yeah," Shane said, slanting a look at Rachel only to find her gaze on him. "It must be."

A second or two of silence stretched out between them and hummed with energy until even Maeve was affected by it. As she looked from one of them to the other, one perfectly arched brow lifted slightly. Delicately she cleared her throat until she had her son's attention again.

"I'll let you get back to work now, Shane darlin'," she said. "I'm just on my way to see your father and force him to take me to lunch."

Shane tore his gaze from Rachel and scrambled for equilibrium. Blowing out a breath, he took his mother's arm and said, "Why don't I join you? You can tell me all about the new Elliott."

"That would be lovely," she said, lifting one hand to touch his cheek. Then she turned to Rachel. "Would you like to accompany us as well, Rachel?"

"No," she said quickly, with a shake of her head. "I'll, um, just stay here and get a few things finished."

"Shame," Maeve said thoughtfully, then walked from the office, her son and Rachel right behind her.

With Shane gone for at least an hour, Rachel did something she'd never done before in all the four years she'd worked at *The Buzz.*

She rifled Shane's desk.

"For pity's sake, where would he put the blasted thing?" She yanked open the first two drawers in his desk, quickly thumbed through the folders and looked under the books and magazines stored there.

Nothing.

The bottom file drawer yielded no happier results.

She zipped through the stacks of folders atop his desk, her fingers flipping through the pages as her gaze swept the printed pages. But the new Tess column was nowhere to be found. Which left only one possibility.

Her gaze drifted to the locked drawer on the bottom left of the big desk. There was no way for her to get inside it. And if she *did* lose her mind and try to pick the lock, Shane would notice and then the jig would be up, anyway.

"How could I have been so stupid?" she wondered aloud and just managed to keep from thumping herself in the forehead with the heel of her hand.

Shane would read the column, know exactly who wrote it and would probably fire her on the spot. Of course, since she'd already resigned, it wouldn't carry a lot of weight. But oh, God. The embarrassment quotient was just too high to think about!

Mentally she raced back over the other columns she'd turned in for publication. All the times she'd talked about her boss in less than stellar terms. All the times she'd complained about his too active social life.

Her toe stopped tapping against the floor and her mouth dropped open. And the last column, where she'd admitted to feeling too much about him.

"This is a *disaster.*"

Dropping her head into her hands, she wished for a hole to open up under her feet and swallow her.

By the time Shane returned from lunch, tension bubbled inside him like a thick, poisonous brew.

Luckily enough, Rachel was gone from her desk, probably taking a late lunch herself. Just as well. He was in no mood for yet another stiff, polite exchange of empty pleasantries.

Especially after spending the last two hours dodging Maeve Elliott's questions.

God knew he loved his mother, but there was nothing the woman liked better than digging into her children's lives. Whether they welcomed it or not.

He'd been able to dodge her thinly veiled questions about his and Rachel's relationship—but just barely. And if his father hadn't insisted on talking about the company, Maeve wouldn't have given up until she'd pried every last ounce of information from him.

He stepped into his office, closed the door behind him and gratefully went back to work. At his desk, he unlocked the bottom drawer, pulled out the latest columns sent to him by Production, and leaned back in his chair to flip through them.

When he found the Tess column, he smiled to himself, put the other articles aside and started reading. After the first paragraph, he was frowning. At the second, he was muttering to himself.

And by the third paragraph, the words were blurring beneath the red haze covering his vision.

Heart jumping, stomach twisting, temper spiking, Shane crumpled the edges of the paper in his fists and forced himself to keep reading.

Sex with the boss is never a smart move,

Tess wrote,

> but in my case, it was imbecilic. I've spent the last year or more writing about how hard it is to work with a man who never sees you as anything more than an especially fine tuned piece of office equipment. But now that Shane actually has seen me—naked of all things—the situation is completely untenable.
>
> So here's a word of warning for all of you assistants out there. When the boss smiles and says "Let's celebrate," remember that celebrating usually means hangover.
>
> Or worse.
>
> For your own sakes, if the boss starts looking too good to you…run.

"Rachel," he muttered thickly, staring at the page in front of him as if he still couldn't believe what he'd read. "All this time, it's been her. All this time."

He swallowed hard, choking back the knot of fury in his throat. When he thought he could speak without growling, he snatched up the phone on his desk and punched in a number.

"Circulation and archives."

"This is Shane Elliott."

"Yes, sir," the female voice snapped out, and he could almost see the woman jerking to attention in her chair.

"Get me a copy of every one of our magazines that contains a Tess Tells All column."

"Oh, sir, I just love that column."

"Great," he muttered, thinking now about all of the people who'd read every word Rachel had ever written about him. Hell, people all over the *world* had been laughing at him for more than a year.

And he'd wanted to give the mysterious Tess a raise!

"I want those copies here in thirty minutes."

"Yes, sir."

Shane tossed the receiver back into the cradle, gave up on trying to rein in the temper nearly strangling him and started reading the most recent column again.

Ten

When Rachel came back from lunch, she was feeling a little better. She'd done a little Christmas shopping, wandered through the windy, cold streets and lost herself in the crowds.

Hard to keep feeling sorry for yourself when you're reminded that you're simply one cog in a very large wheel.

Now, back at *The Buzz,* she was simply determined to survive the rest of her two weeks notice and then move on with her life. Smiling at the people she passed, she headed right for her desk and noticed Shane's door standing open.

As she glanced inside, she saw that he'd been watching for her. And he didn't look happy.

"Everything okay?"

"Not really," he said, waving one hand at her. "Would you come in here please?"

A quick twist of apprehension tightened in her belly before she made a titanic attempt at smoothing it out. *Oh, God. He saw the column.*

Her brain raced, coming up with explanations, excuses, *anything*. She'd had a glass of wine at lunch, knowing that this confrontation would be headed her way. Now she wished she'd had two.

She paused long enough to deposit her purse in the bottom drawer of her desk, then steeling herself, walked into Shane's office and closed the door behind her. "What's going on?"

A brief, hard smile crossed his face. Standing up, he walked around the edge of his desk. Then folding his arms across his chest, he sat on the corner of the desk and watched her through narrowed eyes.

Rachel now knew how a rabbit felt staring down a snake. Fire flashed in his eyes and a twitch in his jaw told her he was gritting his teeth. No point in pretending ignorance any longer, she thought, and spoke right up. "You've seen the article."

"Not even going to try to deny it?"

"No."

"So you *are* Tess."

She smoothed the fall of her skirt, then clasped her hands together at her waist. Her fingers tightened until her knuckles went white. "Surprise."

"I can't believe this." He shook his head in disgust. "I don't even know whether to be insulted or flattered that you've been writing about me all these months."

"I didn't mean for you to find out like this."

"You mean," he corrected, pushing off the desk to stalk across the room toward her, "you didn't mean for me to find out at all."

"Well," she hedged, "yes."

He walked a slow circle around her and Rachel turned slowly, keeping her gaze fixed on him. "Did you enjoy watching me trying to find out ways to identify you? Did you get a laugh out of lying to everyone here? Lying to *me?*"

She huffed out a breath and mentally scrambled for the right thing to say. But she kept coming up empty. "I wasn't trying to lie to you, Shane."

"Ah, so that was just a happy side benefit."

"I don't know why you're making such a big deal about this," she said, deciding to go on the defensive. "You *loved* those columns."

"Yes," he snapped, coming to a fast stop. "When I thought they were written about some nameless, faceless *jerk.* I *don't* love finding out that *I'm* the jerk."

She held up one hand. "I never called you a jerk."

"You might as well have," he countered, spinning around and walking back to his desk. He picked up a thick manila file and waved it at her. "I've been going over all the old columns. And now that I think about it, I believe I'm more insulted than anything else. You made me look like a fool."

The knot of tension inside her started to loosen and

with it, came a burst of outrage. "I did not. All I did was write about the day-to-day job of working for you."

"And about the women I date."

In her own defense, she pointed out, "I wouldn't have had to write about that if you hadn't put *me* in charge of buying your make-up gifts, your break-up gifts. Ordering flowers. Making reservations for you and the Barbies, Bambis and Tawnys of the world."

"Tawny," he muttered. "That's her name."

"You're the one who dragged me into your social life, Shane, so you're hardly in a position to complain about it now, are you?"

"You're my assistant. Who the hell else would I ask to do all that stuff?"

She hitched one hip higher than the other, folded her arms under her breasts, cocked her head to stare at him and offered, "Oh, I don't know…*yourself?*"

He tossed the folder onto his desk and the columns inside scattered across the gleaming surface. "If you hated your job so much, why didn't you just quit?"

"I did," she reminded him.

"I mean before," he blustered, throwing both hands high. "If I'm such a bastard to work for, why did you stay this long?"

Rachel dropped the angry pose, walked forward and dropped down into one of the twin chairs opposite his desk. Looking up at him, she said, "You were never a bastard to work for. And I enjoyed my job. I just got…"

"Jealous?" he asked.

"No." She jumped to her feet again. "Not jealous, just—I don't even know what. I started writing those articles as a way to vent my frustration. And hey, apparently there are a lot of admins in the city who know just what I'm talking about."

"Yes, but—"

"You said yourself only last week that Tess Tells All is the most popular column in the magazine. You wanted to find her. To offer her—me—a weekly column. You wanted to give her a huge raise and bring her—me—on staff." She watched him and noted the relaxing of his jaw muscles and the tension dropping out of his squared shoulders. "So what's changed, Shane? Only the fact that you found out who Tess really is."

"That's plenty," he snapped.

"From your point of view, I guess so," she acknowledged. "But you have to admit that you laughed at my columns as hard as anyone else."

"That was before. Now..." He turned from her and walked to the windows. Staring out, he said, "You wrote about our nights together."

She swallowed hard and met his gaze when he looked over his shoulder at her. "Yes."

"Why?"

She shrugged and knew that wasn't an answer. But she wasn't sure she had one to give him. "I don't really know."

"I think I do," he said, turning back to face her again. "I think you wanted me to find out that you're Tess."

"Oh, I don't think that's it," she said, shaking her head slowly.

Shane walked toward her and noted that she took a half step back, as if trying to keep a safe distance between them. Wasn't going to work. He'd had time to think about this. Time to reread her columns with a clear eye.

"You wanted me to know, Rachel. Otherwise you never would have made the mistake of putting my name in the most recent article."

"That was a mistake."

"A Freudian slip."

"Oh, please," she said, backing away as he got closer.

"You wanted me to know because you don't want to quit your job. You don't want to leave *The Buzz.* You want your own column. You want to stay here. With me."

She laughed shortly. "I already turned in my resignation, Shane. And you accepted it."

"Reluctantly."

"Whatever. The point is, it's done."

She glanced around the room, keeping from looking at him, avoiding meeting his gaze. Shane actually enjoyed watching the usually unflappable Rachel display telltale signs of nervousness.

"No, it's not," he said. "I don't want you to quit, Rachel. I'm willing to offer you the same deal I was going to offer your alter ego."

Finally she looked at him. "You *want* me to keep writing about you?"

"No," he admitted. "But you're very talented. You're funny. And our readers love your columns. I'm guessing you could find something else to write about. Life in Manhattan. Interviews with other admins. Anything you want."

She thought about it for a long moment and Shane found himself wishing to hell he could read her mind, since nothing of what she was feeling was visible on her features.

"Well?" he prodded, anxious for her answer.

"Tempting," she admitted, backing up again. "But no. Thanks for the offer, but I'm leaving *The Buzz,* Shane."

Speaking up quickly, he offered her more money. Up to twice her present salary. Her eyes popped, but still she shook her head.

"It's not about the money and it's insulting to me that you're acting as though it is."

"You want to talk insulted?" he countered hotly. "You've made me a laughingstock all over New York for the last year."

Her lips thinned into a grim slash. "If you hadn't behaved like an idiot, I wouldn't have had so much ammunition."

"Oh, that's perfect."

"Look, Shane," she said, making a heroic attempt at controlling her temper. "You have the CEO position you wanted, but I can't be around you anymore. I just can't do it."

Disappointment gathered in his chest, warred with anger and tightened until he could hardly draw a breath. "Because of what happened between us."

"Partly," she said, nodding. "We can't just go back to our old working relationship, Shane. We can't pretend we didn't…"

Hell no, he couldn't pretend nothing had happened between them. Every waking minute she was there, in his mind. Every time he closed his eyes, he saw her. Felt her. Tasted her. She haunted him and he knew that even if she left, her memory would stay with him. Always.

"So let's just leave things as they are and part friends, all right?"

His gaze locked with hers, he tried to find some way to change her mind. To make her stay. He knew damn well that without her, he might never have won the competition with his siblings.

And he couldn't imagine trying to run all of EPH without Rachel's advice and common sense and humor. Damn it, she couldn't just walk out.

But she did.

She left him standing there staring at her back as she walked away.

The next couple of days, Rachel buried herself in the preparations for the big charity event that EPH sponsored every year. The rich, the famous and the infamous would gather in the ballroom atop the Waldorf-Astoria and donate enough money to keep several children's shelters running for a year.

She already had the flowers arranged for and the

caterers and band. Then she spent half the morning on the phone with security experts, lining up the extra guards they'd need on the doors. Running her finger down her list, she made several check marks and only frowned once.

Santa.

She still needed a Santa.

The one she'd used the year before was already booked and she couldn't hire just anyone to hand out gifts to children. Flipping through the phone book, she looked up several numbers for casting agents in the city. Somehow or other, she'd find the perfect Santa.

Her last job for EPH was going to come off perfectly even if she had to work herself to death to make sure of it.

When her phone rang, she reached for it automatically. "Shane Elliott's office."

"Ms. Adler?"

"Yes." Frowning, she sat back in her chair.

"This is Dylan Hightower at *Cherish* magazine."

"Oh." She straightened. *Cherish* was a celebrity homestyle magazine she'd applied to just last week. Good news. When she left EPH, she wanted to be able to go right into a new job.

"I wanted to call you and explain why we're unable to offer you a position."

She blinked, stunned. She was *perfect* for the job of executive assistant to the editor-in-chief. Her computer skills were excellent, matched by her organizational abilities and her work ethic. "I see."

"No, I don't believe you do," Hightower said

abruptly. "And frankly, I'm only calling to warn you that publishing is a very small business. Liars don't go undiscovered for long."

"I'm sorry?" Her stomach was spinning.

"You should apologize for wasting my time, Ms. Adler. I checked with your references and I have to say I was shocked when Shane Elliott told me the real story behind your leaving your present position."

"He did." Temper boiled and bubbled in the pit of her stomach and she was forced to take deep, even breaths to steady herself out. "What exactly did Mr. Elliott have to say, if you don't mind my asking?"

"Not at all. He informed me that you were quite possibly the worst assistant he's ever had. And the fact that you're not a team player and actually go out of your way to foment dissension in the ranks..." He paused for breath. "Let me just say that your reputation is less than stellar."

The edges of her vision went a blurry red. She could hardly speak she was so furious and it took all she had not to slam the phone down on Mr. Fabulous Hightower.

"I understand," she finally managed to say.

"I hope you do," he retorted and hung up.

Still clutching the phone, while a dial tone buzzed in her ear, Rachel shifted a look at Shane's closed door. Inhaling sharply, she slapped the phone into its cradle and stomped across the floor toward it. She didn't bother to knock, just shoved it open, slammed it shut behind her and advanced on her boss with blood in her eye.

"Rachel?"

"How *dare* you?" She slapped both hands on his desk and leaned in toward him. "How dare you submarine my chances at a new job."

"Now wait a—"

"Mr. Hightower just called to explain personally why he wouldn't be hiring me."

Shane's gaze snapped to one side and he scrubbed one hand across his face. "Oh."

"Yeah, *oh.*"

He looked at her again, but couldn't quite meet her eyes. "Now, Rachel—"

"I can't believe you did that, Shane. My God, are you really that petty?"

He jumped to his feet. The cityscape stretched out behind him, snow falling softly against the windows, blurring the edges of his silhouette. The silence in the office was profound.

"It wasn't that. It was—"

"What, Shane? What could possibly have been the motivator for you to tell people lies about me?" She pushed up from the desk, folded her arms across her chest and tapped the toe of her shoe against the carpet. "Four years I've worked for you and in all that time have I ever screwed up?"

"No."

"Fomented dissension in the ranks?"

"No."

"Then why?" she asked, shaking her head and

looking at him like she'd never seen him before. And indeed, this side of Shane was a mystery to her. Never before had she seen him so embarrassed. Ashamed.

He blew out a breath, shoved both hands into his pockets and rocked back on his heels. "I thought if I could slow down your job search you might change your mind about leaving."

"By lying about me. Amazing."

"A bad idea. I see that now."

"Well, congratulations," she snapped. "A breakthrough. You're finally willing to admit that not everything in the known universe is about Shane Elliott. Other people have their little lives and problems, too."

"Rachel, I'm sorry, I—"

"Forget it," she said, stepping back from his desk but keeping her eyes on him, as if expecting him to stab her in the back again. "It's a lesson learned, that's all. I'm sure I'll grow from the experience."

"Damn it…"

"You can have personnel send me my last check, Shane. I'm leaving now."

"You can't. You gave me two weeks notice."

She'd reached the door. Snaking her arm behind her, she turned the knob and pulled it open. "If you can lie," she said quietly, "then so can I. Goodbye, Shane."

Eleven

The dining room at The Tides, the Elliott family home, was elegant but warm. Deep burgundy walls, with cream colored trim and crown moldings gave it an old-world feeling. A polished to perfection walnut table that could easily sit twelve stood on a thick Oriental carpet. Original oil paintings dotted the walls and a hand carved buffet sat against the far wall.

When Patrick and Maeve Elliott hosted dinner parties, this room sparkled with fine crystal and fragile china. But Shane remembered all the years growing up in this house and he could almost hear the memory of his brothers' and sister's voices echoing off the walls.

The estate was palatial—seven thousand square feet of turn-of-the-century home, surrounded by five acres of meticulously cared for grounds, situated on a bluff overlooking the Atlantic Ocean in Long Island. And though the house could be intimidating to visitors, to the Elliott children it had simply been home. And a great place for spur-of-the-moment games of hide-and-seek.

The roar and hush of the nearby sea pulsed in the background, almost making the old house seem alive. Shane loved this house. But at the moment, he wished he were anywhere but there.

"Your Rachel is certainly a lovely girl," Maeve said, taking a tiny sip of white wine.

Shane snapped his mother a warning look. "She's not *my* Rachel and yes, she is."

"I sensed a bit of—"

"Mom."

He should have tried to get out of dinner tonight. But to do that, he'd have had to come up with a damn good explanation and at the moment, Shane just wasn't up to it.

Hell, even *he* couldn't believe how he'd sabotaged Rachel's attempts to leave EPH. It had seemed like a good idea at the time. Downplay her abilities, make her seem a little less employable and maybe she'd stay with him.

He hadn't meant to— Damn. Yes, he had. He *had* meant to screw things up for her. So what did that make him? A bastard? Or a desperate bastard?

Either way, he'd lost her.

She'd gathered up her things and walked out of the building right after leaving his office. And for the rest of the day, walking past her empty desk drove needles of guilt into his skull, making his head ache and his temper spike.

He could still see the expression on her face when she'd faced him down just a few hours ago. Shock, betrayal, fury. If he could have, he would have kicked his own ass. He never should have given into the temptation to sabotage her job search.

His own fault. He'd let Rachel become too important to him over the years. She'd become such a part of his day, he could barely imagine *not* having her there.

That thought irritated him more than a little and he scowled to himself.

"Fine, fine," Maeve said, having another sip before setting her glass down on the linen draped table. "Far be it from me to interfere in my children's lives."

Shane snorted a laugh and his mother's eyes narrowed on him.

"Well," she pointed out, "if you and your brothers and sisters would talk to me about what's bothering you, I wouldn't have to pry now would I?"

"Ah, so it's our fault."

"Darlin'," she said, a soft smile still curving her mouth, "I can plainly see that there's something bothering you. Won't you tell me?"

For a moment or two, he considered it. Just unloading on his mom. Then he thought about how

Maeve would react when she discovered what he'd done to Rachel and thought better of it.

"I spoke to Rachel this afternoon," his mother said into the silence.

"Really? About what?"

"The charity ball," Maeve reminded him. "She wanted to say that despite the fact she no longer worked for you, she would continue to oversee the preparations."

"Ah." Of course she'd do that. Rachel was the most responsible human being he'd ever known. She took her duties seriously and once she'd given herself up to a project, she never quit.

Not even when she had more than enough reason to.

"Idiot," he muttered, rubbing his eyes in an attempt to ease the headache pounding behind them.

"Aye," Maeve said, the Irish accent she'd never quite lost dancing in her tone, "apparently you are, dear. Would you like to explain to me why you've fired that lovely girl?"

"I didn't fire her."

"She quit?"

"Yes."

"Why?"

He slanted Maeve a look and wished he hadn't. He was thirty-eight years old, the newly crowned head of a Fortune 500 company and one steely glare from his mother could completely cow him.

Thankfully he was saved by an interruption.

"What're you two talking about?" Patrick asked

as he walked into the room, heels clicking on the marble floor, and took the chair at the head of the table.

"Not a thing, my love," Maeve said, patting his hand. But the look she sent Shane told him that this wasn't over.

"Hmm." Patrick wasn't convinced, but he was willing to let it go. Focusing his gaze on Shane, he asked, "Before dinner arrives, why don't you tell me what your plans are for the company?"

"Patrick," his wife said, "can't we have a single meal without discussing business?"

"No," Shane said quickly, eager to talk about anything but Rachel. If he could keep his mother's mind off of that subject, he just might be able to get through dinner and escape before she could corner him again. "It's fine. Actually I'd like to get Dad's opinion on a few things."

Maeve picked up her glass of wine and took a sip, focusing her gaze on her son. Shane pretended he didn't feel that hot stare and concentrated instead on his father.

The next week was a blur of activity.

Even though Rachel was now officially unemployed, she was busier than ever, coordinating the charity function. Keeping in touch with the event planner at the Waldorf, Rachel had her finger on every hot button.

Nothing was getting past her; she wouldn't allow it. If this was going to be her final task for EPH, it was going to be one that people would be talking about for years. She'd arranged for a ten-foot pine tree to be delivered and professionally decorated. There would be a champagne fountain, a chocolate bar and enough hors d'oeuvres to keep even the most famished guest satisfied.

Every table at the event would boast its own tiny tree, complete with twinkling lights, and garlands of holly and mistletoe would be wound around the perimeter of the elegant room.

This ball was going to be organized smoother than a military coup. There wouldn't be a single hiccup.

She took a bite of her maple scone and shifted a look out through the window of the coffeehouse at the street beyond. Dark clouds hovered over the city as if waiting for just the right moment to dump another few inches of snow on the already slushy streets. People were bundled up, colorful scarves wound tightly around their mouths and necks. And the wind whipped down the high-rise canyons, snatching up trash and twirling it through the air.

Made her cold just looking out at it. So she turned back to the paperwork spread out over the table in front of her and got back down to the business of running a charity event.

Her cell phone rang and Rachel rummaged in her oversized purse for it. A perky little tune played louder as she grabbed it, and a few of the patrons in the coffeehouse glared at her. "Hello?"

"Honey, how's it going?" Christina's voice came across in whispered concern.

Rachel leaned back in her chair, picked up her latte and took a drink. She'd only spoken to her friend once since leaving EPH and Rachel had really missed her. "It's going *great.*"

"Uh-huh."

"Really." She put every ounce of conviction she possessed into her voice, but clearly it wasn't enough to convince Christina.

"Oh sure, I believe you."

"Fine," Rachel muttered, shooting a glare at a bearded man hunched over his laptop. What was up with him? He was allowed to type and clatter but she couldn't have a conversation? Honestly, some people.

Focusing on her friend, Rachel said, "I'm working myself to death to keep from thinking about Shane."

"That's what I figured. So if you're still so nuts about him, why'd you quit?"

"What other choice did I have?" she demanded a little too loudly and glared right back at the Beard. Lowering her voice, she said, "I couldn't stay there after—"

God, she couldn't even think about those nights with Shane. It was hard enough to lie there in her bed and remember him lying alongside her. To imagine the hush of his breath, the sweep of his hands on her body, the taste of his mouth on hers.

She took a gulp of hot coffee and burned her mouth. Good. Nice distraction.

"Okay," Christina said, "sex with the boss would make things a little…sticky."

"Yeah, just a touch. But it's more than that, too."

"You mean it's because you love him?"

Rachel winced. "Oh God. *Yes.* I do. And it's hopeless and pitiful and ridiculous and all of the above at once." She shook her head and trailed the tip of her index finger around the circumference of her coffee cup lid. "He's never going to see me like that. Never going to love me back. How could I stay there?"

"I guess you couldn't," Christina said on a sigh. "But I really miss you around here."

"Miss you, too. Heck, I miss my *job.* I was good at it, you know?"

"I know." There was a long pause and then Christina lowered her voice so much Rachel could scarcely hear her. "Would it help to know that since you've been gone, Shane's been miserable?"

Instantly Rachel cheered right up. "Really? His new admin isn't working out?"

"Doesn't have one."

"No way." Surprise made her voice a little louder again and this time Beard actually lifted his index finger to his mouth and warned, "Shhh." Rachel sneered at him.

Shane hadn't hired someone to take her place? Why not? She'd been gone a week. And heaven knew the man couldn't keep track of his own appointment schedule. He needed someone highly organized or he'd never get anything done. And that thought brought a small smile to her face.

"It's weird. Your desk sits there empty," Christina

said, "like the elephant at the cocktail party that nobody wants to talk about."

It shouldn't have made her feel better that Shane hadn't replaced her, but it did. She should be letting him go, getting on with the life she'd promised herself to find. But how could she, when every other minute Shane's face kept popping up into her mind?

"So who's doing all the work if he hasn't hired somebody?"

"No one. That seems to be the problem."

"Oh boy."

"Exactly. And he's not a happy camper these days. Shane's got every department head hopping. Jonathon even threatened to quit yesterday!"

"No, he didn't."

"Oh, yes, he did and Shane backed off quick. I mean, he's crabby, but he's not stupid. If he lost you *and* Jonathon, he'd really be up the proverbial creek. And to top it all off, Shane slams his office door so often, the doorjamb's coming loose."

For a moment or two, Rachel indulged herself, pretending that it was *her* he missed. But in reality she knew better. Right now he was angry because she hadn't fallen into line with his plans. He was feeling a little ashamed of himself for ruining Rachel's job opportunity and he was, no doubt, frustrated because his office life wasn't running as smoothly as usual.

"He'll survive," Rachel said firmly, "and so will I. I hope."

"You hang in there, honey," Christina said. "How about you and I meet for dinner tonight?"

"I'd really love to," Rachel assured her, "but I can't. I have to go to my folks' house for the annual What's Wrong with Rachel holiday discussion."

"Man. You just can't catch a break, can you?"

Actually she *did* catch a small break.

Another storm was rushing toward the city, so to avoid having to drive in a blizzard Rachel made her excuses and left her parents' house early.

Not nearly early enough, though.

She flipped on the rental car radio and tuned it to a soft rock station. The windshield wipers slapped against the glass, keeping time with the rhythm of the song. Nearly hypnotized, Rachel started talking to herself, more to stay alert than anything else.

"A podiatrist. *This* is the dream doctor Mom wants me to hook up with?" Okay, he was a perfectly nice man and not too bad looking in that "probably has back hair" kind of way. But could the man *be* more boring?

"Feet. That's all he talked about all night—feet." Rachel was willing to admit that in the grand scheme of things, feet were a fairly important body part. After all, they made walking a lot easier. But she now knew way more than she'd ever wanted to know about corns, blisters, calluses and warts.

"That's it, Mom," she swore and slapped one hand against the steering wheel. "No more fix-ups. I absolutely refuse."

Her cell phone rang and she reached one handed into her purse, on the passenger seat. Keeping her eyes on the road, she didn't even look at the screen, just opened the phone and said, "Hello?"

"Rachel."

Chills swept up and down her spine, ran along her arms, across her knuckles and back up to swirl in a happy little clog dance in the middle of her chest. God, would the sound of his voice always have that effect on her? "Hello, Shane."

He smiled at the sound of her voice, even though it was less than welcoming. Ever since leaving his parents' house, Shane'd been thinking about Rachel. Hell, he hadn't been able to get his mind off of her all week. Every time he passed her empty desk, he was reminded again of what an idiot he was.

The nights were the worst, though. He glanced around his apartment and found no pleasure in the stark, designer furnishings. White couches, hardwood floors and a lot of glass and chrome, much like the offices at *The Buzz*. His home had all the warmth of a dentist's office. And, at the moment, about the same appeal.

He kept remembering being at Rachel's place. A small, cozy place that she'd made warm and friendly. He could see her, all curled up in one corner of the couch, her blond hair lying loose in soft waves. He heard her laughter and remembered the passion in her eyes.

He couldn't stop thinking about carrying her into her bedroom and how she'd looked in the pale glow of the streetlight shining through the window. He couldn't seem to sleep without tasting her again, reaching for her, like a blind man fumbling for a life rope he knows is there, but can't find.

During the last week, he'd been forced to admit to himself just how important Rachel really was to him. And the question Gannon had asked him a couple of weeks ago kept replaying over and over again in his mind.

Do you love Rachel?

He'd spent so many years avoiding that particular word that now a part of him recoiled even at the thought of it. But the more he missed Rachel, the more he was forced to acknowledge that maybe love had sneaked up on him.

Maybe.

But how was a man supposed to *know?*

The only way he could think of was to get Rachel to come back to work at *The Buzz,* so that they could spend more time together. And then maybe what he was feeling would start to make sense to him.

He walked across the living room of his spacious apartment overlooking Central Park and stopped opposite the terrace doors. Behind him, a fire roared in the hearth, in front of him, a storm was blowing in off the Atlantic, threatening to shut the city down this time.

And he was oblivious to everything but the woman on the other end of the line. He held the phone to his ear in a white-knuckled grip and asked, "Is this a bad time, Rachel?"

"Actually…"

He'd only said that to be polite, so he spoke up

fast. Couldn't risk her hanging up on him. He figured it was best if he went straight to the point. "Rachel, you've gotta come back to work."

"What?"

"I mean it. The place is falling apart, nothing's getting done."

What he didn't say was that it wasn't just work that concerned him. The real problem was *him.* He couldn't think anymore. Without seeing Rachel every damn day, it was like part of his life—the most important part—was gone.

"Not my problem anymore."

He slapped one hand on the icy glass of the French doors and tried to keep his voice calm, steady, without betraying any of the panic he was beginning to feel. It wasn't easy. "Damn it, Rachel, without you there, nothing works right. Nothing is what it should be. I need you, Rachel."

For some reason, something his father had said to him just a couple of weeks ago came flying back into his brain. *Winning doesn't mean a damn thing if you've got nothing to show for it but the victory.*

The old man was right, he thought. Without Rachel to share things with, the victory he'd won over his brothers and sister was an empty one.

There was a long pause where all he heard was a radio playing softly. He stared out at the swirling snow and noted the lamps and the blazing fire behind him reflected in the glass. He waited what seemed like forever for her answer and when it finally came, it wasn't what he wanted to hear.

"You don't need *me,* Shane," she said, her voice sounding sad and weary. "I really wish you did. But what you need is a good admin. There are plenty of them in New York. Find one."

"Rachel, wait—"

"Goodbye, Shane."

Twelve

She wasn't coming back.

Shane scrubbed both hands across his face and blew out a shaky breath. He looked around his office and tried to find the excitement, the old sense of pride being here used to give him. But there was nothing.

Nothing at all.

The work went on.

The world went on.

But nothing was the same.

Rachel was gone.

And he didn't know how to fix it.

When the phone rang, he almost ignored it. God knew he was in no mood to talk to anyone. But the shrill rings sliced into his head, accentuating the headache already pounding behind his eyes. So he grabbed it and snarled a greeting.

"Well, Merry Christmas to you, too," a familiar female voice said.

"Fin." He sighed, plopped down into his desk chair and spun around so that he was facing the windows and the cold, dark world beyond the glass. Outside, the sky was gray and heavy. New York had been getting quite the winter this year and it looked as if it was going to keep right on snowing through Christmas.

Christmas. Only about ten days away and he still didn't have any shopping done. Another example of just how much he missed Rachel. She'd have made damn sure he got out to the stores.

Pitiful, he thought. He couldn't even Christmas shop without Rachel in his life.

Just pitiful.

"So," he said, "you coming home for Christmas?"

"I don't think so," Fin answered. "I sort of want to start our own traditions this year. But I'll definitely be there for the New Year's party."

Disappointment flared briefly to life inside him. He hadn't realized how much he'd been looking forward to seeing his sister again.

Shaking his head, he forced a smile into his voice and asked, "So how's life in the Wild, Wild West?"

Fin laughed again and Shane saw her in his mind. His twin. His best friend. Like a younger version of their mother, Fin was short and slender with auburn hair, green eyes and a few gold freckles across her nose. Her smile could light up a room and he was grateful that lately, his twin had had so much to smile about.

Fin might be living on a ranch in Colorado these days, but clearly their connection was still strong. She'd chosen just the right time to call him.

"You really need to get out of Manhattan more often, Shane," she said, still chuckling. "You know, we really don't have gunfights in the center of town and desperadoes hardly ever hold up the stagecoach anymore."

"Cute," he said, nodding, "and the ranch was a great place to visit but I think the West Village is about as west as I really want to go."

His sister sighed a little. "I know you're not the outdoorsy type, Shane, but I know you enjoyed yourself."

The Silver Moon ranch, just outside Colorado Springs, was mainly a cattle ranch, but according to Fin, her new husband ran quite a few horses, too. Enough to make her happy anyway.

And it wasn't as if his city born and bred sister was roughing it. She and her husband, Travis Clayton, lived in a huge, two-story log home, surrounded by tall pines and open spaces. Shane had seen for himself how happy she was there. And that was good enough for him.

"I did. And I'll come back," he promised. "This spring. In the meantime, how're you feeling?"

"Good," she said, a little less enthusiastically. "I could live without the morning sickness, but otherwise, I feel great."

Shane smiled. "I'm glad. And damn, it's good to hear your voice."

"Yeah," she said wryly, "you sound thrilled."

"Been a bad couple of weeks," he admitted, leaning his head against the chair back.

"Not the way I hear it," she said. "You made it, Shane. You're the new CEO. This is a good thing."

Should have been, he told himself. Now it didn't mean a thing to him. How could it when the woman who'd helped him win the damn thing was gone?

His silence must have told her there was something wrong.

"So do you want to tell me what's going on?" she asked.

"I wouldn't know where to start," he admitted.

"Most people say start at the beginning," Fin said and he heard the smile in her voice. "I say start with what's upsetting you and work backward."

"Upset?" he repeated. "Small word for what I'm feeling." Hell. What *was* he feeling? He couldn't ever remember experiencing this kind of emotion. The feeling that his chest was too tight. That his heart was empty.

That he might never be *warm* again.

"Talk to me, Shane."

"It's Rachel," he blurted. "She's gone."

"What do you mean gone?"

He frowned at the phone. "How many things could I mean?"

"She quit?"

"Yeah." He bit the word off and tasted the bitterness of defeat.

"Why?"

He rubbed his mouth, closed his eyes and said, "Because I'm an idiot."

Fin chuckled. "She's known that for a long time, but she just now quit, so what else happened?"

"We—" He caught himself and shook his head. "None of your business, Fin."

"Well, *yahoo,*" she crowed. "It's about time."

"What?"

"You slept with her."

"Like I said, none of your business." And why was his twin, the one person in the world who should be on his side at all damn times, so excited by his misery?

"So did you tell her you love her?"

He sat up like a shot and noticed the horrified expression on his reflection in the windowpane. "Who said anything about love?"

"Oh, Shane, I love you, but you really *are* an idiot."

"Thanks for calling," he snapped.

"For Pete's sake, everyone but you has known for at least a year that Rachel's nuts about you."

"What?" If that was true, why hadn't he known about it? Why hadn't someone told him? Hell, why hadn't he *noticed?*

"And you feel the same way."

He shook his head firmly, decisively. "I'm not in love."

"Really?" his sister prompted. "Then why don't

you tell me how you're feeling now that Rachel's gone?"

He scowled and his reflection glared back at him.

"Be honest," she said and her voice softened in sympathy.

"I feel like hell," he finally said, admitting what he'd been keeping inside for too long. "Nothing feels right without her here. Nothing's working. I can't work. Can't think. Can't sleep. Damn it, Fin, I wasn't looking for this."

"No, you weren't. You just got lucky."

"I'm *lucky* to feel this bad?"

"No, Shane," she said on an impatient sigh. "You're lucky to have the chance at something amazing. Most people never find what you have. Don't blow it."

He shook his head, as if he were going to try to deny his sister's words. But he couldn't. "I already *have* blown it. Fin, she won't talk to me. Won't see me."

"Then it's up to you to find a way to make it happen."

"Easier said than done."

"Nobody said it would be easy. Nothing worth having comes easily, Shane." A long pause and then her voice dipped even lower. "Trust me on this one. I know."

Fin had gone through so much in her life to reach the happiness she'd finally found, he knew she was speaking from experience. But just because she and Travis had found each other didn't mean that he and Rachel were destined to find the same thing.

Did it?

Was Fin right?

Was it all so simple after all?

Was this overpowering emotion nearly choking him *love?*

"Shane," Fin said quietly, and he focused on the sound of her voice, "for too long, I was living only for the company. I forgot about actually having a life. But now, I've got a wonderful life, with a man who loves me. I've found my daughter and I have a new chance at being a mom."

"I know and I'm glad for you—"

"I want the same kind of happiness for you, Shane," she said, interrupting him neatly. "Don't let Rachel get away. Don't miss your chance at love."

When he finally hung up with Fin, Shane was thoughtful. Everything she'd said played over and over again in his mind, as if the words were on a permanent loop. Love. Rachel. Chance at happiness.

The silence in his office pushed him to leave it. As he wandered through the deserted hallways of *The Buzz,* his footsteps echoing in the quiet, he felt the underlying pulse of the business his father had built. Everything that he himself was now responsible for. And weirdly, he felt both fulfilled and empty.

This place was where he belonged, but the woman who belonged *with* him wasn't there.

And without Rachel, he knew suddenly, none of this was worth a damn. Fin was right. If he didn't act quickly, do *something* to convince Rachel to take a chance on him again, he'd end up just like his father—a lonely man with more regrets than anyone had a right to.

Patrick Elliott loved his wife madly, but he'd so buried himself in the business he'd created, that he'd missed much of the life they could have had. He'd been a stranger to his children and a phantom presence in his own house.

Shane didn't want the same kind of life.

He didn't want to be a man whose only happiness lay in the profit margins of his business. He wanted to be happy. To love and *be* loved.

He wanted Rachel.

Now, all he had to do was convince her that she still wanted *him.*

The Waldorf-Astoria hotel was decked out in all its grandeur for the Elliott Charity Gala. Towering floral centerpieces sat atop gleaming tables that lined the marble foyer where elegantly dressed attendees mingled, enjoying appetizers and champagne.

Crystal chandeliers shimmered with quiet light and led the guests along the marble hallway toward the elevators that would take them to the grand ballroom. Upstairs, the long, narrow room was ablaze with strings of white lights. A DJ stood along one wall, playing a selection of Christmas music that had feet tapping and a few couples twirling on the dance floor.

In one corner of the room, a gigantic blue spruce tree stood proudly, its limbs bowing under the weight of lights and ornaments. At its feet were dozens of gaily wrapped packages awaiting the crowd of children here representing those this fund-raiser would be assisting.

Rachel smiled and nodded to those she passed as she listened with half an ear to the voices coming across the earpiece/microphone she wore. Keeping everything running smoothly was enough of a task that she didn't really have time to think about Shane. Or the fact that he wasn't there.

She'd missed him desperately the last week or so. Missed going into work every day and seeing him. Missed teasing him and hearing him laugh. Missed working with him and sharing the victories and defeats of running *The Buzz.*

And every night, alone in her bed, she missed the feel of his arms around her. Missed the sound of his breath in the darkness and the heated touch of his hands on her body.

She closed her eyes and swayed slightly under the onslaught of memories rushing through her. Rachel's heart ached as her gaze swept the crowd, searching for the one man she most longed to see. But he wasn't there and in the ocean of people, she might as well have been alone.

Two hours later, the DJ began playing "Here Comes Santa Claus," and the gathered children erupted in excited cheers.

A voice in Rachel's ear said, "Santa's here, and hey, it's a good one."

"Excellent," she answered and followed the

crowd as the people slowly moved toward the decorated Christmas tree and the "throne" that had been set up for Santa.

Then the man himself stepped out from behind a panel of velvet curtains and paused midstage for a hearty belly laugh. His voice rolled out across the room and sent a chill straight up Rachel's spine.

Her heartbeat quickened and her mouth went dry as her gaze locked on the tall man in the red velvet suit. The red hat, white wig and beard, bushy eyebrows and rectangular glasses perched low on his nose did a good job of disguising his true identity.

But Rachel would have known him anywhere.

Shane.

She wove through the crowd, excusing herself, apologizing, but never stopping. Her gaze on Santa, she headed straight for him. And halfway there, his gaze found hers. She felt the power of his stare slam into her and for the first time in more than a week, she felt wholly, completely alive again.

"Merry Christmas," Santa shouted, his gaze still on Rachel.

The children shrieked and clapped and the gathered adults got into the spirit of the thing, too. Women in diamonds, men in designer tuxes smiled along with the kids, enjoying the thrill of the moment.

Rachel stopped alongside Santa and looked up into Shane's beautiful green eyes. She didn't want to make too much of his being here. Of his playing Santa. Of the quickening jolt of her heartbeat.

But how could she not?

How could she not hope that somehow, someway, they might find each other in the magic of this night?

"Santa's got some work to do," Shane whispered, "but once the presents are distributed, you and I have to talk."

"Shane..."

His eyes actually twinkled. *"Santa."*

She nodded even as one of the kids moved in close and started tugging at her hand. "After, Santa."

Shane grinned and immediately bent down to scoop up the little girl who was staring at him as if he held the answers to all of the universe's questions. Perching her on his hip, he tapped her nose with the tip of one finger and said, "Now, let's see what Santa's got especially for you!"

For an hour, Rachel worked side by side with Shane. His laughter rang out and inspired hers. The kids were awed and touched and thrilled with the gifts the Elliott foundation had purchased specifically for them. The real magic of Christmas hummed in the air as the crowd began singing along with the carols pouring from the stereo.

Outside, the snow started again and turned the ballroom into a picture postcard. And when the last of the children's wishes had been satisfied, Santa took Rachel's hand and pulled her backstage.

"You were wonderful tonight," she said, taking a cautious step back from him even as her heart urged her to move in closer. "The children loved you."

Shane pulled off the hat, wig and beard, then carefully took off his glasses and set them aside before turning to Rachel. "I've never had so much fun," he admitted. "And it's all because of you."

"What?"

"You, Rachel," he said, reaching for her, dropping his hands onto her shoulders and pulling her slowly toward him. "I played Santa tonight because I knew you'd be here. Knew you'd like it. And I hoped you'd give me a chance to say what I should have said a long time ago."

"Shane…" Her throat felt incredibly tight. As if air were just too thick to penetrate it.

"Just listen," he said quickly. "Please."

Rachel nodded because she simply couldn't speak. She locked her knees to keep herself upright and stared into his beautiful eyes.

"I miss you, Rachel," he said, his voice gruff, raw. "I miss seeing you every day. Miss hearing you laugh. Miss the way you nag me into doing what needs doing."

She found her voice at that. "I don't nag, I—"

"You do," he interrupted, "and I need it, God knows. Nothing is right with me, Rachel. Since you left, there's no light. There's no laughter. There's no…anything."

"I miss you, too, but—"

"No," he said quickly, pulling her even closer, tipping her head back until she was staring straight up into his eyes. "No buts, Rachel. Just the simple truth. Without you in my life, I've got nothing worth having."

She swallowed hard and let the tears crowding her eyes begin to fall.

"I love you, Rachel," he said, his fingers digging into her arms as if holding on to her meant life itself. "I think maybe I've always loved you. I just never knew it until you were gone." He bent his head, kissed her gently, lightly, then said, "You're everything to me, Rachel. You make me want to be a better man. A man who deserves you."

Her heart thundering in her chest, Rachel could hardly believe she was hearing him say all the things she'd dreamed of hearing. Her soul lit up like Christmas morning and hope for a future filled with love swept through her.

"If you let me," he said, hurrying on as if unwilling to stop talking long enough to hear her answer, "I'll spend the rest of our lives proving to you just how much I love you."

"What are you saying?" The words squeaked out of her throat. She was pretty sure what he was getting at, but she wanted no mistakes. No misunderstandings. Not about this.

"I'm proposing, Rachel!" He dragged her tightly against him and wrapped his arms around her, holding her in place. "For God's sake, haven't you been listening?"

Rachel laughed and nodded. "Yeah. I really have. But I don't think I've heard an actual question yet."

He gave her a brief smile. "I'm getting to it. This isn't easy for a man, you know. What if the woman you're asking says no?"

She smiled back at him. "Just a chance you're going to have to take, I guess."

"Well," Shane said, "a very wise woman I know told me recently that nothing worth having comes easily."

"I like her already," Rachel said, loving the feel of Shane's arms around her, there in the dark. From the room beyond, Christmas music drifted on the air and conversations came muted, as if from a distant planet.

"Yeah," he said, "me, too. But this is about us."

"Us," Rachel echoed. "I like the sound of that, too."

"Glad to hear it," Shane said, lifting one hand to smooth her hair back from her forehead. "Marry me, Rachel. Let me marry you."

"Yes."

His smile was quick and broad. "Just like that?"

"Just like that," she said, nodding. "Although, I'm not going to work for you anymore."

His smile faded abruptly. "Why the hell not?"

"Because," she said, "I'm going back to school. I always wanted to be a teacher. I think I'd be a good one."

"I think you'd be a great teacher," Shane said, dipping his head for another quick taste of her. "I'll miss having you at the office, but as long as you come home to me every night, I'll be a happy man."

"I do love you, Santa," she said, going up on her toes to meet him for another kiss.

His glued-on, bushy white eyebrows wiggled expressively over his twinkling green eyes. "Then how about a sleigh ride?"

Epilogue

The tree was still up, the garlands and lights still twining around the great room at The Tides. And with all of the Elliotts gathered at the family home for New Year's, the noise level was pretty impressive.

Shane wandered through the crowd, listening to snatches of conversation and smiling at the sudden bursts of laughter that shot up and flavored the air. He glanced across the room, caught Rachel's eye and felt again the punch of sheer joy that was a constant companion these days. With Rachel's love he could do anything. Face anything. And he looked forward to a future of loving her and the children they were already trying for.

The stereo was suddenly turned off and each of

the gathered Elliotts turned to look at the older man standing beside the roaring fire in the hearth.

"I think it's time for a speech," Patrick Elliott announced, lifting a glass of champagne to his family.

"Now, Patrick," his wife chided, "'tis no time for one of your long talks. The family's here, we should be celebratin'."

Shane watched as his father dropped an arm around his wife's shoulders and pulled her close.

"You're right, Maeve," Patrick said, "as always. But, the idea was for Shane to give the speech. As the new CEO of EPH, it's only fitting."

Around him, applause erupted and Shane grinned. Gannon slapped him on the back and gave him a shove toward the front of the room. Erika held their baby daughter as if she were made of spun glass and smiled up at her husband.

Tag had his fiancée, Renee, trapped under a ball of mistletoe and the lovely woman showed no signs of trying to escape. Michael stood beside the chair where his wife, Karen, practically glowing with her very short hair, sat enjoying the fun.

Shane kept walking, stopping long enough to snag Rachel's hand and drag her along with him. He grinned at Summer and her rock star Zeke, huddled with Scarlet and John, no doubt planning the double wedding that Maeve was already fretting over.

Outside the living room, the night was cold and moonlit, pale silvery light glancing off the mounds of snow, illuminating the grounds. Inside, warmth filled the gathered Elliotts and touched Shane more deeply than ever before.

Fin lifted a glass to him and gave him a wink. He grinned at her and her husband, Travis, who'd flown in from Colorado with Bridget and her husband, Mac, just for this traditional party. In a corner of the room, Daniel and Amanda were cuddling, ignoring everyone else. And to round out the crowd, Jessie and her husband, Cade, were talking with Liam and his fiancée, Aubrey, about their upcoming wedding at their Napa winery. Collen and Misty were cuddled up together, as if they were alone on an island. And Bryan and Lucy were kissing under the mistletoe. The family was together and happy. A great start to a New Year.

Finally, though, Shane was at the head of the room and as his parents stepped to one side, he pulled Rachel close against him. His heart swelled as she leaned into him.

"I'm a lucky man," he said, lifting his glass to the faces turned toward him. "I found the woman I was meant to love and the work I was meant to do."

"Hear, hear!" Gannon shouted and was quickly shushed by Erika.

"But," Shane continued, looking from one beloved face to another, "I think this year we all got lucky. When Dad started his little contest, I thought he was trying to drive a wedge between us." Shane glanced at his father and smiled. "I should have known better."

Patrick smiled and kissed Maeve.

Renee gave Tag a friendly slap and stepped out from under the mistletoe to listen.

"The Elliotts have come together this year," Shane said, lifting his champagne glass even higher. "We've rediscovered our family ties and forged the bonds that connect us one to the other, even tighter than they were before. We've passed our own tests, we've faced our fears…" He paused to nod at Michael and Karen. "And we've come out the other side. We've found love and we've found each other."

Liam whistled and Fin applauded.

"Old wrongs have been righted," Shane went on, with a nod at Fin and Jessie. "And the future stretching out in front of us looks bright."

"Well said," Patrick called out.

"To the Elliotts," Shane shouted, "together, we're invincible!"

And as the family celebrated, Shane pulled the love of his life into the circle of his arms. Together, they shared a kiss that promised a future filled with all the love and hope anyone could ask for.

* * * * *

Take a quick look at the second book in
THE MILLION DOLLAR CATCH,
Susan Mallery's sexy new mini-series.

What happens when Willow Nelson meets the one man who doesn't want *to be rescued?*

Find out in

The Unexpected Millionaire

pn sale December 2007.

The Unexpected Millionaire

by

Susan Mallery

"I don't get it," Willow said. "I'm not your type."

"You said that before. How do you know?"

"I'm not anyone's type."

Kane shook his head. "I don't believe that."

"It's true. I have the sad, painful romantic history to prove it. I'm the best friend, the one guys confide in."

"I don't confide in anyone," he told her.

"You should. It's very healthy. Sharing problems make them seem more manageable."

"You know this how?"

"I read it in a magazine somewhere. You can learn a lot from magazines."

His dark gaze never left her face. "Go back to bed. I'll take you home in the morning."

No! She didn't want to be sent to bed like a child. "But then where will you sleep?"

"You're in the guest room. I still have my own bed."

"See, that was flirting. I was flirting. Wouldn't it be nice if you just went with it?"

He moved so fast, he was like a human blur. One second he was several feet away and the next he was right in front of her, one hand on her waist, the other wrapped around her hair. He eased forward that last inch, so they were touching everywhere.

She had the feeling he was trying to intimidate her and it would have worked, except she couldn't seem to be afraid of him.

"You won't hurt me," she whispered.

"Your faith is foolish and misplaced. You don't know what I'll do."

He bent his head and claimed her with a hard, demanding kiss. He pushed into her mouth and stroked her tongue, then sucked on her lower lip.

She wrapped one arm around his neck and gave as good as she got, stealing into his mouth and dueling right back. She felt him stiffen with surprise. He pulled her hard against him and she went willingly. The hand holding her hair tightened, drawing her head back.

He broke the kiss and stared into her eyes.

"I am dark and dangerous and I don't play the games you know," he said. "I'm not anyone you want to get involved with. I'm not nice, I don't call the next day and I'm never interested in more than a single night. You can't fix me, reform me, heal me or change me. You are so far out of your league, you don't know enough to run scared, but you should. Trust me on that."

His words made her tremble.

"I can't be afraid of you," she told him again.

"Why the hell not?"

She smiled and rubbed her index finger against his lower lip. "I'll agree that you're tough and you probably scare other people, but Kane, you rescued me and kittens and you were nice to my mom and my sister and when you put me to bed, you didn't even think about taking advantage of me. What's not to like?"

He closed his eyes and groaned. She had a feeling the sound wasn't about being turned on.

He opened his eyes. "You're impossible."

"I've heard that before."

"You're just about irresistible."

She sighed. "That's a new one. Can you say it again?"

He backed her up until she was trapped between him and the wall. She felt his body—and his arousal—pressing against her.

"I want you," he said in a low growl. "I want you naked and begging and desperate. I want to bury myself inside of you until you forget who you are. But you're a fool if you take me up on that. This is not a fun trip to the dark side. If you expect anything of me, you *will* be hurt. I'm going to walk away, Willow. I can walk away now or later. It's your choice."

She saw the truth reflected in his eyes. Once again the sensible part of her brain pointed out that the guest room was the best option. Only Willow had never met anyone like Kane before and she was unlikely to ever again. He claimed to be incredibly tough and maybe he was, but she had a feeling there was more to him than he wanted her to see.

Walk away? Not possible. Maybe he would hurt her, but maybe he wouldn't. She was willing to take the risk. She had to. There was something about him that called to her.

Besides, the guy could make her quiver with just a look.

"For a man so intent on insisting he doesn't care, you're

going out of your way to warn me off," she said. "Maybe you should stop talking and kiss me instead."

"Willow."

"See? You're doing it again. I understand the rules, I'm willing to play by them and you're still talking. You know what? I think it's all an act. I don't think you have any real intention of doing anything at all. I think—"

He grabbed her and kissed her. There were no preliminaries, just him wrapping his arms around her as he claimed her mouth with his own. He kissed her deeply, passionately, with no pause for breath or social niceties. He took, sweeping past her lips to stroke her tongue, circling her, claiming her. His possessive acts thrilled her and she freed her arms so she could hang on for the ride.

There was no fear, she thought as her body heated and her muscles lost their ability to support her. However much he threatened, he still held her gently. His hands moved up and down her back, exploring her, touching her, but there was nothing harsh about the contact.

She put her hands on his shoulders and leaned into him. His body supported hers. The combination of hard muscles and warmth thrilled her. She tilted her head and closed her lips around his tongue so she could suck.

He stiffened, then took a step back and stared at her. There was shock, pleasure and need in his eyes—an irresistible combination.

"I don't scare easily," she said with a shrug.

He shook his head, then bent down, gathered her in his arms and carried her down the hall.

They moved into a bedroom illuminated by a single lamp on a nightstand. Here the design was totally masculine with large pieces of dark furniture lining the walls. The bed could sleep twenty, and suited Kane completely.

He set her on the mattress and looked at her.

She felt the challenge of his gaze and refused to look away—even when he began unfastening the shirt he wore. When he'd removed that, he pulled off a T-shirt, exposing his bare chest.

Her breath caught. He was as muscled as she'd first thought, but there were also scars...dozens of them. Small irregular circles and long, jagged lines. Scars from surgeries and from wounds that made her ache inside.

What had happened to this man? Who had hurt him and why?

But there was no time for questions. He pulled off his loafers, then his socks. Trousers quickly followed, along with dark briefs.

And then he was naked. Beautiful and hard and ready. His body should be immortalized in marble, she thought. A master should sculpt him. Not that Kane would ever agree to pose.

He put his hands on his hips and stared at her. "You can still run," he told her.

"Not with my ankle."

"You know what I mean."

"Yes, I do. And I'm not going anywhere."

* * *

Don't forget The Unexpected Millionaire *is on sale next month!*

BRIDES OF PENHALLY BAY

Medical™ is proud to welcome you to Penhally Bay Surgery where you can meet the team led by caring and commanding Dr Nick Tremayne. For the next twelve months we will bring you an emotional, tempting romance – devoted doctors, single fathers, a sheikh surgeon, royalty, blushing brides and miracle babies will warm your heart…

Let us whisk you away to this Cornish coastal town – to a place where hearts are made whole.

Turn the page for a sneak preview from
Christmas Eve Baby
by Caroline Anderson
– the first book in the
BRIDES OF PENHALLY BAY series.

CHRSTMAS EVE BABY
by
Caroline Anderson

Ben crossed the room, standing by the window, looking out. It was a pleasant room, and from the window he could see across the boatyard to the lifeboat station and beyond it the sea.

He didn't notice, though, not really. Didn't take it in, couldn't have described the colour of the walls or the furniture, because there was only one thing he'd really seen, only one thing he'd been aware of since Lucy had got out of her car.

Lucy met his eyes, but only with a huge effort, and he could see the emotions racing through their wary, soft brown depths. God only knows what his own expression was, but he held her gaze for a long moment before she coloured and looked away.

'Um – can I make you some tea?' she offered, and he gave a short, disbelieving cough of laughter.

'Don't you think there's something we should talk about first?' he suggested, and she hesitated, her hand on the kettle, catching her lip between those neat, even teeth and nibbling it unconsciously.

'I intend to,' she began, and he laughed and propped his hips on the edge of the desk, his hands each side gripping the thick, solid wood as if his life depended on it.

'When, exactly? Assuming, as I am, perhaps a little rashly, that unless that's a beachball you've got up your jumper it has something to do with me?'

She put the kettle down with a little thump and turned towards him, her eyes flashing fire. 'Rashly? *Rashly?* Is that what you think of me? That I'd sleep with you and then go and fall into bed with another man?'

He shrugged, ignoring the crazy, irrational flicker of hope that it was, indeed, his child. 'I don't know. I would hope not, but I don't know anything about your private life. Not any more,' he added with a tinge of regret.

'Well, you should know enough about me to know that isn't the way I do things.'

'So how do you do things, Lucy?' he asked, trying to stop the anger from creeping into his voice. 'Like your father? You don't like it, so you just pretend it hasn't happened?'

'And what was I supposed to do?' she asked, her eyes flashing sparks again. 'We weren't seeing each other. We'd agreed.'

'But this, surely, changes things? Or should have. Unless you just weren't going to tell me? It must have made it simpler for you.'

She turned away again, but not before he saw her eyes fill, and guilt gnawed at him. 'Simpler?'

she said. 'That's not how I'd describe it.'

'So why not tell me, then?' he said, his voice softening. 'Why, in all these months, didn't you tell me that I'm going to be a father?'

'I was going to,' she said, her voice little more than a whisper. 'But after everything – I didn't know how to. It's just all so difficult – '

'But it *is* mine.'

She nodded, her hair falling over her face and obscuring it from him. 'Yes. Yes, it's yours.'

His heart soared, and for a ridiculous moment he felt like punching the air, but then he pulled himself together. Plenty of time for that later, once he'd got all the facts. Down to the nitty-gritty, he thought, and asked the question that came to the top of the heap.

'Does your father know it's mine...?'

She shook her head, and he winced.

'Have you had lunch?' she said suddenly.

'Lunch?' he said, his tone disbelieving. 'No. I got held up in Resus. There wasn't time.'

'Fancy coming back to my house and having something to eat? Only I'm starving, and I'm trying to eat properly, and biscuits and cakes and rubbish like that just won't cut the mustard.'

'Sounds good,' he said, not in the least bit hungry but desperate to be away from there and somewhere private while he assimilated this stunning bit of news.

She opened the door, grabbed her coat out of the staff room as they passed it and led him down the stairs.

They walked to her flat, along Harbour Road and up Bridge Street, the road that ran alongside the river and up out of the old town towards St Piran, the road he'd come in on. It was over a gift shop, in a steep little terrace typical of Cornish coastal towns and villages, and he wondered how she'd manage when she'd had the baby.

Not here, was the answer, especially when she led him through a door into a narrow little hallway and up the precipitous stairs to her flat. 'Make yourself at home, I'll find some food,' she said, a little breathless after her climb, and left him in the small living room. If he got close to the window he could see the sea, but apart from that it had no real charm. It was homely, though, and comfortable, and he wandered round it, picking up things and putting them down, measuring her life.

A book on pregnancy, a mother-and-baby magazine, a book of names, lying in a neat pile on the end of an old leather trunk in front of the sofa. More books in a bookcase, a cosy fleece blanket draped over the arm of the sofa, some flowers in a vase lending a little cheer.

He could see her through the kitchen door, pottering about and making sandwiches, and he went and propped himself in the doorway and watched her.

'I'd offer to help, but the room's too small for three of us,' he murmured, and she gave him a slightly nervous smile.

Why nervous? he wondered, and then realised that of course she was nervous. She had no idea what his attitude would be, whether he'd be pleased or angry, if he'd want to be involved in his child's life – any of it.

When he'd worked it out himself, he'd tell her. The only thing he did know, absolutely with total certainty, was that if, as she had said, this baby was his, he was going to be a part of its life for ever.

And that was non-negotiable.

* * * *

On sale 16th November 2007

The Unexpected Millionaire *by Susan Mallery*

Dark and dangerous Kane Denison has a one-night only rule – but Willow Nelson is hard to forget. When Willow falls in love with him will he take a chance on her?

To Claim His Own *by Mary Lynn Baxter*

Cal Webster had come to claim his child, but his son's beautiful guardian was not giving up to this seductive stranger without a fight.

Bunking Down with the Boss *by Charlene Sands*

Caroline Portman's new employee, Sam Beaumont, seemed like a man used to being in control. And when he set his sights on Caroline, she knew she was about to bed down with the *real* boss.

Holiday Confessions *by Anne Marie Winston*

Lynne Devane was finally confessing who she really was, but gorgeous Brendan Reilly was wary of trusting her. If she wanted him, she would have to prove it!

Bending to the Bachelor's Will *by Emilie Rose*

Having been pressured into buying him at a bachelor auction, the last thing Holly Prescott expects with Eric Alden is romance. But their passion gives them no choice…

Secrets in the Marriage Bed *by Nalini Singh*

Pregnant Vicky Callaghan demanded absolute honesty from her husband, Caleb. But that was the one thing that he couldn't give her; some secrets have to be kept.

Available at WHSmith, Tesco, ASDA, and all good bookshops

www.millsandboon.co.uk